THE SHORT CUT

THE SHORT CUT

Mark Pepper

Hodder & Stoughton

First published in Great Britain in 1996
by Hodder and Stoughton
A division of Hodder Headline PLC

10 9 8 7 6 5 4 3 2 1

British Library Cataloguing in Publication Data

Pepper, Mark
The Short Cut
1. English fiction - 20th century
I. Title
823.9'14[F]

ISBN 0 340 68220 5

Typeset by Avon Dataset Ltd, Bidford-on-Avon, Warks

Printed and bound in Great Britain by
Mackays of Chatham PLC, Chatham, Kent

Hodder and Stoughton
A division of Hodder Headline PLC
338 Euston Road
London NW1 3BH

DEDICATED WITH LOVE TO
MY PARENTS
AND
MY BROTHER, DAVE

ACKNOWLEDGEMENTS

Thanks to my friend and agent, Merric Davidson; Stephen Powell and Kirsty Watt at Ringpull; Jim Middleton; Lisa Pickford; and especially Jeannifer Blankanette, for her love, strength and guidance.

'Wickedness is always easier than virtue,
for it takes the short cut to everything.'
SAMUEL JOHNSON

PROLOGUE

The moon was full. The time was midnight.

Nathan Lake did not see the first, or know the second.

He felt more alive this evening than in his entire life. The power of anger filled him, elemental and brutal.

But he was alone in the flat. No one to talk to or shout at.

So he closed his eyes and spoke a livid, wretched prayer for his salvation.

'God, why have you forgotten about me? I'm a good person. I'm good at what I do. So why is nothing happening? I thought you were meant to care. Well, show me you do. I want success. Give it me. Please. I can't cope with this. God . . . someone . . . anyone. I don't care. Just make me famous.'

1

He came from the Underground.

London once again. Oxford Street.

December now. The dark month.

He stopped at the exit. The hordes surged up the steps and past him, spilling out into the street. None of them touched him, though he stood in their way. They split and flowed around him, avoiding him like an island of unspoilt beauty none of them had the nerve to invade. Or like a leper colony.

With indifference, he noted a flutter of female eyes turning his way. He was used to it.

Conrad Dreave was unmissable. From his swept-back, white-blond hair atop his six-five frame, to his cream suit over white turtleneck, down to his cream shoes, he oozed a level of class such ostentatious attire had every right to negate.

But even on a cold winter's afternoon, with the light fading, his effect was nothing short of mesmeric.

He watched them through his black wrap-around glasses. He hated their lives. He hated their lack of life. But he smiled to himself.

One of them was calling him. One who desired a life, who was dying within for the lack of it, and was about ripe to embrace anyone who could give him that life.

Nathan Lake stared hard at the cinema screen. Through narrow, hateful eyes he watched the adverts, the previews of coming attractions. His right hand fed popcorn into his face like an automaton. In his left hand was a ticket stub, crushed by an unconscious, steely clench. When he finished eating, his teeth would resume their constant, rigid grit, as though lock-jawed in combat. He saw the film classification appear, announcing the certificate, and he shook his head.

Eighteen. Another reminder he didn't need, could barely stomach.

His mind flew back to the main event of his eighteenth year; the event he had thought would be the launch-pad for the rest of his life.

He no longer had it in him to smile at the memory of RADA. He had smiled a lot at the time, though. Eighteen years old and accepted by the élite Royal Academy of Dramatic Art. Three years' training, then fame and fortune guaranteed. Forget the cynics, their talk of naïvety. Nathan Lake was going all the way, and fast.

It could all make a man wonder what the hell had gone wrong. Lake certainly wondered, now he was thirty and still living in the same one-bedroom flat of his RADA days.

Of course, he told himself, there were people worse off. Contemporaries who had long since abandoned hope, given up and taken regular work. Or grown up and got a life.

At least he still had an agent. He still acted. Bits and pieces, here and there. Sometimes.

But never the break. Never even close.

So now it was a form of torture, going to the cinema; a reminder of how the dream remained unfulfilled. He didn't replace the actors on-screen with himself, not any more. It was simply an exercise to get him out of the flat for a couple of hours. He took no real notice of the film, or who was in it. It didn't matter. It wasn't him up there, and it never would be.

2

The freezing night air cut through his thin sweatshirt like an ice pick. The living-room window had been open for ten minutes. Each time he breathed in, his whole body juddered.

Common sense told him to close out the chill and dive into the warmth of his bed, but a deeper sense warned him to keep himself exposed. The cold calmed his anger, but it was more than that. It was the experience of something outside himself that mattered. An attachment to a force unmoved by his own failure and perception of futility. The world was bigger than him, if only for the brief period he shivered in its palm. Sealed in his centrally heated flat, he would be by himself, with no connection to anything beyond his own problems.

He checked the wall clock above the television. Nearly ten p.m. He looked out, up into the sky. No cloud cover. The moon was full; he noticed that tonight.

Lake smiled awkwardly as he recalled his little speech to the heavens the previous night. He felt vaguely ashamed of himself, pleading so pitifully to powers he had never really believed in. It seemed somehow squalid, underhand.

To hell with it, he thought, no one ever listens to me.

That night Lake had a dream, and even as he slept, he was aware of the massive bearing his dream would have on his crumbling life when he eventually awoke. It possessed a quality of absolute credence.

He was in no doubt: it was a message sent to save him, to prevent his slide into a depression with suicide at its base.

5

He was in the foyer of RADA. The place seemed ageless, never changing, always inviting. The grand stone staircase swept up and out of the entrance hall, splitting and curling round either wall to the first floor, past huge, dark paintings in heavy gold frames, and bronze busts on tall columns.

Someone tapped his shoulder. He turned to find Ben, his closest friend from RADA, standing beside him. His light, freckled features were soft and dispassionate. He was in a white shroud. He had been dead for years. A car had hit him outside the Academy in the final term.

Ben said, 'You're dreaming, Nathan.'

'I know.'

'But I'm not a part of your dreamscape, I'm real, and you must listen to me. I'm your guide, but I can't answer questions. I can only tell you and show you certain things. You must discover the essence, learn the central lesson for yourself. If you learn the lesson, you beat the Dark One.'

'Dark One?'

Ben did not illuminate. He indicated the small lift beside reception. 'In,' he said.

Lake pulled open the door, slid back the grille and went in. Ben followed and closed them into the compartment.

'We take the Light Path first,' Ben said.

The mechanism clanked and whirred overhead and the lift began its ascent, but it was so slow, hardly moving at all. Lake felt agonised by its lack of progress. Each floor inched down to meet them with yawning lethargy.

The ascent lasted a full hour of genuine sleep, so within the peculiar time-scheme of dreams it seemed like years. Lake hated the journey for the age it took.

At the top floor, he was led out of the lift towards a photograph on the opposite wall.

The picture contained a white Cadillac stretch limousine standing outside a plush hotel. It was night-time. A red carpet led from the car door into the building. A man in uniform and top hat stood beside the vehicle, white-gloved hand outstretched to the door. Press photographers were poised on the sidewalk. Barriers and American police officers held back an excited throng, eagerly calling for the black windows to give up their secret.

'And action,' Ben whispered.

The picture came to life. The crowd began jostling and screaming. The man in the top hat opened the limo door. A young woman emerged, slim and slinky, dressed to thrill, then a man in a black tuxedo. Lake could not see their faces. The press closed in, flashguns popping. The limousine pulled away. The couple walked down the red carpet towards the building, favouring their public with nods. The press followed, urging them to turn for a static photo opportunity. At the entrance, the couple obliged. The man in the tux was Lake. The woman was currently one of Hollywood's rising stars. The flashguns lit the scene like sheet lightning before the couple waved and resumed their sweep into the building. Another gleaming stretch limousine swished in. The crowd swung as one fickle entity, directing their screams at more darkened windows. The press returned to the sidewalk. The doorman leant in to release the hidden occupants.

The photograph had returned to its original composition.

'And cut,' Ben said, and the picture froze.

Lake stood silently transfixed.

'It's your future along the Light Path,' Ben explained. Then he walked back to the lift and stopped just outside. He beckoned. 'Come see the Dark Path.'

They re-entered the lift and Ben sealed them inside.

Lake prepared himself for another snail slither down the lift shaft.

The mechanism clanked overhead and the lift began its descent.

And Lake's mouth flew open, only no sound emerged; fear had taken it. The lift was dropping as though a great fist had punched the roof and was rocketing down the shaft above them, pushing harder, faster. Lake's feet lost contact with the lift floor. His stomach was on the ceiling.

He found a voice, but it was nothing more than a doggy whimper.

They stopped instantly.

The descent had taken only seconds in dream-time. Ben offered no apology.

Outside the lift window, it was black. Black as hell with the fires out. Lake pressed his nose against the cold glass. Nothing to be seen. But the black space beyond the glass was palpable. It had a texture, a smoothness gone sickly awry, like velvet brushed backwards. There was a depth to it all, as though there were no end to its Stygian gloom, no boundary a person might breach to escape. It could house whole

7

generations across the wastes of time, and no one would ever roam far enough or long enough to meet another. Down here were the husks of old human life, but no humanity, no souls but those who mourn, and absolutely no light.

Strong hands circled the back of Lake's head. Thumbs dug into the softness at the base of his skull. Fingers clawed into his hair. He was held firm at the glass.

'You must watch,' Ben softly insisted. 'So you know.'

It came flying at him, a figure carried by the unseen transport of the dark. Lake first saw it only the second before it was right there, inches from the window. He tried in vain to pull away.

Its skin was bubbly, waxen white, like burnt, cold candle. Its face was struck with an expression of perpetual, untold horror, like that of a man buried alive, scraping fingers down to bone on the underside of a coffin lid. It was hairless. Its ghastly eyes were pure black: shark eyes.

The figure came closer, touching its nose to the glass directly over Lake's, like inmate and lover on Death Row, eskimo-kissing the glass. Dead, black pupils bored into his soul. The figure pulled back from the glass and spat. A lump of black saliva struck the window and hung there. The figure retreated suddenly, lost from Lake's abominable TV screen. Then white, stubby digits slapped an object at the glass.

Stuck there by the black spit was a photograph, a smaller copy of the picture that had come to life along the Light Path.

The picture began to move, and Lake watched.

Its short story was identical.

Ben said, 'It's your future along the Dark Path.'

Instantly, Lake was back up in the foyer with Ben.

'But . . . I don't get – what's it mean?' Lake protested.

'I can't answer that, except to tell you this: your call for help has been answered. Your future is now assured. It has been decided. The power is yours to achieve your every desire.'

Lake's excitement swamped the fear he had felt in the Dark Land. 'When do I get it? When's it start?' he said.

'Your path will be set by the time of the next full moon.'

'A month?'

'You must have learned the lesson by then if you are to walk the Light Path.'

'One month?'

'The lesson is simple but far from easy.'

'I have a month?'

'I'm sorry, Nathan, it's not within my power to give you any more time.'

'No, I don't want any more time. I only want a week.'

Ben winced. 'Take the month, Nathan. It is the only concession the Dark One will allow. I advise you to accept it.'

Lake ignored his dead friend. 'That's really my future? What you showed me?'

Ben nodded.

'I'm really going to be famous?'

'You are.'

'And rich?'

'That, too. Take the month.'

'No.' Lake was adamant. 'I haven't come this far to faff around now. I'll take a week. I'll learn the lesson by then. It can't be that hard.'

Ben's expression was pained. 'I don't want to see you walk the Dark Path.'

'I won't,' Lake insisted. 'I'm not a bad person. Ben, you know I'm not. You know me.'

'But do you know yourself?'

'Oh –' Lake grimaced. 'OK, if it makes you happy, two weeks.'

'My happiness is not at stake, Nathan. Yours is.'

'Then I'm happy with two weeks. I'd be happier with one but I'll take two.'

'Nathan –' Ben began defiantly, but then his voice softened into one of reluctant resignation. 'No. No, it's not my place to argue with you.' He nodded. 'Two weeks it is.'

'Thanks, Ben.'

'Don't thank me,' Ben said quickly. 'Never thank me for this. This is far bigger than me. By your own design and by universal circumstance, you have drawn a great power to your cause.'

'Well, isn't that good?'

'It can be, but that is entirely up to you. At the moment its nature is malign.'

'What . . . evil?' Lake asked, his excitement gone.

'Pure and true,' Ben said. 'Finally, you understand. And that is why you must learn the lesson. Remove the malignancy. Beat the Dark One.

Cheat him of yet another victory in this world of yours.'

'Walk the Light Path,' Lake said quietly.

'Walk the Light Path,' Ben agreed.

'I understand.' Lake nodded gravely. 'And I've got a month?'

'Two weeks. Your choice.'

'Right.'

'Think hard,' Ben said. 'Make the next choice more wisely.'

3

Lake woke up thinking hard. What was the lesson he had to learn?

He had taken the dream as Ben intended; as an intangible expression of a concrete truth. He didn't know whether to feel elated or petrified.

But why should he be scared? What did he have to fear from the Dark Path? He was a good man at heart, and two weeks was plenty of time for a good man to learn a simple lesson. One would have been enough.

Lake regarded his face in the bathroom mirror. He looked into his dark eyes, ran a hand through his unkempt, spiky black hair and across his stubbled chin, then frowned. Something was odd. After a moment he realised with amusement that his skin was simply flushed with the bloom of life. His blood was up. For the first time in years he felt himself bursting with physical energy. Not quite believing what he was doing, he bobbed into the bedroom, stripped and changed into an old black track suit. He rolled his door keys into the top of one sock, left his flat, ran down the four flights to street level and tore from the building as though it was ablaze.

Regent's Park was two minutes away. Lake picked up the pace and recalled his days as a regular jogger during the RADA years, and for a couple after, before unemployment took its toll and sapped his energy. He realised it was all psychosomatic, but that made its effect no less real.

Today he cruised effortlessly in top gear. He went into the park at the first gate on the Outer Circle, by Park Square Gardens. He ran through to Broad Walk, a path which cut down the east side of the park to the zoo.

All the way, he sensed within him a rapture. He absorbed the trees,

11

bare and spidery, like Indian ink sketches against the clear sky; the conifers, stubborn in their greenery. And although the flowerbeds in the neat lawns would be empty of colour for some months yet, they too brought him a yearning kind of pleasure, for he knew the passage of time would finally bring good things to his door, and not just leave him older and more bitter.

He ran on, and his ears began to burn.

On the sturdy wooden benches either side of the path, lovers sat huddled in each other's arms, two pink faces, cheek to cheek, swaddled as one by their winter woollens, but properly insulated only by the lunatic happiness of love fully aglow.

Lake experienced a great twinge of sadness. Not since his last girl-friend, Suzy, had he known real love, and that had been six long, empty years ago. The six years they had spent together, she had witnessed him float sky-high through his course at RADA and then plummet into a depression she could not ultimately handle. She had left to save her own sanity. He couldn't blame her, but, even now, the memory stung.

Once across Chester Road, he ran into the main expanse of the park. To his left, public playing fields were criss-crossed by footpaths and lone joggers. To his right were the lawns he headed for during the hot summer days, which were all too infrequent.

The tree-lined path he moved along was still flanked by benched lovers. They looked like clones, one identical pair after the other, and Lake thought once again of Suzy, how he had spent so many similarly lazy, frivolous hours on those very benches with her.

Pretty soon, his body began steaming inside his clothes, his muscles rubberising inside his legs, and the run that was to last the whole day became a finite proposition; to the north end of the park, the zoo, then back, more sedately.

As he plodded home, Lake re-examined last night's dream: the lift taking him the two paths to his future, and Ben's warning to learn the lesson. Still he failed to make sense of it, but he questioned whether it really mattered if his future worked out the same.

Then an image of the floating thing from the Dark Land came to him, and it focused his mind perfectly, making him shiver in his sweaty warmth.

The Dark Path was to be avoided.

He would search earnestly for the answer, strive to learn the lesson, delve within himself to find the fork that split the paths up and down. Firming his commitment to do just that, he faltered in his shambling semi-jog.

It wasn't, was it?

He sped up but slowed again, pulling up to a walk, wheezing deeply and clouding the air with hot breath. He stopped, moved over to the side of the path, but didn't turn back to look.

It couldn't be, could it?

He sensed he was being watched. Slowly, he glanced back over his shoulder.

She was a solitary figure on a bench, watching him.

No. Was it? Suzy? She smiled timidly at him. Suzy.

He grinned, his tired legs weakened further, and his burdened heart pattered excitedly. He walked towards her, feeling decidedly wobbly. He wanted to run like Heathcliffe but he walked, and as he drew nearer she stood up to greet him.

A maroon cashmere coat hung to her ankles. Her hands dug deeply in the pockets. Black leather boots piped up into the coat.

He thought she looked tearful, but decided that must be the cold. And still he could hardly believe it was her.

She had changed little. Her chestnut hair was cut differently, in a wavy bob, parted on the left, but the face was the same, untouched by the years. A cheeky face and sexually dirty; big brown eyes, full of improper fun; a thin nose with a slight snub; lips that were both delicate and cruel; and a fresh, clear complexion. At five foot nine, she was an inch shorter than Lake, but her slender frame made her appear taller than she was. Twenty-eight years old. Twenty-two when he had last seen her.

Face to face, Lake experienced a quaint shyness.

'Hi.'

'Hi.'

He did not expect she would feel it her place to, so he leant in and pecked her cheek.

'Been far?' she asked.

'Too far.'

She smiled. 'Sit down, have a rest.'

'Actually, can we walk?' he asked. 'I don't want to catch a chill.'

'OK.'

'I mean, if you've got time,' he added. 'Only if – you know.'

'I don't mind. I can take a long lunch.'

At Chester Road, Lake instinctively took gentle hold of Suzy's arm. A car passed and they crossed.

'I do know the Green Cross Code,' she said with a smile.

Lake released her. 'Sorry, I know, of course, I didn't mean—'

'No, it's sweet.'

They walked on, his head bursting with six years of intimate questions, but their conversation was an exchange of simple pleasantries.

Conrad Dreave watched from a distance as his prospective assignment left the park. He liked to see what the poor sods looked like.

When he turned his gaze upon the female at Lake's side, a brief flicker interrupted the smooth skin of his brow. Something about her. She reminded him of someone; a woman he should have forgotten from a past he barely remembered.

The physical similarity was striking. And Dreave couldn't help but wonder if the resemblance extended inwards. Could she be as black-hearted as his companion of old? Could he have found another soul-mate after all this time?

Dreave shook himself and made a conscious effort to curb his enthusiasm. There were two weeks yet. It was always possible that Lake might solve the riddle in time, and then he and his girlfriend would no longer be of any concern. Mmm. Dreave scowled at the thought.

Then a cheery grin. On the other hand, he mused, if Lake *did* screw up, the girl could easily be drawn into things. A nice little sideline in corruption.

Yes, she would make a splendid hobby.

Out of the park, Lake walked with Suzy down Euston Road and crossed opposite Great Portland Street Underground. This time Suzy offered her arm. As they turned into Conway Street, in the shadow of the Telecom Tower, Lake suddenly suspected he was being a bit presumptuous. He stopped.

'Sorry,' he said, 'I'm taking you back to the flat. I didn't mean—'

She chuckled. 'It's OK. I could do with a coffee.'

Lake nodded eagerly. He prayed to be calm, not frighten her away. Twice in one lifetime would have destroyed him.

* * *

Once in the flat, he took Suzy's coat from her and said, 'Sit down. Make yourself at home. I'll get the coffee.'

He opened the cupboard in the living-room wall that contained all the kitchen appliances and flicked the kettle. All the while he prepared their coffee, Lake could think of nothing to say. Small-talk seemed false and pointless, but how to broach anything more searching? Behind him on the settee, he imagined Suzy to be in a similar state. And that damned kettle had a malevolent streak with the time it took to boil.

Eventually, coffees in hand, they sat beside each other. They smiled foolishly at the carpet and gave tutting little shakes of the head, as though they had to overcome their disbelief at meeting before they could talk properly. Lake finished his coffee while it was way too hot; anything to occupy his mouth. It was all starting to look like a big mistake. What had he expected would happen?

'Have you bought the place?' Suzy asked suddenly.

'I wish,' Lake said.

'Oh.'

'No, I still rent.'

'Right.'

'Still,' Lake echoed.

Suzy made no reply, and Lake felt sure he was doing it all over again, making her miserable with his damned self-pity. He thought he could read her mind: that nothing had changed with him. But it had, he knew it had, he just didn't know how to tell her. So what if he'd had a bloody dream? How could he explain to her, to anyone, that it really meant something?

'I should be able to afford it soon, though,' he blurted.

'I'm sorry?'

'The flat,' he said. 'If everything pans out. As it should.' He wondered desperately if the internal cringe he felt was visible on his face.

'Really?' she said, her voice chirping up noticeably.

He nodded, then tried to drink from an empty mug.

'Will you make it a home then?' she asked.

Lake surveyed the walls and shelves, unspoilt by picture or possession. He nodded again, and said, 'When it's mine.'

Suzy smiled and seemed genuinely pleased for him. 'I'd like to see that.'

15

'I'd like it too,' Lake said, before he was caught by a sneezing fit.

'D'you want to take a shower?' Suzy asked him.

Understanding came a fraction too late to stop a lecherous grin spreading across his face; she wasn't coming on to him, she just didn't want him catching cold.

'Good idea,' he said, jumping up. 'You'll wait, won't you?'

'I'll make another coffee,' she replied, stifling her amusement.

He disappeared into the bedroom and stripped off. Suzy did not walk in on him. It would have been nice, but he didn't really expect it. He figured she had to be long-term attached or married by now. He hadn't noticed a ring, but that did not preclude the possibility.

His thoughts were a jumble as he stepped into the shower and opened the jets. Things were simultaneously great and terrible. He believed she now accepted he was not the loser of six years ago, and that was great, but he had convinced her on the basis of nothing more than a sleeping fantasy, which was terrible. And though he had total faith his life was about to turn, which was great, he could never explain why that was so without inventing a complete fabrication of prior events, and that was terrible. The best he could hope for, he concluded, was that she was happily married. That way it could all end there and then, and be neither great nor terrible. Problem was, that thought made him feel miserable as sin, and, damn it, he was getting a hard-on remembering their past sexual exploits, and imagining her stepping in with him right now, naked and beautiful as ever he knew her.

All clean and calm and back in the bedroom, he spent all of three seconds at the open wardrobe door, decided, and put on some black clothes, as black was about all his wardrobe contained. It suited his features, his hair, and his mood for the most part, and it made dressing in the morning a blissfully thoughtless task, if somewhat monotonous.

'Still a flashy dresser,' Suzy said when he came in.

'Ah, but you don't see my pink velvet undies.'

'You actors, you're all poofs.'

He laughed, and too many emotions instantly spilled inside him. 'I've missed you,' he bluntly announced.

Suzy looked down at her lap.

He apologised. 'Forget I said that.'

She shook her head, still downturned. 'No, I don't mind.' She was fiddling with the belt buckle of her blue wool dress.

Lake found the glimpse of knee between boot top and dress hem absurdly arousing.

When she finally looked up, he saw tears in her eyes.

'Oh, Suze,' he said, going over to sit beside her. 'What is it?'

She didn't start crying, but her voice had a sob in it. 'I didn't mean to hurt you, Nat. Never.'

He placed an arm around her shoulders, and was surprised to feel her snuggle against him. 'I know that. You got out of a nut-house, that's all. No one could blame you for that. Least of all the resident nutter at the time.'

She giggled, but it didn't last. '*I* can blame me.'

'You shouldn't.' He squeezed her shoulder. 'Really. You did everything for me.'

'Except stand by you.'

'No. No, I'd have destroyed you given time.'

She didn't argue with him.

He bit his tongue, but said it anyway, 'It wasn't a waste of time, you know. It's happening for me, Suze.'

She pulled back a little to fix his eyes. 'The career?'

He nodded. That was it. The invention was on track and rolling. If he derailed it now, it would wreck his chances with her for ever. He was going to the end of the line with it, and would just have to hope true success hopped aboard before it got there.

'How?' she wanted to know. 'What's happening?'

'I don't want to tempt providence by talking about it.'

'But it's good?'

'It will be.'

'A film? A series? What?' she persisted, with clear delight.

He screwed up his face apologetically.

'OK,' she said, 'I'll shut up.'

'I have missed you, you know.'

'Yeah. It's not been easy.'

Lake's heart went crazy. 'You mean . . . you mean . . . what do you mean?'

'You know what I mean.'

And he did. He could see it in her eyes: the old love still alive.

'Can I kiss you?' he asked.

'Please. But I have to tell you something first—'

17

'No.' He held a hand up. 'You don't have to tell me anything. Not a word. Not now.'

To make love with someone he had loved and lost, and found again after six long, empty years, felt to Lake like the ultimate waking dream.

They showered together afterwards and did dirty things as they got clean.

Once dressed, Suzy had to talk to him. They sat together on the sofa, bathed in a bar of light from the harsh winter sun.

She began, 'I hope you know how I feel about you, Nat.'

'I'd like to hear the words. You haven't said them.'

'Sorry. I love you. I do. It's just—'

'You're not married? Engaged? You're not wearing any rings.'

'No, but I have been seeing someone.'

Lake tried hard to stop his new world falling in on him. His guts filled with the gnawing rats of jealousy and began cartwheeling. Still, she had tried to tell him, he couldn't blame her.

'He's a police officer—'

'Oh, fantastic, and don't tell me, he's an expert marksman and jealous as hell. Bye-bye, Nathan.'

The impulse to laugh beat her.

'What?' Lake said. 'He is?'

'He's an AFO in an ARV.'

'A what in a what?'

'An authorised firearms officer in an armed response vehicle.'

'Great. I'm dead. Do you love him?'

She appeared to consider for several seconds. 'In a way. But it's not like our love. Do you understand?'

'You love two people?'

'Do you understand?'

'Not really. I've only ever loved you.' Designed to draw sympathy, he realised his comment had served only to dredge up years of guilt from her mind.

Suzy's expression became severe. She got up and began to put her coat on. 'Perhaps this shouldn't have happened,' she said coldly.

Lake went to her. 'Don't say that. I don't want to lose you again. I'll do anything.'

She stopped buttoning up and peered seriously at him. 'Can you be happy?'

He reached out and took her hands. 'You're joking. I'm *ecstatic* with you.'

'It's not enough,' she said. 'It wasn't before and it wouldn't be now. I mean be happy with yourself. Love is great but it's only one part of life, and it doesn't make up the slack in the other areas. Love doesn't conquer all.' She gently extricated her hands and pulled her mitts on. 'It didn't conquer your depression.'

'Suze. Please don't get tough on me. Give me a chance. I've told you, I'm on my way. I'm happy, I am.'

Suzy went and sat down. Lake remained standing. If he had to block her exit, he'd be ready. Love wasn't walking out on him again without a struggle.

'I don't want to seem mercenary, Nat,' she said, not meeting his eyes, 'but it's the old thing, the biological clock ticking away. I'm not looking for kids and stuff now, but some day I will be, I know. I don't want to have to start a dating game when that happens, it's too crude. I want you, Nat, I always have done. But I couldn't bear to see you fade away again, because this time you'd take me with you. You'd take my best years from me.'

Lake was quiet, thinking.

'Does that sound mercenary?' she asked.

He shook his head. 'Perfectly fair.'

'Do you understand, I have to be sure this time?'

'Yes.'

Looking up at him, she said, 'It's not to do with money. I'm not waiting on you getting rich and famous or anything like that. I just want to know the old Nat isn't going away this time.'

Lake smiled inwardly. Yesterday the old Nat wasn't even around. Yesterday she would have met the world's most bad-tempered man, and said hello and goodbye at the park bench. Then again, he believed this could not have happened yesterday, before the revelation of his future.

He chose his words carefully. 'The old Nat you loved is now the only Nat.'

'Good. That helps clarify things.'

His guts were still twisting jealously like a love-sick Medusa. He had

19

to give voice to his fear. 'You won't go to bed with your copper friend again, will you?'

Suzy flushed. 'Difficult . . . we live together.'

'Oh, shit, no.' Lake began pacing around the room. The pain was almost physical.

'Sorry,' she muttered.

He dropped to his knees in front of her. 'Move in here. Now.'

'I can't. I've got to be sure. I've too much to lose.'

'Like what, if you don't really love him?' He knew he was making things very difficult for her, but what did they say about desperate times?

'He's . . . dependable.' She squirmed a little, then told him, 'He proposed. Last night.'

Words deserted him.

'I didn't take the ring,' she said quickly. 'I told him I needed time to think. That's why I was in the park. Trying to exorcise your memory.'

'Right. I was trying to exercise my body.' It was an extremely poor joke, and he was surprised he found it within him to joke at all, but it had the most startling effect.

Suzy laughed and swept him into her arms and held him very tightly. 'Oh, I love you!'

'So leave him,' he urged.

'Please understand, Nat. Let me get to know you again first; be sure.'

She was not about to be swayed, and if he pushed he would lose her.

'OK,' he said. 'But, please, when you go to bed with him, if you have to do anything, don't make love with him, just . . . have sex.'

She gave no indication she would or could comply.

Lake made her write down his telephone number, though she said she still remembered it. Suzy gave him her office number, kissed him on the mouth and said she'd call.

He watched through the window as she left the building. She turned in the street and blew a kiss to him.

As she disappeared from sight, Lake remembered Ben's words: *The power is yours to achieve your every desire.*

———◆·◆·◆———

4

The next morning, Friday, Lake's agent phoned just after eleven a.m.

Lake was in a deep and disturbed slumber. Some spiteful corner of his mind had been hissing away all night, telling him it was all a dream, that Suzy wasn't really back in his life. As the ringing telephone brought him to, the semiconscious seconds of uncertainty between sleep and wide awake, where fantasy and substance swirl together, had become a nightmare all of their own. But then he had known – her perfume on the pillow.

'Hello?' Lake said thickly into the receiver.

'Morning, my dear,' said Billy Banbury, in his camp way. 'Audition, next week, Wednesday.'

'Oh, hi, Billy. Hold on, I need a pen.' Lake didn't like the sound of that: *audition*. That meant theatre. For television you were called to 'interview'. And it was television he wanted. TV work got you noticed, made you famous. He discovered a pen sandwiched between two directories. 'Go on.' He opened the cover of the upper directory to jot down the information.

'Next Wednesday, the fifteenth. The Actors' Centre, that's—'

'Chenies Street, I know.'

'Chenies Street. At three-fifteen. You'll be meeting a fellow named Trystan Walton-Streckman.'

'Do what?'

'Beg pardon?'

'Never mind.' Lake scribbled: *Wed – 3.15 – A C.*

Billy gave him the lowdown. 'It's nine months' work. A production of *Oedipus* for The Touring Company. A coming little troupe. Attracted a lot of attention, rave reviews. It could be quite a springboard. It'd be good for you.'

'OK. Do I need to prepare anything?'

'A nice lasagne.'

Lake recognised one of Billy's inane attempts at a wacky sense of humour. 'Very good. No speeches?'

'You'll be asked to read from the script.'

'Oh. My Greek's a bit rusty.'

'They'll have a translation, dear.'

'No, Billy, that was . . . never mind.'

'What?'

'Nothing.' Lake squeezed some gratitude into his voice. 'Well, thanks for that.'

'Welcome. Tatty-bye.'

'Yeah, bye.' Lake hung up, and felt like he'd swallowed something quite revolting.

Shit. *Oedipus*. Silly clothes, illicit sex, hatred, depression, screaming and suicide. And that was just the actors. Ha-ha. Lake made himself chuckle but it wasn't funny. A Greek tragedy was nothing to laugh at. Obviously not, it was tragic. But touring to some of the draughtiest arse-ends of the British Isles, regurgitating the same stuff for months on end . . . that was the real tragedy. Touring a comedy would have been bad enough.

It did bode well, though, a call so soon. It lent credence to the promise of his dream.

Lake thought: days remaining. Thirteen. No. Damn, only nine. Weekends. Dead days. No chance of a call.

Well. Still plenty of time.

But Lake noticed he'd been doodling – squares, cross-hatched down to blackness, and one word repeated: HELL.

At lunchtime, the telephone rang again.

Lake was daydreaming at the lounge window, his favourite perch. Outside, the weather had changed. Silver needles of rain cut steadily through the grey sky.

He raced for the phone.

It wasn't news of work, but he wasn't disappointed.

It was Suzy.

'Sorry, Nat,' she began, 'but I have to go to Manchester for a week or so and I've got to leave right away.'

'Why?'

'Business.'

'What are you doing these days?'

'I'm an office manager. I rent out office facilities in a building in Soho.'

'Right. And what are you doing in Manchester?'

'Overseeing the closure of our north-west operation.'

'Sounds ominous.'

'It is,' she said. 'We're going to the wall.'

'You mean you'll be out of a job?'

'Barring a miracle.'

'I'm sorry.'

'Could you love a dole-ite?' she asked.

'Try stopping me.'

'I do love you, Nat.'

'I love you too.'

For the next five minutes, Lake's handset was magnetically repelled by the cradle. Try as he might to replace it, it kept popping back up to his face, and he felt their love-sick exchanges could have lasted indefinitely, and he would have been blissfully happy had they done so.

'Put the phone down,' she finally told him, then swore her love once again.

'I love you too,' Lake said again. 'You put the phone down.'

Over and over, the same oaths.

Eventually, they agreed to hang up on a count of three so neither one would feel bad for cutting off first. Such was the nonsense of love. On the fourth attempt, they succeeded.

Lake moved around in a warm glow for the remainder of the day. The actor's diet of continuous television, he absorbed even less than usual. There was a vague, uncomfortable recollection of watching crap Australian soap for hours on end, as though it had taken over the broadcasting networks for the duration of the afternoon. Then he remembered: it had.

No more calls came in that day. Lake occasionally picked up the receiver to check for the tone, just in case Billy was trying to get through when the line was down, but the unit was in order.

23

Dinner was beans on toast. His food was as his clothes, for the same reason: simple, requiring minimum thought. Occasionally it was also black, but that was a mistake. After eating, he lay down for a short snooze.

He didn't wake up until Saturday lunchtime.

His weekends were lazy. Lake didn't know how to make them any different. He supposed he ought to enjoy it before the work began flooding in.

Saturday and Sunday were such dead days. He dreaded them. He was the antithesis of working man.

Suzy kept her promise, calling both days, twice on Saturday, four times on Sunday. Lake rang her hotel room a total of nine times.

The hands of his wall clock slowly swiped away the useless weekend hours. The television blared out its mainly banal weekend fare. It was company, if nothing else, and Lake did what any self-respecting out-of-work actor does in front of a television set: bitch.

Bed was never more welcome than on Sunday night. His head was dancing to a confused tune that robbed his thoughts of all their rhythm. It worried him to think so, but he was almost as depressed now as before his dream of Ben. He put it down to missing Suzy, but it was more sinister than that. He was worried there would be nothing more than *Oedipus*, and he didn't know how to make himself happy about it. He believed Ben's prophecy. But if *Oedipus* was the springboard, it still distanced him from real fame by at least nine months.

Monday.

The leaden feeling in his guts began to settle in at about four p.m., as though a hideously screeching alarm clock had gone off in his soul. There was a time-system to interviews, and very rarely was there less than a two- or three-day gap between receiving the agent's call and the interview itself. Apart from commercial interviews, which could be for the next day, a call on Monday or Tuesday would be for Thursday or Friday. From Wednesday on, the interview would generally land the other side of the weekend.

For Lake, four p.m. felt like a daily watershed. He had received plenty of calls after that time, but it still made his heart sink. It was like a death knell for his telephone, a curse of silence. Prepare to give up hope for yet another day . . . not long now.

Suzy's call at five p.m. was only a thin ray of sunlight through a darkly threatening sky.

He hoped she wouldn't ask, but she did. Lovers did ask. He didn't want to lie, but he was in too deep already. 'Yeah,' he said, 'I've heard something. It's good. I don't want to say too much, you know?'

She wasn't fooled. 'That's wonderful, Nat, but . . . are you all right?'

'I miss you, Suze.' No lie there, but not the truth.

'I hope you do, but I'll be back soon.'

'I know.'

'So cheer up.'

Lake made himself smile broadly, a purely physical exercise, but it was difficult to sound miserable with a mouth that shape. 'Yeah, you're right. I can't wait.'

'That's better. Listen, I've got to go. I'll call tomorrow.'

'Take care.'

'You too. And, Nat?'

'Mmm?'

'I only think of you. D'you understand?'

'Yeah. Good. Love you.'

'And you. Got to go. Bye.' She blew a kiss and hung up.

Lake felt very bad about lying to Suzy down the phone, but he was more concerned about seeing her face to face. If nothing apart from *Oedipus* had turned up by the time she returned to London, could he con her up close that he was pleased? He didn't think so. And if she saw his distress, she might get scared. Where was the old Nathan? The happy Nathan?

She would never trust him again.

Tuesday. Lunchtime. Bugger.

Come on, Billy . . . *CALL!*

The phone trilled.

'Yes?' It was no more than an eager expulsion of air.

'Hello?' Billy asked uncertainly.

'Yes?'

'Nathan?'

'Yes?'

'Yes, tomorrow's audition, they've changed the time. Is five o'clock a problem?'

25

Lake was, thankfully, immensely disappointed. Anger would have made him very rude.

'Nathan?'

'Uunng.' No known language.

'Five o'clock tomorrow?'

'Fantastic.'

'Tat—'

Lake hung up, then immediately called back.

'Greetings,' Billy answered.

'Yeah, listen, Billy, has nothing else come in apart from the Greek thing?'

'No. It's very quiet at this time of the year. You know that, Nathan. You've been in the business long enough.'

'I know, but . . .' *I was told by a dead friend that I was on the road to Hollywood.*

'Nathan, dear, what do you want from me?'

Lake couldn't answer.

Billy carried on, 'I can only do my best, you know. Have you thought perhaps that a new agent is more what you want?'

'*What?*'

'Only, an agent–client relationship *can* run its course. Another agent will have different contacts, people I know but who don't necessarily favour me. All the people I have close ties with . . . you've met. It's something you should think about.'

'You're dumping me?' Lake's head was swirling.

'I don't dump clients, dear, I let them go.'

'Same thing.'

Billy's voice gained a cool, professional edge. 'Not to me. I'm merely suggesting it as an option we should both consider very carefully.'

'And while I'm considering, you'll stop looking for me, eh?' Lake clenched the handset with white knuckles.

'*If* we part company, I will handle anything that comes in for you until you sign with someone else.'

Lake squeezed his eyes shut, trying to find peace in the darkness.

Billy ended the conversation. 'Think about it, Nathan. Call if you want to talk. Cheerio.' The line broke.

Lake replaced the receiver with a strange, studied gentleness, defying the desire to lose all control.

* * *

Suzy was sitting in the foyer bar of the Manchester Holiday Inn, in one of the luxurious leather seats that were physically difficult to get out of. She was sipping her third gin and tonic at the end of a tiring day.

She noticed a man enter from the street into the plushly carpeted foyer, and something positively primeval awoke in her.

He was about forty and very tall. He didn't walk so much as glide up to reception. In his white turtleneck, cream suit and cream shoes, he could have looked quite ridiculous. He was, however, the perfect figure of a gentleman. His features were classically sculptured: a jawline of impossible definition; high cheekbones; a strong, straight nose; a commanding mouth; an intelligent forehead. His hair was white-blond, swept back without grease. In short, Hitler would have creamed himself. He wasn't having a too dissimilar effect on Suzy. His eyes were hidden behind black wrap-around glasses – a potentially ludicrous touch, particularly at the death of a dull December afternoon – but they simply added to his tantalising mystery.

She had the shock of her life when the receptionist he was talking to pointed over his shoulder directly at her. He spun on his feet and gave a little nod. Suzy flushed hotly and, as he returned to the receptionist to no doubt thank her, Suzy tipped her glass and emptied it down her constricting throat. She watched as he started towards her, a smile breaking and widening on his perfect face.

He came over and towered above her. His teeth were dazzling in his open grin. He silently requested her hand, which she offered. He bent at the waist in a bow and kissed it. She half expected him to click his heels together and say, 'Fräulein.'

He straightened up and announced himself. 'Conrad Dreave. Pleasure to meet you, Miss Cooper.'

There was an accent, but it was indistinct. Mid-Atlantic, maybe.

She got up, merely to wipe out some of the height deficit. It was unnerving. She knew her expression was puzzled, and that was natural, but she also felt the warmth of a fresh bloom in her cheeks, and not a little awe in her eyes. She guessed he had experienced that reaction in countless women, but it still embarrassed her.

'I'm sorry . . .' she said, quite thrown.

'I will reveal all in a minute. First, would you like a refill? Gin and tonic?'

'Yes, thank you.'

He smoothed up to the bar and ordered. Suzy tried to place the accent. Not mid-Atlantic. Australian perhaps? South African? Not really. Very odd.

'There you are, Miss Cooper,' he said as he handed her a clinking tumbler. She suspected the excess ice in her glass was a disguise. Had he got her a double? 'I got you a double,' he said. 'May I sit?'

'Of course.'

He settled opposite her, across a low table, and set his drink down. He was colour-coded to the last detail: a tall glass of milk.

'Before I begin,' he said, 'I must apologise for my dark glasses. I do not mean to be rude, but I have a rare eye disorder; bright light causes me considerable distress. I hope I am not too off-putting like this.'

Suzy smiled. 'No, I understand.'

'If you would prefer, I will remove them. I appreciate it is not exactly dazzling in here, but I really prefer not to test my tolerance.'

She wanted him to take them off. A face without eyes spoke in fables; the truth was within. But she said, 'No, don't worry.'

'Then to business. You rent office space in London. I may well be in a position to require your services in the very near future.'

Suzy shifted in her chair. Her split dress rose and gaped from her movement and she made no effort to adjust it. 'Could I ask how you found me?'

'I have contacts all over the world, Miss Cooper. I can find anyone I want.' He gave her a disarming smile.

Suzy sensed he knew precisely the power of attraction he wielded. And what on earth was that accent? Scandinavian? East European? Nuances even of West Indian? That was pure madness in a man so wholly white.

'I see,' she said, but she didn't. He had not answered the question. 'Can I ask something else?'

He nodded, then sipped his milk.

'What's your accent? I can't place it. It's intriguing. A real mixture. I thought mid-Atlantic at first, but—'

'That is a most preposterous expression, is it not, mid-Atlantic?'

Suzy frowned and went scarlet again.

'My apologies, Miss Cooper. I do not mean to imply your use of it is preposterous, merely the expression. Surely anyone with a genuine mid-Atlantic accent would drown on their first attempts to use it.'

Suzy giggled.

'In answer to your question,' he said, 'I would say I have a multi-national accent. I have spent many years travelling, and have found much to enjoy in every tongue. I am fluent in most languages, and passable in the rest, and I carry a spark of each in whichever one I find myself presently speaking.'

Suzy found his use of the English language oddly formal. She also thought he was a consummate bullshitter. Fluent in most languages? Sure.

'I will not demonstrate,' he said, reading her expression. 'You would no doubt think less of me for showing off than you already do believing me to be a liar.'

'No, I . . . I just . . . I've never met anyone so . . . lingual. I didn't mean—'

'I understand. Now, should I wish to rent office space?'

'Hmm. Right. Ah.' She was in an agony of unprofessionalism. 'Well, what size office would you require? How many staff?'

'I would need the entire basement space. It would help my eyes to be away from natural light.'

She wasn't really listening. She was entranced by the strength of her attraction to the man. 'Oh, that's fine,' she told him.

His black glasses glared at her. 'Hmm.' He took his milk and drained it. 'Good. And I would not require any staff.'

'What? Oh. The receptionist puts through all calls from the switchboard.'

He repeated, 'I would not require any staff. I will pay for her services if that is the norm, but I would require a private line to my office.'

She considered. 'I can arrange that, but you would be charged for the connection.'

'Cost is not an issue.'

'Fine.' Then she grimaced. 'Sorry, did you say the whole of the basement?'

'I did.'

Her face screwed up; she didn't want to deny this man anything. 'Someone's renting there at the moment.'

Dreave smiled and waved a manicured hand dismissively. 'Move them.'

'I beg your pardon?'

Dreave dipped a hand inside his jacket and brought out a bulging white envelope, which he offered to her. 'For you.'

She gingerly accepted it, tore an end off the envelope and pulled the contents partly out. For a moment, she didn't speak.

Dreave let the silence maintain itself.

'This is a lot of money,' she said, fingering the fifties secretively in her lap, her eyes darting shiftily around the bar.

'Not really. Ten thousand pounds. Down payment. Yours unconditionally, whether or not I choose to avail myself of your facilities.'

'But if you don't rent, the company obviously won't—'

'It is not for the company, it is for you. I said yours unconditionally. Yours. To clear the basement for me on your return. I take it you do not have a full complement at the present time.'

'Uh, no,' she said, absently caressing the tips of the bank notes.

'Then there should be no problem, should there?' he reasoned. 'And if I find I am not required in London, you can apologise for inconveniencing your client, and you have the sum of ten thousand pounds to alleviate any feelings of personal guilt pertaining to the removal of said client.' He leant forward in his seat. 'If I do make the trip south, I will pay whatever is the going rate for the rental of one whole floor, the basement. The ten thousand is still yours. It is simply to concentrate your attention on my personal requirements, which, I admit, must appear quite unusual.'

Suzy didn't know what to say. Or, rather, she did. She just didn't know how to say it without sounding too easily bought.

'In my experience,' Dreave said, 'poverty and moral sensibility are indissoluble from one another.'

Suzy's eyes flicked around the bar. She wasn't breaking any law, but neither was she indulging in normal business practice. She felt vaguely like a crook. It was really quite exciting.

'Don't be shy,' Dreave told her. 'Ten thousand pounds. Put it in your bag, clear your conscience, and clear your basement.'

She pushed the notes back in the envelope, unzipped her handbag and put the package inside.

'Thank you,' she said.

'One thing, though, Miss Cooper.'

'Please, call me Suzy.'

'I will. And you may call me sir.'

Suzy felt her mouth drop open.

'I jest,' he said. 'Call me Conrad. Yes, just one final thing. The money I have given you is not to be spent until after my business in London is concluded. Naturally, if I have no business in London, that proviso will not apply. The reason for this is that the nature of my work is extremely sensitive. I want no unwelcome attention brought to my presence in town, and if you spend the money, someone will ask where it came from. The fewer people who know I am here, the better.'

'Sounds fascinating.' Suzy grinned, feeling the effects of the drink. 'Do you work for the government or something?'

Dreave gave no response.

Suzy made a face. 'Ooh. Sorry. Shouldn't have asked.'

'Let us just say,' Dreave confided, 'that I work for one of the world's great powers.'

'Gosh. Well.'

'Mum's the word.' Dreave smiled.

'Absolutely, Conrad. Right.'

'Splendid. Then I shall be in contact.'

'When will that be?'

'Whenever I need you. Wherever you are.'

He rose from his chair. Tipsily, she followed suit. He kissed her hand again.

'A true pleasure,' he said, straightening up. Then he was away.

Suzy's system was in meltdown. She slumped back into the chair and checked her bag. It was in there. Ten grand in fifties. He had left her ten grand.

She wriggled her bum a little. Ten grand and the horn.

Four p.m. had long since passed and the curse on Lake's phone had held. Even Suzy had not yet called, though he wasn't especially bothered. He would only have to lie again if she asked about work.

Six p.m. signalled the death of hope. Only three calls in nine years after that time.

He sat at his window seat, but didn't let in the cold. Outside, the orange sodium flare of the streetlamps hovered lowly in the heavy night sky.

He thought of his future, the one Ben had revealed to him. The limo, the young actress, the adoring fans, all the trappings of fame and fortune.

He believed it. He did. But it all seemed so far away from that moment in time. If *Oedipus* was the springboard, it was nine months away at the very least. How could he make himself happy about that? How, when it felt like a prison sentence? A weak panic sickened his system, like a low-grade fever.

His conversation with Suzy that night was oddly muted. Love-talk exchanged itself as usual, but it was half-hearted, automatic. He had no need to lie about work; she didn't ask. She sounded as preoccupied as he felt. He didn't ask why, but if he could have seen her in her Manchester hotel room, he would have understood.

Suzy was lying naked on a bed of fifties, watching the soft-porn channel on satellite and stroking herself. Dreave was in her head and he was no longer being a gentleman.

The mind of Conrad Dreave went to work. It worked thoroughly. It knew the contacts it had to make and it knew how to reach them. They had to believe in him; had to think they'd believed in him for many years. If it turned out they were not, after all, required, they would never know contact had been established. The mind of Conrad Dreave, waiting at the edge of their minds, would simply drop away.

But Conrad Dreave had to be ready if called upon to set up his business.

So his mind went out, calling cards at the ready.

It settled here, there, with him, with her, a vulture mind alighting as a black shadow, waiting on a soul's demise.

———◆———

5

Lake set off at four-thirty, Wednesday afternoon.

Chenies Street was a ten-minute walk. He shuffled through the death of another miserable day, darkness above him already, a dragging punchline to the swift joke of winter's daylight hours.

He almost wished his wardrobe had contained something bright.

Festive decorations hung and twinkled in shop windows: trees, baubles, gaudy gold encouragements for a 'Happy Christmas' and, looped across each shop window, seemingly fed through each shop wall, a mile of glittering tinsel. Christmas had not touched Lake since childhood. This year was no exception.

Lake was familiar with the Actors' Centre. It was entered through a bland door in a bare wall on Chenies Street, just around the corner from RADA. It occupied the third floor on the corner of Chenies Street and Tottenham Court Road. That the Actors' Centre was directly above the Reject Shop was, in Lake's opinion, one of life's little ironies.

He pulled open the door and trudged reluctantly upwards, then headed through the Centre's coffee shop to the audition rooms.

Behind a desk was a permanently smiling middle-aged woman who had mistakenly adopted the current young fashions in clothing and hairstyle. Lake gave his name, took a script, sat down and perused the part.

He was up for the lead. The auditions were running late; as always. Two other candidates sat in the waiting area, their faces crucially involved with the lines they read.

Some beaming young hopeful, evidently fresh from drama school, emerged from a room opposite, gushing drivel to an unseen director. Lake noted the lad's expression, an unscarred naïvety, but nothing the switchblade of bitter experience would not carve up a treat.

A minute passed and a young woman came out and checked on attendance with the list at the desk. She then called for the next actor, inviting him in with impossible jollity. Lake put his nose back into the archaic script, practically bored to tears by it already. After another minute he decided he would cock up the audition – come across all bolshy, or simply give an atrocious reading.

Then someone tapped his arm, and Lake inclined his head to the actor next to him.

'What do you think?' asked the actor, indicating his script and giving a conspiratorial wink.

Lake thought he'd found an ally. 'Give me an advert any day of the week.'

'*What?*' the actor whisper-shrieked. 'This is the core of our profession! This is where theatre began! If you don't want the part, why don't you go home and leave it to those of us who do?'

Lake couldn't answer that one. 'Because . . .' he began, but he had no idea why he was sitting there when he wasn't interested in the job.

Except, perhaps that was the lesson he had to learn. Assuming that he got the part, he would never be able to enjoy nine months of further obscurity – in fact, he'd hate every minute – but maybe if he refused to wilfully screw up the audition, he would be learning a great lesson in life: to make the most of a bad lot.

That had to be the answer.

Lake smiled. He had told Ben he would need only a week.

Ten minutes later, another name was called. Lake received a final withering look from the actor beside him, who then flounced indignantly across the floor and into the room.

For Lake, that moment was the clincher. No way would he be beaten by a bloody luvvie. He would be as nice as pie to the director and deliver the best reading of his professional life.

The audition-room door clicked shut and Lake began to study his script with fresh interest.

The part was his. He didn't want it, but it was his.

* * *

Lake badly needed a drink. As a final parting comment, Walton-Streckman had said, 'Thank you, Nathan. You'll hear very soon,' which was as close as any director ever came to letting on that the outcome would be favourable. Rejected individuals were left hanging for days, or weren't told at all. No news was almost always bad news.

Lake couldn't believe it. He had just consigned himself to nine months of living hell.

He really did need a drink. So he had ten.

By the time the landlord prised him from his barstool, Lake had forgotten where he was. Only outside in the street did he remember which pub he'd been in, and thus which direction was home.

He talked to himself as he made his way up Tottenham Court Road, weaving the entire width between gutter and shop front.

'Snot-nosed little toe-rag,' he mumbled, referring to the actor he'd had words with at the audition. 'Well, matey boy, I'm going to the top. Me. Nathan Lake. Not you. Me. And I'm having Oedipus. He's mine. You're not bloody having him. Dip-stick.' He smiled sickly. 'Seriously, though, folks, I'd like to accept this Olivier Award for my portrayal of Oedipus in memory of Ben, my mucker, who taught me . . . What are you bloody staring at?'

The couple in love at the bus-stop stopped looking at him.

'Where was I? Yes, my mucker, who taught me the value of brown-nosing and taking whatever shit comes my way, even if it does involve a whole nine months with a lot of insufferable luvvies. So I thank you, Ben. I have learned the lesson and now accept my place on the Light Path.'

He began laughing and continued to stagger home.

When the keyhole eventually kept still long enough to accept his latch key, Lake entered the building and climbed on all fours up to his flat. After another game of catch-the-keyhole, he stumbled into his living room and went to the kitchen sink for some water, but threw up before he could get his mouth round the tap.

Before crashing out on his bed, fully clothed, he had the foresight to switch on his answering machine. He'd be dead to the world tomorrow morning. Didn't want to miss Suzy calling to say she loved him, or Billy's call to confirm he had *Oedipus* in the bag.

* * *

35

There was no hope for the boy.

Conrad Dreave knew. He had seen it before. His prospective assignment would never learn the lesson. Not in two weeks. Not in a month. Not in a million years. And as Lake had originally requested one week, in taking him now, Dreave would be giving the boy only what he had truly desired.

The time had come.

From his palatial suite at the Dorchester, he made the telephone call to secure his new business premises, then really got down to business.

He closed his eyes and concentrated.

Near and far, far and wide, the mind of Conrad Dreave began breaking through to its chosen contacts, and their minds received it unawares.

He had stolen into their lives. They would think of him as an old acquaintance. When he bid them, they would serve his needs.

All to serve the needs of the newcomer.

Darkness.

Sleep was a black cavern and Lake slipped in quickly. He floated sightless through its blind passageways.

And the passageways were endless . . .

———◆·◆·◆———

6

. . . endless . . . endless.

Lake woke up crying. Such a profound sobbing. He recalled no dreams, no reason to cry, but the tears streamed nonetheless.

His alarm clock indicated one-twenty-six p.m. Outside his bedroom window the day was bright and blue. Strangely, he had no trace of a hangover.

As soon as his feet hit the carpet, he rushed into the living room. For some reason, he believed he could sense his telephone message light silently calling for attention.

He was right. Only it was positively screaming at him. He counted. Fourteen quick red flashes then a gap, then the same sequence. In one morning? He frowned. Was the machine on the blink, mechanically as well as literally?

Then wonderful understanding dawned in his eyes. He had learned the lesson and this was his reward. All the acting powers-that-be were backed up on that micro-cassette, queueing to bid for his services.

He started to laugh. He hadn't heard a single ring from his telephone. Hangover or not, he certainly had been dead to the world.

He touched replay. The machine beeped and began.

'This is Billy at five past eleven, Thursday morning. Well done, dear, you got *Oedipus*. Call me. Tatty-bye.'

Beep.

'Billy again at twelve-fifteen. It never rains . . . Interview for you. I'll give you the details when you call, but it sounds exciting. Tatty-bye and well done again on *Oedipus*.'

37

Beep.

'Hiya, darling, it's Suze. Call me after six at my hotel room. Can't wait to see you tomorrow. Love you, Nat. Bye.'

Beep.

'Nathan? Billy. Five-fifteen, Thursday afternoon. The Touring Company would like a decision. And don't let this other interview get away—'

Lake stopped the tape and his eyes shot to the wall clock, but he knew it was only lunchtime. What was the silly sod on about? *Five-fifteen?* He rewound a bit and replayed.

' . . . don't let this other interview get away from you. Call soonest, Nathan. Tatty-bye.'

Beep.

'Where've you got to, darling? Hope everything's OK. I'll be going to bed soon. Call before midnight or I'll speak to you when I get back to London. Lots of love. Bye.'

Lake stopped the tape again. He made a queerly annoyed face at the machine as though it was ridiculing him. *Going to bed soon? Midnight?* He let the tape continue to talk its nonsense.

Beep.

'Nathan? Billy. Friday lunchtime. The Touring Company want a decision by tonight. And ditto with that interview. Last day of seeing people is Monday. I might add, this is highly unprofessional of you. Anyway, dear, call soonest.'

The machine beeped and Lake sank to the carpet in the wake of a fear that tore his head apart and left him mentally paralysed.

'This is Billy, your nearly ex-agent. Nathan . . . what are you playing at? I've just had a call: *Oedipus* has gone. I said I'd call back on that television business by the latest five-thirty. You leave me in a very awkward situation. I'm sure you want it, but I'm not arranging interviews only to break them. You must call and confirm.'

Beep.

Lake began giggling insanely.

'It's me, Nat. I'm back in London. I'll call tonight. Love you.'

Beep.

'Nat, where are you? I'll come around tomorrow morning. Please be in. I want to spend the weekend with you. Love you.'

Beep.

'It's me. It's Saturday morning. I'm calling from a payphone around

38

the corner. I've just been buzzing your flat. Where are you? I hope I haven't done anything to upset you. I can't think of anything but . . . Oh, I'll try later.'

Beep.

'Nathan, don't treat me like this. This isn't fair. I'm sorry my situation's as it is, but I only asked for a bit of time. I thought you understood. Phil wants an answer from me and you're helping me decide against you. I'll call tomorrow, the last time, then it's up to you. I've spoken enough to this stupid machine.'

He stopped the tape.

He was going mad. It was simple. He was going mad. Yep. Sounded about right. He fluctuated between briefly feigned comprehension, longer spells of utter bewilderment, and extended stretches of maniacal giggling. Yep. He was going mad.

Going?

Gone. Going going gone. Ging gang gooligong going going gone. Absofuckinglutely.

Might as well hear the rest.

Beep.

'This is Billy. Remember me? Monday morning, Nathan. Well done. You've now lost *Oedipus* and the TV interview. Incidentally, that was for a BBC series. And guess what? Another two interviews have come in for you this morning. A film and a commercial. If you check this thing by the end of the day, call me. Otherwise, I'm killing the interviews and concluding our relationship. Sorry, but I don't think I need to chase clients to offer them work. You should be checking messages every few hours, even in a lull. You know how things can suddenly pick up. Anyway, I don't know why I'm bothering with the lecture, this is sheer irresponsibility on your part. Goodbye. Oh . . . if you've expired, I apologise for speaking ill of the dead, but if you do phone, anything short of that excuse won't cut the mustard.'

Nothing more from Billy. Wednesday had the weekly call from his parents, and a final curt message from Suzy.

'Nathan. I've said yes to Phil.'

Just then, the whole mental truth of it screeched to a halt in front of him.

He had asked for only one week and, as Ben had said, his every desire was now his for the asking.

The night of his *Oedipus* audition he had made his choice of paths, obviating the need for further contemplation. Thus he had slept right through his second week: Thursday, Friday, Saturday, Sunday, Monday, Tuesday, Wednesday. It was now Thursday morning. In name, the day after he lay down to rest. But it wasn't. It was a week later.

Hold on, Lake thought, that's nuts. A week's sleep? He'd be starving hungry by now, and he wasn't even peckish. His message tape had to be a clever practical joke. Had to be.

Yeah, clever. Very clever. Impossibly clever.

Shit.

He dashed from the flat, leaving his door and the building door wide open. As he ran, he kept thinking, *It's the sixteenth, the sixteenth. Today's the sixteenth. Yesterday was the fifteenth, so today's the sixteenth.*

Round the corner, in the newsagents, he grabbed the first daily paper to hand. The date on the front page announced itself like the chimes of Big Ben: THURSDAY, 23rd DECEMBER.

He rocked on his feet and dropped the paper back on the pile. He wanted to scream, but he was struck dumb.

His second week had passed. His path was set. His journey had begun.

Conrad Dreave stepped through the glassed entrance of Studio House on Wardour Street in the centre of Soho. Suzy welcomed him into the building. He was dressed impeccably, and identically to the last time they had met. As he kissed her hand, thoughts of Lake were instantly banished from her mind.

She waited politely as he took time to scan the reception area, a smile resting subtly on his lips. He clicked a heel down on the white marble floor and seemed gratified by the sound. He ran a long finger over the cream walls, faintly flecked with hairs of blue paint, and Suzy heard a sound of endorsement purr in his closed mouth. The uplighter wall lamps and tiny gold-rimmed spots in the high ceiling met with similar approval.

'The building echoes the class of its manager,' Dreave enthused in his silky, kaleidoscopic accent.

Suzy grinned sheepishly. She felt like a silly schoolgirl.

'Did you encounter any problems in freeing the basement for my occupation?'

'No, not at all. I hope you don't mind, but I told my client about your . . . your eyes, you know, how sensitive they are, and he was happy enough to oblige.'

'If you deemed that to be the simplest way, of course I do not object.'

'Christine,' Suzy said, addressing the receptionist, 'this is Mr Dreave, who'll be renting the basement for a time.'

No reaction whatsoever. In fact, nothing short of a nuclear cataclysm could have shaken Christine from her gawping awe of Conrad Dreave. It was a remarkable picture, Christine aroused. She was a pretty girl, a natural blonde, but she lacked confidence in the social world, and was ambivalent about sexual talk when she deigned to join an office booze-up.

Suzy tried again. '*Christine.*'

Dreave smiled benignly at the mesmerised receptionist. Suzy apologised for Christine's temporary loss of manners.

'No matter,' he told her. 'I am quite sure that Christine and I will be communicating with each other in no time. May I go downstairs now?'

'By all means, Mr Dreave.'

'Conrad.'

'Yes. Conrad. Please, follow me.'

Dreave was empty-handed: no briefcase, files, ledgers, nothing.

The basement was set in a square around the central lift and staircase that descended into it. The décor was the same as in the reception area, except that the floor was covered in light blue carpet tiles.

'Is this all right for you?' Suzy checked.

'Exactly as I pictured it, thank you, Suzy.'

'Is there anything I can get for you?'

'Nothing, thank you.'

'OK.' She produced a bunch of keys from her jacket pocket. 'Can I go through these with you?'

Dreave extended an open palm. 'I know about keys.'

'Er, OK.' She handed them over. 'The building doesn't have an alarm system for you to worry about—'

'I do not worry about alarms, Suzy. I know about alarms.'

She laughed nervously. 'Good. It's just that we don't have one because clients work different, sometimes late, hours. We'd have all sorts of problems if—'

'Ssshhh,' Dreave interrupted softly, but with power. 'I understand. If

I had wanted an alarmed building, that is what I would have sought.'

'Right, well, if you do have any valuables, we have a safe.'

'People do not steal from me.'

'Right.' She shifted on her feet. 'So, come and go as you please.' She knew she sounded too cheerful; freaked. She lowered her tone. 'And as requested, your telephone line is direct into the basement. Incoming calls will come straight through, but you need to—'

'Dial 9 for an outside number,' he finished.

'Yes, of course,' she said without really thinking, 'you know about phones.'

Dreave regarded her very seriously for a second, then a dazzling grin cracked his face. 'You have the measure of me already, Suzy.'

Somehow, Suzy doubted that very much. 'That's it then,' she said.

'You are most kind. And if I should want you?'

'Street-facing office at the end of the second-floor corridor. Or dial 21.'

'Splendid. And may I dim these lights?'

'Ah. They don't actually dim.'

He nodded, smiling. 'Yes, they do.' He didn't add that he knew about lights. He didn't need to.

She smiled at him. 'OK,' she said, then turned and slowly climbed the stairs.

God, Dreave was a funny one. She remembered the call he had made to confirm his booking – just after midnight Wednesday, one week ago.

Crazy. Who made business decisions at that time?

Once alone, Dreave focused his thoughts on the electrical circuitry hidden in the suspended ceiling above his head. The lights in the basement began to dim. At their lowest ebb of virtual darkness, he freed his mind from the task and removed his glasses. He pinched and rubbed the bridge of his nose, then moaned in appreciation of the gloom.

'Much better,' he said to himself.

There were two shopping days to Christmas. There should have been nine.

In Lake's missing week he had lost a job, a girlfriend, an agent and the best work prospects in nine years.

The chasm of loss he experienced was so deep, the voice crying from within was itself so lost it could not be heard. The truth of his world was so unreal it hardly registered.

His mind dealt with matters quietly, subconsciously, like an inner chamber of some secret courtroom deliberating on items of such weighty importance that the public could never know of them for its own protection.

The inner chamber discussed damage limitation.

Item One: Suzy. Gone. OK. Best treat the whole affair as just another bizarre dream.

Item Two: Agent. Gone. Bad. With the state of the business, how would he ever find another?

Item Three . . .

Item Three . . .

Apparently, Item Three was off the agenda. There was an Item Three, his mind knew that, but even the inner chamber of his secret courtroom would not presume to answer the question posed by it. Anyway, surely he'd precluded the question eight days ago, when he had resolved himself to succeed at the audition in spite of his objections. Yes. Which meant there was no question to answer any more. Right. No Item Three to discuss. However things had turned out with Suzy, Billy, the jobs, it would all be for the best. He wasn't a bad man. He could only walk a good path.

His mind flew ahead to his future: Hollywood assured. When he came back to himself, he was imbued with a new sense of calm. He felt incredibly powerful. It was nothing he had known before. It was not a physical energy, or the excitement of a mind high on personal dreams. It was just strong, as though no one could touch him any more to hurt him, mentally, emotionally, physically – no one would even dare contemplate such a thing; as though a higher authority had overseen his rite of passage to a better place.

He believed his future was bright, and the path which would lead him there was light.

Dreave sat in the dimmed atmosphere of his office. The door was shut. The blinds down the vertical glass pane at the side of the door were open. His glasses were off and his eyes were closed. His posture was correct and relaxed. Perfect Alexander Technique. He knew about Alexander Technique, even before Alexander.

His telephone chirped. He tapped the button for hands-free operation. 'Yes, Suzy?'

'Hi, this is –' A nervous cough. 'Settled in all right?'

'Yes, thank you. You wish to discuss payment of rent.'

There was a pause before Suzy answered. 'If you're not too busy.'

'Not at all. Pop down when it suits.'

'Right, thank you.'

Dreave tapped the phone dead, put on his black wrap-arounds and waited.

Suzy stopped at the top of the basement stairs. She pulled down her blouse so it hung neatly off her breasts, aware of what she was doing, then descended.

At the left-hand bend of the L-shaped stairs she stopped again. Below her, the basement was practically black.

However, as she gingerly took each of the lower steps, the light grew brighter, as though greeting her arrival.

Dreave was standing outside his office, waiting for her. 'Ah, Suzy,' he said.

She half-smiled; the other half was masked by a lack of understanding.

He led her into the office. 'I have a remote for the lights,' he explained, which did not explain how he knew she was arriving at that precise moment.

'I see,' she said.

He pulled out the top drawer and gave her an envelope. It was bulging. 'That is to cover this month's rent,' he said. 'But it is not a month's rent. The extra is for you, and there will be more to follow, I promise.'

'Thank you.'

'Mum's the word, remember?'

'Our official secret?' she punned.

'My kind of girl,' Dreave said. 'Scruples are so tedious, are they not? They only prevent us from taking what we know we really want. Now, I will allow you to spend a little over the festive season, but no large amounts. Just sufficient to cheer yourself up.'

He regarded her with a light smile. It was either kind or mocking, she couldn't tell.

'What do you mean?' she asked.

44

'I am afraid your suffering is easy to read.'

'I'm not suffering,' she lied. 'I've just got engaged as a matter of fact.' She knew she probably sounded too defensive.

'Then I am wrong and I apologise.' But he continued looking at her, pressuring her.

'No, I am suffering actually,' she admitted. 'I'm not marrying the right man. I thought I'd met the right man, but . . . I don't know what happened.' She perched on the edge of the desk, puzzled by her openness before a relative stranger.

He drew his chair out from the desk and sat in it, swivelling to face her, then walked it towards her and lay a hand on her thigh. 'Never fear, Suzy. You will work it out. In my experience, things always work out in the end. Do you believe me?'

She nodded rather than speak. An open mouth would have let out nothing but a moan; his warm hand on her thigh. She was wearing tights but wished she wasn't.

'Yes, you believe me, Suzy. You trust me.' He let go of her and tapped the envelope she held in her hand. 'We have our secrets, you and I. We can talk to each other, be honest. True?'

Another nod. She thought if he hadn't removed his hand from her thigh, she would have proved her openness; she would have taken it and urged it beneath her skirt. But from the cruel curl of his lips, she guessed he knew that already.

She moved unsteadily to the open office door. She smiled at him and nodded, blushing and frowning madly. She still couldn't trust herself to form any coherent sentence or even say goodbye to the man. She scurried away and up the stairs, and the light dimmed behind her.

On the second floor, she went straight to the loo and locked herself in. She tugged her skirt upwards and yanked down her knickers and did something she'd never before done at the office.

7

Christmas was a non-event for Lake.

As always, it was spent at his parents' large, ivy-covered house in Chislehurst, Kent, in the time-honoured way of the family get-together. As usual, they carried on the traditional seasonal business, and it was open house at the booze cabinet, but Lake felt apart from it all. His missing week was something of a nagging ache at the back of his mind, but it was not times past or opportunities missed that caused him to feel distant, it was the promise of times to come, and Christmas was an unwelcome stopover on his journey to that future. It was nothing more than an extended weekend; dead days masquerading in paper hats and tinsel as a time of lively celebration.

'Come on, Nathan. Open your presents,' urged Ronald Lake on Christmas Morning.

Lake looked at his father, a silver-haired gentle giant of a man, and managed a smile. He loved his dad, and was disturbed to feel so out of sorts at such a time, so he dutifully obeyed the instruction and proceeded to tear open a veritable mound of gifts, all labelled for his attention.

It seemed fairly clear to Lake why he was spoiled at Christmas and birthdays: it was a symptom of his father's profession. A surgeon for twenty-five years, he had to be acutely aware of the transient nature of life, how a person could slip away in an instant, and how each death left a gaping hole in a family just like his own.

At times, it seemed his father suffered more for Lake's lack of progress in his chosen career than Lake did himself. Lake wanted

47

desperately to tell both his parents that the good times were coming, but it seemed less hurtful to keep them in the dark than to make them feel sorry for his apparently continuing delusion.

So he feigned feeling under the weather, and went to bed early to avoid a tipsy, three-way heart-to-heart.

He returned to his flat after Boxing Day. His machine did not want to talk to him. No one called for the remainder of the year. Again and again, he went over in his mind the bizarre events preceding Christmas, and could only conceive that he had chosen correctly at the fork of the Paths.

The locked core of his mind stayed locked. With the light out. Airtight. So he continued to believe in the only notion that could keep him sane: a Bright Future along a Light Path.

New Year's Eve ended early, a little after ten-thirty. Sleep was ready for him, took him swiftly. He missed the chimes of Big Ben, didn't care; resolved nothing new for the coming year, was not inclined to; failed to celebrate another round of 365 days because he had no need to. Success was no longer in time; it was in him.

The New Year was nothing next to the New Lake.

Suzy spent a disturbed Christmas with her new fiancé, AFO Sergeant Philip Cage. AFO Cage was partly responsible for this upset, having to disappear in the afternoon of Christmas Day to work a shift, but Suzy was mostly to blame, and the disturbance was inside her own head.

Meeting Lake again had provided a measure of how lacking in true passion was her love for Phil.

Then there was Conrad Dreave. A queer fish who swam in a dark sea. He had the most profound effect on her of any man she had ever met, including Lake. When she was with him, she felt naked of soul and yearned to be naked of clothes. At home in the evening, she couldn't wait for the next morning to see him again. Her reaction to him was so real, so alive and exciting, her lust in his presence so animal, primeval, so alien in its intensity, that she thought she would scream inside for the loss of it when he eventually left the building for good.

Christmas was not a time for Conrad Dreave. Though its true origin was pagan, the festival was now too often commandeered by rather unsavoury elements. There could be no celebration for him.

It had not always been this way. He remembered times, places, in ages past, when he had not been constrained by his dark duties, when he had been a simple man. But simple men had access to evil as surely as any tyrant king, and there came a time when incessant evil in a soul was recognised, plucked out of time and set to work with an agenda.

Conrad Dreave knew. To LIVE was to face the dark mirror of EVIL.

And to have LIVED, sinfully, over and over, was to step through the mirror and become the reflection.

8

First working day of the New Year and lo, Lake wasn't working.

He wasn't worried, though. Ben had said, *Your call for help has been answered. Your future is now assured*, and his lost week was ample proof that Ben's words were not simply the hollow promise of a pointless dream.

However, that was the Light Path, and this was the Borough of Camden, and there were people out there who did worry that he wasn't working. Like the staff at the Unemployment Benefits Office, who would interrogate him again very soon concerning his inability to find regular work.

The whole business galled Lake. He didn't think there was anyone on this earth who wanted to work more badly than he did. He never stopped sending his details out to casting directors, and the photographs weren't cheap. But the staff at the UBO were no longer interested in his futile quest to become a famous actor. He had been told umpteen times that long-term employment was the goal, in whatever form it came. The message was: forget acting.

Accordingly, Lake searched the papers and wrote off for all manner of jobs. Why not? He figured at thirty years of age with no work experience outside the one profession, he wasn't in much danger of being offered anything. Only now the staff at the UBO couldn't argue with him. He was fulfilling their requirements. Occasionally they stuck him on a government course, supposedly to help but more, he suspected, as a form of punishment. The aim was to get him on to another course, this time vocational, and hence off the unemployment figures. Lake

51

deemed it utter madness that while he was being forced towards joinery or teaching or bricklaying, there were people on his very course, qualified in those very professions, who had hardly worked in years.

Nonetheless, he had to play the game, so he picked up his *Evening Standard* and sat down with it, knowing exactly the sort of thing he would find inside. Perhaps he was becoming an old cynic, but the wording of the adverts never ceased to amaze him. *Applicant must be highly motivated and have a keen interest in all aspects of corrugated plastic mouldings technology.* Yeah, right. *Wanted: Sewage Worker. Must have a keen interest in shit.*

He opened the paper and leafed through, stopping to look at the Larson cartoon. Two devils in hell were looking with evident disappointment at one of their lost souls, who was going about his hellish chores whistling a happy tune, oblivious to his surroundings. One devil was saying to the other, 'You know, we're just not reaching that guy.'

Lake smiled and flicked through to find the Situations General section of the Employment pages. He didn't get that far. Instead, a full-page advert caught his attention.

Lake could hardly credit the words he read:

LONG-ESTABLISHED AGENT TO THE STARS
SEEKS UNDISCOVERED TALENT.
TO JOIN CONSTELLATION
CONTACT:

CONRAD DREAVE
STUDIO HOUSE
WARDOUR STREET
LONDON W1

Surely this was it. To be first in the queue, he ran all the way there.

The days since Christmas had been dark and wet. Daylight never managed to completely make it into the sky. It clawed upwards at its appointed time but with only a half-hearted effort – a grey diluted night.

Lake stood on the pavement outside Studio House. His chest heaved from his exertions, and sweat trickled uncomfortably beneath his clothes in the damp, cold atmosphere. His face was hot, slick with perspiration.

Drab figures passed by, collars high, hats low, side-stepping, avoiding, courses set, noticing nothing. Traffic flowed weakly along the street, like diseased blood through clogged arteries.

His eyebrows felt icy. He took an old tissue from his pocket and blotted the chill beads of sweat from beneath the fine hairs. After a minute his pores began to close.

He pressed the intercom. There was a click, then a female voice.

'Yes?'

'I'm here to see Conrad Dreave.'

'OK, come in.'

The door buzzed and Lake entered. He approached the receptionist, but before he could ask her to inform Conrad Dreave of his arrival, an oddly accented voice swam across the reception area.

'I am Conrad Dreave.'

Lake spun around. Conrad Dreave was a sight to behold. He should have been in the movies himself.

'And who might you be?' Dreave inquired.

'Nathan Lake. I'm here about the advert.'

'Of course you are.' Dreave approached and forced a handshake.

Lake experienced nothing untoward. He felt simply an assurance, a sense of relief at having found someone to help.

'Come down to my offices,' Dreave said, opening out a pressed cream arm in the direction of the stairs.

'Thanks.'

Lake followed Dreave, and he had the oddest idea that the basement grew lighter as he descended into it.

'Take a seat,' Dreave said as he sat behind his desk. He hadn't closed the door. Lake suspected this was not a man who needed the protection of a door against interruptions.

It was a large office, clean and light, with cool, pale blue walls. Immediately apparent was the absence of normal business paraphernalia: no computer, no files, no folders, no desk clutter – apart from a solitary telephone, the desk was bare of objects. Lake looked back at Dreave and had a brief moment of fear that he was in the presence of a man even more deluded than himself.

Dreave pulled open a drawer in his desk and brought out a Milk Can and a tall glass.

53

'Coffee or tea?' Dreave asked.

'No, thanks.'

'Well, do excuse me.' He opened the old-style ringpull and tore it off, slipping it onto the little finger of his right hand, like a cheap novelty trinket. He poured out the drink and took a long draught, then produced a cream handkerchief and dabbed at the corners of his mouth. Lake hated such affectation, and Dreave's dark glasses were beginning to annoy him.

Dreave inclined himself towards Lake and said, 'I want you to be clear at the outset, Nathan. I am in a position to advance your career like no one else. You are ready for that career advancement, but you must take me seriously. You see a man in dark glasses in a cream suit and you have doubts that I am anything more than just another pretender. You see another ridiculous figure in a ridiculous profession. True?'

'No, no, it's not . . . um, I'm just—'

'You are just another loser, Nathan. You are a deluded fool in a profession full of them. You have no future in a world where futures do exist, and for the lack of that future you will die a sad and unfulfilled old man.'

Lake felt tears brim. 'What?' he said very softly, then found a voice. '*What?* How *dare* you speak to me like that. You don't know me from Adam, you big cream fuck.' He stood up and the chair fell over behind him, but as much as he wanted to walk away, he couldn't move.

Then Dreave began smiling, and laughing, and began to applaud, and it seemed to Lake that it was all sincere, that it was not further ridicule. He sat down, and landed on the floor where his chair had been, and started snivelling.

'Get up, Nathan.' Dreave's voice drifted over the desk and down to him like a magic waterfall to soothe his pain. 'For the last time in your life, find the strength to get up, and I promise you will never fall again.'

Lake wiped his face and pushed himself off the floor. He righted his chair and sat down. 'You're wrong,' he whispered, 'what you said.'

'I know.'

'But—'

'I need you to believe in me, Nathan. I was only making the point that what we see is never all there is to see. Underlying all we see is a deeper meaning: the truth. You have lost, but you are not a loser. And you have failed, but you are no failure. In the same manner, how I appear to you is not my essence. Do not take it as such. I am not a self-obsessed agent who spends more time on my wardrobe than my work. I am not concerned with image, certainly not my own. I am deadly serious where work is the issue. Others can make of me what they will. And there is, believe me, a very good reason for my dark glasses that has nothing to do with idiot notions of what is, shall we say, *cool*. I have an intolerance to light. It is a rare but . . . grave affliction.'

Lake said nothing.

Dreave went on, 'I see in you what you know to be within yourself. Your defence, while not exactly eloquent, was forceful, but only right if you are to attain the heights. So you believe in yourself. Good. But if I am to work for you, you must also believe in me. If not, you will not do as I say, and that is essential. Will you agree to do as I instruct?'

Lake felt hope bloom inside him and when it reached his skin, it appeared as goose bumps and he nodded. It seemed he had been taken on, though Dreave had not seen a curriculum vitae or anything more than the tantrum of an unemployed actor.

'Good for you,' Dreave told him. 'Really. That is very good for you. The reason I ask is that my methods are somewhat unconventional. Does that disturb you?'

'As long as they work, I'll have no problem with them.'

'They most certainly work, Nathan. There are people living in the most luxurious houses Beverly Hills has to offer, earning the highest sums Hollywood can afford, who can vouch for my methods. Of course, my modesty and their privacy forbid my revealing their identities, you understand?'

'Oh, yes. No, I understand. But . . . what is it you do that other agents don't?'

'Hmm. The best I can do is liken it to insider-trading in the stock market.'

Of course, that did not help Lake's understanding one bit, but he still said, 'Aah, right,' as though it had.

'Now, to what you must do.' Dreave stood up from his desk and began pacing leisurely around the office. Lake sat up straight in his chair. 'After you receive instructions to go for an interview, you must first prepare yourself. This you must do in the following fashion. If the interview is for, say, the role of a soldier, you must seek out a serving member of the army and talk with him. Is that clear?'

'It's like the Method, then? Stanislavsky and all that?'

'Only on the surface,' Dreave said, circling behind Lake, his cream suit swishing softly. 'For one thing, the Method requires you to ask questions of your subject. That is not necessary. As the instinctive actor I suspect you to be, you need only *meet* with your subject to gain what you require. Your subconscious will retain the vital insights that will inform your mind and body in interview and cause you to create the impression in the subconscious of the interview panel that you possess the exact qualities they are looking for.'

'Wow! What? You mean they'll see me as a soldier if all I've done is *meet* a soldier? Just said hello?'

'Precisely, Nathan.'

'Is it some new thinking from America?'

'Down under, actually.'

'Oh, right, Australia.' With eager eyes, Lake fixed his new agent, who was settling back in his chair. 'So I just try to meet someone who does the same thing as my character?'

'You do not try, Nathan, you succeed. Because if you do not succeed, you can forget the interview, safe in the knowledge that you would not have succeeded there either.'

'Yeah, sorry, right.'

'And, Nathan, you must always shake hands when you arrive and depart. That is essential. Always shake hands, Nathan. Always. A long, firm handshake. Trick of the trade. Remember that. Physical contact. Silent communication. Do you understand?'

Lake nodded. Of course he didn't understand.

Dreave smiled at his new client. 'For my part, I will now put all my energies into the process of . . . insider-trading, and I shall be talking to you presently. If you could give me your telephone number.'

Lake reeled it off. Dreave did not write it down, but Lake felt sure it was safe inside that strikingly handsome blond head.

Damn, if he hadn't known better, Lake would have thought he was sexually attracted to the man.

'Splendid.' Dreave finished his glass of milk, then rose to his feet in a majestic lengthening.

It was time for Lake to leave. He stood up, and a question popped into his head. 'Er, just out of interest, how many clients do you have on your books?'

Dreave began visibly thinking, counting. After fifteen seconds, Lake's heart began to sink. If there were that many, how attentive could Dreave be to any one of them?

Then Dreave's perfect features snapped into sudden realisation. A joke expression. He tutted. 'How silly of me. There is only you, Nathan.'

'Only me?'

'I am not in this for the money, Nathan. I have no need of money. I will take no commission from your work. I will only take pleasure in seeing a deserving soul elevated to greatness. You have my undivided attention. I will think only of you.'

Again, Lake felt a slight sexual tug, and was a little disturbed that it didn't bother him unduly.

'So –' Dreave extended his right arm.

A long, firm handshake. That was the way. Lake grinned, and grasped Dreave's smooth hand, squeezing firmly. Dreave responded in kind, a crushing grip.

The childish excitement in Lake's grin flickered and was gone, chased away by a split second of uncertainty, followed by a lengthy distortion of pain. Something had sliced into his palm. He yelped and tried to pull his hand away. Dreave didn't loosen his grip; in fact, he seemed momentarily to tighten it.

'*Aaah, let go!*' Lake cried, and suddenly had the answer: the curled aluminium tear of the ringpull which had been in Dreave's palm was now well and truly in his.

Dreave opened his hand and Lake jumped away, inspecting the wound, which was welling with blood. It was only a small cut, but it stung like hell, and Lake shivered inside, sensing he had somehow been deeply violated.

'What have I gone and done now?' Dreave chided himself. 'Let me see.'

Without hesitation, like a child called to mummy, Lake came to him and held out his palm, and Dreave took a gentle hold of it. Lake could not see the offending piece of metal on Dreave's finger or anywhere else. His dumb face turned up and questioned his agent, but of course there were no answers to be gleaned from a face devoid of eyes.

Dreave produced his cream silk handkerchief. He put it to his lips and touched a spot of milky saliva onto the material, then dabbed gently at the bloody cut.

That Lake had not uttered a single word of objection now became oddly apparent to him, but far from feeling like withdrawing from Dreave's influence, he felt something very much like gratitude towards the man; a creeping, slithering gratitude that verged on the worshipful.

Dreave closed Lake's hand around the handkerchief and Lake held it tightly, gratefully.

'You are with me now, Nathan Lake,' Dreave said so quietly it almost wasn't real. 'And I am for you.'

Lake was still wrestling with his insane desire to thank Dreave.

Thank Dreave? For cutting him, causing him pain, making him bleed, delivering alien saliva into an innocent blood? Thank Dreave for that?

'Thank you,' Lake said.

Christine watched Mr Lake leave. She thought of saying goodbye but decided against it. He looked as though he wouldn't hear if she did speak, or care if she didn't. What had happened downstairs to make him look so vacant? It was a mystery.

But she was more than intrigued by the basement world of Mr Dreave, she was besotted with the man himself. He gave her feelings she had never known before. She didn't have a boyfriend at that moment, and had little experience of the opposite sex, and certainly not *that* type of experience, but she was lately filled with strange urges. She would every so often catch herself rubbing gently between her legs. She'd feel ashamed but carry on anyway, until some other task diverted her attention. Then without realising, she'd wind up doing it again. It wasn't right. She was proud to be pure at twenty-five, and wanted to remain so until the right man came along, but each dispatch rider who came in with a parcel was ever closer to getting himself raped. She had never been more sexually alive, or more brightly aware of the dark denial inside her.

The reception telephone disturbed her thoughts and she answered.

'Yes, that's right, sir,' she said. 'Would you like me to send you a fact pack?'

Once again her free hand absently crept across her thigh and down.

'Of course you can come in and look around, sir. If you'd like to give me a time that's good for you.'

She busied her naughty hand with the appointments book.

'That's fine, sir, no problem. Look forward to seeing you then. Bye.'

She replaced the receiver and thought that was another unexpected turn of events: the amount of interest suddenly flooding in from companies wanting to rent in Studio House. If even just half moved in, it would fill the building, and save the company.

Suzy returned from lunch just after two p.m. She checked with Christine before going up to her office.

'Anything for me?' she asked.

'Interest from four more companies just while you've been out,' Christine told her. 'I don't know what's going on.'

'The dole office recedes,' Suzy said with a relieved smile.

'Let's hope.'

'Anything happening with the man downstairs?' Suzy asked, trying to sound casual.

'Why?'

Suzy picked up a defensive tone in Christine's curt response, and gave her receptionist a quizzical look. 'Because I'm asking,' she said, slightly on her dignity.

'Someone came by to see him.'

'What about?'

'How should I know?' Christine snapped.

'Christine, I'm just asking.' Suzy studied her receptionist's expression, a mix of fluster and guilt. 'I'll come back when you're in a better mood. Can I have my appointments book?'

Christine closed the thick desk diary and thrust it at her boss.

Suzy said, 'I hope you're not this miserable on the phone.'

'Sweetness and light,' Christine chirped facetiously.

Suzy backed away from the reception desk, scowling at her underling, and took the lift to the second floor.

Sealed in her office, she sat down and closed her eyes. In stillness and silence, the restlessness inside her became almost a physical wash coursing from head to toe. It had plagued her for days now. An erotic desire, to be in nothing more than a G-string on the most exotic beach, under the most caressing sun. Alone until the man of her dreams strolled up. Then, without words, they would go to a beach house where the breeze flapped gently inside lace curtains across bedroom doors that opened onto the beach. And there on cool white sheets they would dispense with their triangles and lie naked, stroking and kissing, until the time came when they would couple and become one. Hours they would take. Days. Dozing and waking and making love.

Her yearning was so intense, and she had to admit to herself that love need not come into it. Love, in fact, could only complicate the simplicity of their pleasures. Making love sounded nice, but it was a euphemism. All she really wanted was some great sex that lasted as long as she desired it to. Her mind placed her in a beach house – the idyll – but she would have taken it across the office desk if that was the way it came.

The first call brought his phone to life almost as soon as Lake had left the office.

Dreave answered. 'Conrad Dreave speaking.'

The content of the call was no more than he had expected. A casting director who believed she had been acquainted with him for years was casting a new series and required a male lead. Dreave knew that if Lake followed instructions, he would be able to fill any role, but Dreave regretfully informed his interested party that at the present time there was no one available to fit the character breakdown.

Conrad Dreave knew. There was a fast track in every business and a fast train to run along it. Simple fear of missing out caused most to take the first available transport. Movement of some sort, however slow, could always be justified by looking back at those who were still stationary.

Lake clearly wanted to hop aboard a fast train, and those on a straight-line express always overtook those who had left earlier on a slow train down a winding track.

So Dreave turned down the offer.

And the next one.

They would always call again if they happened across the exact job Dreave required for the newcomer. They would always call. As long as he needed them. They had no choice. Their minds were not free to discount him. The virus of Dreave's own mind was in them.

9

Robert Trapes, Senior Claimant Adviser, met his final claimant advisee in the form of Nathan Lake. Robert Trapes was not due to retire that day. He was not actually due to retire for another twenty years.

He enjoyed his work. That was a rare thing these days. Work was rare, but enjoyment of work was rarer still. The first led to the second, of course, as claimants had to ultimately take what was offered. Enthusiasm for any given job was a sham display of exaggerated smiles, half-truths and downright lies.

It had never dawned on him that he was unsuited to his own job, but he was, desperately so.

In truth, he didn't want his claimants to find work. In fact, familiar faces made his day. It was pure joy to him that he was working and they were not. Of course, the quirks and bullies of childhood that had set him on such a mean path had been put from his mind. He ruled the playground now and the football was always his.

Occasionally, Trapes's euphoria was skewered by a claimant like Nathan Lake. An individual's conviction of his own true vocation in life was anathema to Trapes. It smacked of a freedom of choice he had never known, nor thought fair. Perversely, Trapes did want Lake to find work: bar work, shop work, warehouse work, or any damn work that wasn't what he felt he *had to do.*

Trapes had felt himself winning with Lake over the past year or two. The actor's conviction was crumbling, his vocational commitment dulled by the dole. Basically, the actor wasn't acting.

So it was quite a shock to see Lake's expression as he walked through the door. Certainly it was a major disappointment. Trapes watched from his desk as Lake sat in the waiting area. He seemed taller, even seated. There was no despondent slouch.

As Trapes peeked over a mound of paperwork, Lake met his eyes and shone at him. That was how Trapes saw it, a shine more than a smile, and he did not respond. His eyes flicked left, right, down. What was the little bastard up to? Was he working secretly? Breaking the law? Violating rights that Trapes felt were wrong anyway?

He'd have him, never fear.

Lake had forgotten his Restart interview. His mind was elsewhere. It had been a week since his meeting with Dreave. His mind had been in Hollywood, Monte Carlo, Rio, living the high life on the back of his success, amidst magnificently brainless people who all hankered after breathing in the air he had just exhaled; a story they would tell their grandchildren.

Doubt about his new agent or his own future had not entered his head. Dreave would call soon. But, daft as it was, Lake simply couldn't wait to hear his voice. The swimming mix of syllables and stresses, words weaving through the air, each sentence a melting of so many sounds, impossible and perfect, evocative and dreamlike.

So he decided to call. It was as though he craved a hit, as though Dreave was the name of a designer drug that came direct down a phone line. Lake would call and simply exchange niceties for a while. Dreave would understand. It was similar to calling home. He didn't need a reason to speak to his family, and all Lake's senses told him he had indeed joined a family, with Dreave at its head. A surrogate super-dad.

Although Lake had not thought to ask for Dreave's telephone number, he guessed it must have been included in the full-page advert which had first alerted him to the man's presence in town.

He pulled out the uppermost *Evening Standard* from the pile and opened it on the floor. In so doing, he noticed his right palm, how the small cut he had received in Dreave's office that day still hadn't healed. It remained slightly gaping, refusing to knit together.

Ah, forget it, he thought. It's not fatal.

He returned his attention to the newspaper and began turning pages. He passed the Larson cartoon of the two devils, and went through to the Employment section.

It was then that he was reminded of his Restart interview. Today. Imminent.

Lake walked briskly along the Euston Road to the Unemployment Benefits Office and arrived with a minute to spare. He spied Trapes hunched behind the paper mountains of the kingdom of Big Desk. When he had settled in a chair to wait, Trapes's large hooded eyes sought him out, only to panic and dive for cover when confronted by one of Lake's beamiest grins.

Trapes was a good sixty pounds overweight. He broke into a sweat filling out a form. Desk to filing cabinet and back made him huff. Lake thought something had turned inside with Trapes and gone bad. He was not an easy man to like, not appearing to like much himself, except food. He taunted Lake, not directly, but by taking the lowest common denominator and treating everyone on that level, he showed respect to no one. And respect, self-respect, was one thing the unemployed had a running battle to keep alive.

Well, today Lake had an abundance of self-respect, self-confidence, positive self-image. Things had changed. He was with Dreave now, and Dreave was for him.

'Lake!'

Trapes's wheezy bark slapped Lake's ears like an insult. He ignored it.

'Lake!'

Lake wanted to be an obedient little claimant, get up and answer his name, but somehow the name wasn't right, so he sat there ignoring Trapes in spite of himself.

'Lake!'

It was his name, he wanted to respond, but the name wasn't right. He sat still, questioning his refusal to move, and not understanding.

'*Mr Lake!*'

Ah, that was it. The magic word: *Mister.* Respect.

Lake looked at Trapes and cocked a thumb at his own chest. Me? Do you mean me?

A beetroot face nodded once, jangling jowls, then dropped down behind the paper mountains like a livid sun.

'Did you not hear your name?' Trapes asked as Lake sat down.

'I left school a long time ago, Mr Trapes.'

'Pardon?'

'They called me Lake at school. Now they call me Mr Lake.'

'To your claim,' Trapes moved on quickly, opening a bulging file.

Lake could barely submerge a grin. His own last words had tickled him and he didn't know why.

Trapes mumbled gravely to himself.

Of course. Sidney Poitier. They call me *Mr* Tibbs. The grin surfaced.

Trapes winced. 'Mr Lake, have you been working?'

'No.'

'No?'

'No. Why?'

'You seem happy.'

'My apologies. I must make an effort to be more miserable.'

Trapes squinted. 'Mr Lake, your work record is appalling.'

'It's not great, is it? But it won't be long now.'

'What?'

'Work, success, money, fame,' Lake replied seriously. 'All that. Then you'll never see me again, except on telly or at the cinema.'

Trapes sighed heavily. 'We agreed, did we not, last time you were here, that you would look at all areas of work. Yet you still persist in pursuing this acting business. Why?'

'I'm an actor.'

'But you're not,' Trapes told him, leaning forward meaningfully until his belly met and spilled over the desk. 'You only want to be. You don't actually act. I might want to be Prime Minister but I don't go around telling people I *am* Prime Minister.'

Lake made no reply. He stared down at his lap, struggling to rein in his temper.

'Mr Lake?'

Concentration made a response impossible. Something wanted to rise up inside him, and he was resisting it. Some force he had never known before was massing its ranks within him. It was at the same time wondrously liberating and absolutely frightening. Not yet, he told himself, not yet. But what he spoke to was alien, and would it understand? He breathed slowly, deeply for a time.

When he looked up at Trapes, Lake could have sworn he saw a flicker of gleeful anticipation in his eyes, as though he were just waiting to push a bit further and crack his claimant.

When Trapes carried on, Lake knew he was right. Trapes was really pushing, and Lake could guess what he was about to say and how he would phrase it. From his previous encounters with the man, Lake realised the adviser lived by a credo: tell them what you're going to tell them, tell them, then tell them what you've told them. For the truly clueless, it was presumably a great aid to enlightenment. For anyone else, it was simply insulting.

'What I am going to suggest, Mr Lake, is that you endeavour to find work in areas other than acting. So, I think it would be a good idea if you now started to look seriously for employment in other areas, not acting. OK, so that's my advice: have a look at other areas of work outside the acting profession.'

Even though none of this surprised him, Lake still had to bow his head once more and battle the force within him for a second time. It seemed unconnected to rational thought, and although the rising did halt its ascent, it took several moments to do so, as though considering whether to obey.

Lake shook his head in weary agitation as he felt the power sink inside him.

'Mr Lake, are you listening to me?'

The rising stirred, and Lake looked up and spoke fast to interrupt its momentum. 'How long did you train for your job, Mr Trapes?'

'Pardon?'

'How long? Your training? A month? A week? A day?'

'The issue here is n—'

'Three years I trained,' Lake cut in. 'Three years. I beat over two thousand people to get into RADA, and I was naïve. I thought I'd made it there and then. I mean, you beat two thousand people, you think you're on your way. But you're not. It's a foot in the door, and the people on the inside are mostly deaf unless *daddy's in the business*. You can spend ten, twenty years banging away, hoping someone will open up, even if it's just to tell you it'll never happen so you can go off and do something else. But no one does, because there's always a chance—'

Trapes interrupted. 'Would it help if *I* told you you'll never make it?'

Lake fumed. He sensed the strange power inside was very close to revealing itself. 'It wouldn't, no, because I will make it, and when you're still sitting here in twenty years' time – if you're not already dead from a massive coronary – and I'm rich and famous in Hollywood, you just remember this conversation.'

Trapes, his forehead glistening, smiled openly. He picked up a pen and began to scribble something in Lake's file, speaking while he wrote.

'Mr Lake, I want to see you again in a month. At that time I expect to see proof that you have followed my instructions to the letter in the form of correspondence from employers you have approached. My instructions are as follows, and I will write them down for you: first, visit the job centre at least three times a week, arranging interviews; check local papers for opportunities, writing for interviews; and approach local businesses on spec with a view to employment *of any kind*.' The last three words could not have been given more emphasis had Trapes come round the desk and bellowed them into Lake's ear.

He continued, 'I am going to tell you that if I am not a hundred per cent satisfied with your job-search activities a month from now, I will recommend immediate cessation of your income support, with whatever ramifications that might have *vis-à-vis* your housing benefit. So, you should make a supreme effort in the next month to impress upon me your willingness to accept employment in *any* area. So, let us both be quite clear on your course of action—'

'I fucking *heard*! Jesus.'

They were the last words Lake spoke to Robert Trapes. The rising in him would not be denied again. And Lake thought, fine, I've had just about enough of this crap.

Trapes ranted on. 'Mr Lake, it is not my fault that you have failed at your chosen profession, and I *will* not tolerate your attitude any longer. I shall be recommending immediate cessation of your income support—'

Lake heard nothing more. The rising blew up inside him like a nuclear explosion, a gently billowing expansion that belied the power at its core. At its peak, in his vision, was a red mist.

Lake experienced a paradoxical calm as he locked eyes with Trapes; at what he sensed was the instant of his most extreme power, ever, his mind was quiet, removed. Behind Trapes could have stood an army, it would have meant nothing.

In Lake's eyes, Robert Trapes saw it clearly. Death. The eyes before him were devoid of life. But they were not dead. Dead eyes held nothing. Lake's eyes held pure malevolence. The pupils seemed swollen to a blackness that filled the sockets. Not lifeless, but undead. Empty of compassion. Beyond recall to a sentient soul.

Instantaneous, body-filling, orifice-opening, exquisite, complete and ultimate fear took Trapes mid-sentence. His mouth remained slightly open, framing a word that would never emerge; not against Mr Lake, never against *Mr* Lake.

The visual source of Trapes's fear lay in Lake's eyes, but the effect was pervasive. From every molecule in and around Trapes, fear was erupting like a cancer. He had no control to break away.

At the bottom of his vision he was dimly aware of his right hand moving raggedly at something. His left-hand palm ached dully, as though an immense pain there was suffused through drugs.

Still the eyes held him. Undead. Black. Unfeeling.

After a few lifetimes, his right hand stopped moving. He lifted his left palm and turned it to face Lake, but it had no effect.

With a simpering little smile on his face, Trapes began to sob. He wasn't being understood, and it wouldn't end until he was. He looked at his palm. Cut into the skin by the point of his office biro were childish markings, growing more indistinct beneath the blood that was now flowing freely, drenching Lake's file on his desk.

Too much red. Too much blood.

He wiped his palm across his sobbing face, then checked again. The letters were clearer, but the blood would drown their meaning all too soon, and he wanted this to be over. He returned his open palm to Lake. The expression on his dark-smeared face begged comprehension from his last ever claimant.

Somewhere behind Lake, a woman made a sharp noise and began screaming. Quickly, other expressions of horror filled the office. Trapes's name was called several times, but the callers were outside it all and neither Trapes nor Lake paid any attention.

A sliver of Lake's vacated mind came back and focused through his red mist on the letters in Trapes's palm. Just as he got their meaning, Trapes spoke it softly across the desk like a final prayer for a redemption long gone.

'Sorry.'

Trapes had ripped the word SORRY into his skin. The point of the biro had not completed each letter, popping out here and there, but once seen, the apology was clear.

'Sorry,' Trapes muttered again. 'Sorry.' Then he put the back of his injured hand down into the dark, spattered pool on his desk, and with the point of his biro he ended his apology, and his working life, with a full stop punctured deep into his palm after the letter Y.

As he walked slowly down Euston Road, Lake experienced a kind of waking up. The incident with Trapes was clear in his mind, there was no blank space of forgetting, but he had not been involved, not the Nathan Lake he had known for the past thirty years; he had taken a back seat to someone else.

The morality of it all was smudged, indistinct. He had been treated badly and something within him had reacted against it. All in all, it seemed a fair exchange.

For a solid hour after returning to his flat, Lake sat in quiet contemplation of the afternoon's main event. One moment he felt guilt and revulsion, the next a kind of ecstatic pride in his achievement. He wasn't comfortable with either. Was this a part of the baggage he would have to carry on the journey down his Path? He wished Ben was there to explain. He wished there was at least someone who might hear his tale and not judge him for it.

Distraught, he looked down at the carpet.

Lying open on the floor was a copy of the *Evening Standard.*

Now what was that doing there? He couldn't think. Too much on his mind.

Dreave. Of course. Dreave's advert.

He sat up straight, then pushed off the sofa and knelt down.

Dreave would listen to him. He seemed like a worldly man, a wise soul. If there was any sense to what Trapes had done, Dreave might be the person to see it; coolly, rationally, non-judgementally.

Get his number, Lake thought. Give him a call. Tell him everything.

Lake turned one page, then another and another.

The advert would not be easy to miss. A full page.

But miss it he did.

He returned to the centre of the paper and began again. Slowly, he turned one page after another, rubbing them between his fingers in case two had stuck together.

Nothing. At the Sports section he closed the paper and turned it over to start again. This time he scanned every page, still fingering each edge to check it was a single leaf. He arrived at the back page.

Once more through, checking page numbers. All consecutive.

And no advert.

'My! You have had an interesting time today!' Dreave said happily, receiving his one and only client. 'Sit down and do tell!'

Dreave finished pumping Lake's hand, released it and went to settle in his chair. He was beaming from ear to ear.

Lake didn't move, stunned by Dreave's accurate perception.

'Sit! Sit!' Dreave commanded, dripping with eagerness.

Lake did so, then quickly stood up again. The atmosphere was too highly charged. He began moving from foot to foot, twisting his hands together, searching for the right words to begin.

'What happened today?' seemed as good as any.

'What happened today?' Dreave repeated.

'Yes.'

'I am sure I have no idea.'

'Well, what did you mean about an interesting time?'

'Your state is immediately apparent, Nathan.'

'What state?'

'I have no idea.'

'Oh. Do I look odd to you?'

'You look radiant.'

'Radiant?'

'You are sparkling, Nathan, shining at the world, and it is not before time.' Dreave smoothed his right hand over a crease in the cream material of his left arm. The crease evaporated into the cloth; gone.

Neither spoke for some seconds before Lake deposited himself in his chair and said, 'I hurt someone today.'

'Come, I doubt that is the truth.'

'I did.'

'Then I should call the police, should I not?' Dreave suggested, moving in his chair to be nearer the telephone.

'No, I – I did nothing wrong,' Lake said, confusing himself with his own reply.

Dreave sighed deeply. 'Then why be concerned?'

'Well . . .'

'Tell me,' Dreave urged.

So Lake recounted the business at the benefits office as he stared blankly at the edge of the desk before him. When he every so often lifted his eyes to look at Dreave, he sensed the blond man already knew every detail. Dreave had no reaction, audible or visible, to the story as it unfolded, although Lake realised that outside the pages of a splatter novel the whole thing was totally outrageous. Dreave should at least have shown a ripple of disgust at Trapes's self-mutilation, if not a flicker of doubt as to the truth of the tale. But, by his utter non-reaction, Dreave might have been asleep, especially as Lake couldn't even tell whether his eyes were open.

Lake ended his story with a question: 'Have you done something to me?'

'I beg your pardon?'

'I don't know. I'm sure I couldn't have done it a few days ago, before I met you.'

Dreave sat back in his chair and laced his fingers under his chin. Though his eyes were hidden, the impression Lake received was one of intense scrutiny.

Then Dreave spoke, the beguiling accent whirlpooling once more. 'There is more than we see, Nathan. I told you so when first we met. You are currently in the process of claiming your rightful inheritance. In so doing, you release the natural power within yourself. It is well known that some favoured individuals can move objects telekinetically or communicate telepathically. But as to whether I have given you such abilities . . . the notion is preposterous. That a latent power has been awoken in you is altogether a different proposition, although its origin remains within you. If I have offered encouragement which has in any way sparked your deeper awareness, I am glad to have been of service. But really, Nathan, what do you take me for? A wizard? A warlock?' Dreave chortled at his own suggestions, and it was only a grudging effort that forced Lake to respond in kind.

'I don't know,' Dreave said. 'The artistic imagination.'

Lake's head was downcast, his body slumped in the chair. He was desperately confused. Why was Dreave lying? Because he was, through his perfect white teeth. And there was something else not quite right – what was it?

'Oh, yes, Conrad, you know the advert that wa—'

'Goodbye, Nathan.'
'But, you see, it's not—'
'Goodbye.'
Lake hesitated.
'Nathan, t—'
'I do trust you,' Lake said, and left.

10

Conrad Dreave chuckled politely down the line. The casting director on the other end was a bag of nerves, cracking into guffaws for no particular reason. She said it was a privilege to speak with him again, and she thanked him for all the marvellous talent he had sent her way over the years.

Dreave smiled. Suggestible fools. They always said that.

She was also grateful for his help on this particular series. She looked forward very much to meeting Nathan Lake.

'Yes, and thank *you* for thinking of me,' Dreave charmed. 'I am sure you will find Mr Lake ideal for your requirements. Goodbye.'

He tapped the line dead, keeping the receiver to his ear, then called his client.

'Good morning, Nathan. Conrad Dreave.'

'Oh, hi. How are things?' Lake asked at his end.

'For you, splendid,' Dreave said. 'You have an interview. It is to play the part of a young doctor in a British film.'

'That's great.'

'Indeed.' Dreave's tone became very dour. 'Now, Nathan, do you remember my instructions regarding interviews?'

'Yes.'

'Good. Now think hard,' Dreave said, starting to grin. 'Is there anyone you know who works in the medical profession?'

Dreave could hear the amazement in Lake's voice when he answered.

'My father's a surgeon. Is that OK?'

'Splendid.'

73

Dreave gave Lake the interview details and finished by saying, 'So, three days, Nathan. You will see your father in that time, won't you.' It wasn't a question.

'I'll call him straight away to arrange it,' Lake assured him. 'I can't believe the coincidence.'

'Neither can I,' Dreave said.

'Thanks, Conrad, that's really quick work.'

'Well, Nathan, you asked for it.'

As British Rail carried him into Kent, to Chislehurst, Lake conducted an internal discussion with himself.

He had caught his father on a rare day off, which was fortuitous and, he considered, something of a good omen. So perhaps this job was meant to be. But he hadn't revealed the true purpose of the visit. There was no question his father would have been delighted to help, it just seemed difficult to explain how their merely meeting and shaking hands might improve his odds at interview. It wasn't as though he already had the job and required some specialist insight into the part.

The local stopping train clattered beneath him and swayed around him. The stations came and went. Winter sun streamed into his carriage and brought a sense of hope in the stark flood of warm light it lay across his black-clothed body. Outside, remnants of night frost still clung to the west-facing roofs of well-insulated homes, and lent a white crust to shaded back lawns. It all seemed fresh, clean, bright.

Lake's interior conversation persisted and began to irritate. It was the same uncontrollable brain-chatter that had made him a virtual insomniac during the worst times of his life. To hear it now was strange. He didn't feel terribly burdened; in fact, he had reason to be guardedly elated. He thought himself ripe for success and now he had the opportunity.

It was just . . . what was the big deal about shaking hands? What on earth could it do for him? Was he that sensitive to the vibes of another human being that he would carry something essential away with him? Even if he was, would the interview panel be tuned in sufficiently to pick it up?

He couldn't answer these questions. He was acting on blind faith. On implicit trust in Conrad Dreave. Too many wasted years had passed by, and he was ready to try anything to finally make an impression.

Still, he couldn't help feeling a smidgen deceitful. There would be no lie between him and his father, but there would be something unsaid, a pretence played out. For however much he loved his parents, this particular visit had been a business decision, and he wasn't going to tell, because in rational terms it didn't make any sense.

Chislehurst arrived. Lake left the train, passed through the station building, walked down the station approach and started his long trek up Summer Hill, towards his parents' home. This was stockbroker territory. The land of Jaguars, long drives and hidden houses; at least, that was Lake's abiding memory from his childhood.

A deep moan of nostalgia suddenly filled him. The embryonic ambition of a young mind was nearing its triumphant climax. He believed in Dreave. He believed in his own destiny. The dream would be made real, and how appropriate he should return to the place of his childhood to set it all in motion. Perhaps he would make one of his many homes here as a kind of private tribute.

Approaching his parents' house, he began running his right palm along a wall, across the texture of its brickwork, and over the fine, tickling twigs of a leafless hedgerow. Then skimming the roughness of a creosoted fence, a cold concrete post, the wood again.

Until he felt a sharp nick.

He stopped walking and inspected the damage.

The cut he had received in Dreave's office was bleeding. He scrutinised the fence and noticed nothing to have caused it; no nail, no patch of splintery wood. Neither did any foreign object lie in the wound. Around the cut itself, there was no peripheral scratching or redness.

He continued on his way. There was no harm done, really. The damn thing had never healed. What difference would a bit of blood make now?

By the time he reached his destination he had forgotten about the cut. He shook hands with his father at the front door and went inside to greet his mother, who, as always, returned to some apparently imperative household chores and said she'd chat later.

Lake was eagerly ushered into the sumptuous lounge by his father. The room was roaring with heat. The Lakes didn't like the cold and had the means to beat it. Lake shrugged his overcoat onto the back of a large grey velvet chair, eased into it and began perspiring. Ronald Lake sat opposite in a twin chair, and Lake took in the powerful and striking image presented by his father. His huge frame was clad in a long, thick, Prussian blue cardigan. Underneath was a red and white check shirt and green paisley bow-tie. Brown corduroy trousers and white suede moccasins completed the image. Nothing really went with anything, but it all seemed to gel. He regularly dressed this way, even for work, though he did concede to a pair of brogues during his hospital rounds. It seemed to be an attempt to combine the professional, the informal and the friendly; like he might cut people open, but he did it with a smile.

Today, though, Ronald Lake was positively oozing happiness. His gentle brown eyes were twinkling, his entire lined and characterful face beaming madly. Even his full head of prematurely silver hair seemed to exude an unparalleled lustre.

Lake wondered whether his father was taking some of the hospital's happy pills.

'You're hot, aren't you?' Ronald Lake observed, peering at the flushed, trickling face of his son. 'I'll put the heat of the house down.'

'No, it's OK,' Lake said. 'By the time there's any difference I'll be gone.'

Ronald Lake was already rushing to the door. 'No-no-no-no-no-no-no-no-no,' he said, sounding like a kindly machine gun. 'I want to do it.'

Lake overheard his mother and father talking in the kitchen.

'Are you all right, dear?' asked Maureen Lake. 'Is there good news?'

'It's wonderful,' was the reply. 'Nathan's here.'

Ronald Lake bounded back in, gave his sweating son a loving, concerned stare from the doorway, and proceeded to pull the door back and forth in a great fanning motion, wafting cool air across the room. The carpet rasped, and pages of *The Times* separated and fluttered from a mahogany table on to the floor.

'Dad, dad,' Lake said, confused and slightly embarrassed, 'I'm all right, really.'

'Sure?' asked Ronald Lake, stopping for a moment.

'Quite.'

Lake got an insane grin and the thumbs-up, something he couldn't recall ever seeing from his father.

Ronald Lake resumed his seat. Lake wanted to leave. Opposite sat a stranger and he had no idea what to say to him. Ronald Lake didn't have that problem. He began relating the events of his week: the ward visits, the patients, the case histories, the staff, the operations in all their grisly detail. Everything was spoken of with relish and wonderment. Lake felt as though he were listening to a child describing his first school trip.

On the subject of operations, Ronald Lake detailed the hand-scrubbing routine to achieve proper cleanliness. He held his hands out in front of him as though ready to receive surgical gloves from an assistant.

'Oh,' he interrupted himself as he spoke, and screwed up his face at his right palm. He showed it to his son.

In his father's palm was a smudge of red. Lake instantly remembered his cut but said nothing.

'Must have nicked myself somehow,' his father remarked. 'Good job I don't mind the sight of blood, eh?'

The laughter that followed from the mouth of Ronald Lake was out of all proportion to the comment. It was thoroughly hysterical. Maureen Lake entered the lounge and stood there half-smirking, half-frowning at the unprecedented noise from her husband. She looked down at her son, who frowned back and shrugged.

'I'm going to have to make a move,' Lake said, rising to his feet. He sneaked a peak at his right palm. Dried blood lay around the pouting cut, which had filled with a ridge of crusty scabbing. But from beneath the scab, something else apart from blood was just beginning to squeeze out. A white fluid. Lake reached for his coat and put it on, wondering whether he'd somehow managed to infect the wound. Only it didn't really look like pus.

He buttoned up, deciding not to shake hands with his father again. Dreave's method would have to wait for another day.

Ronald Lake quietened down. 'Don't go,' he said with a persuasive bounce in his voice. 'Stay. Stay the night. In fact, come back to us. Move back here. Your mum and I would love to have you.'

Maureen shook her head. 'Darling,' she said to her husband, 'Nathan's got his own life in London. Don't be silly.'

'Make him stay,' Ronald Lake whined to his wife.

'I think your father's playing silly buggers,' Maureen Lake told her son.

'Don't go.'

'Shush, dear.'

'Then come again soon,' Ronald Lake changed tack. 'Any time,

Nathan. Or pop into the hospital. Into surgery. You've never seen me operate.'

Lake wanted to tell his father to stop his grinning nonsense; it was unnerving. For some reason, it made him feel panicky. He hurried from the lounge and tried to get out of the front door to escape. Never mind if it appeared rude not saying goodbye.

He heard his father give a startled 'Oo!', push out from his chair and bolt lumberingly across the lounge. Lake lifted the snick on the front door, twisted and pulled at the knob, but to no avail.

'It's like bloody Fort Knox, this place,' he shouted irritably over his shoulder at his mother, as he simultaneously slid back the top bolt with his left hand, fumbled with the key in the deadlock with his right, and tried to work the base bolt with his toe.

'Safety first,' Ronald Lake announced, bending down to help Lake's foot.

At last the door was open.

Lake felt his right arm being grabbed. His hand was yanked up from his side. Before he could do anything, it was encased in his father's grasp and then pumped enthusiastically.

It didn't last long.

Ronald Lake's grip quickly went limp and his joyful expression sagged into abject depression.

Lake was too keen on running away to more than vaguely note the change in his father. 'Bye, Mum. Bye, Dad,' he said.

On his way back to the station, he found Dreave's silk handkerchief in his coat pocket and pressed it against the cut. He decided his father was due for a long holiday.

11

In the two days before Lake's interview, Studio House received through its doors its last quota of clients.

It was always the same. In they trooped to assess the set-up. Straight away they became shifty, uncomfortable, began to loosen collars, undo buttons, make faces, dart glances back and forth from person to person, wall to wall, floor to ceiling; they wrung their hands, furrowed their brows, closed and opened their eyes, hopped from foot to foot, looked ever more hotly ill at ease with every passing second, then said yes, they'd love to rent facilities. And Suzy rarely had to walk them further than reception for them to make the decision.

Suddenly, Studio House was alive like never before, and Suzy felt her dread of unemployment wither and die.

For this, she was indebted to Conrad Dreave. She didn't really know why she felt that way. There were two tenuous explanations, but even linked together they didn't amount to much. First, the influx had started with him, and, second, he did possess a unique charisma. Against this, there was a phenomenon known as coincidence, and just how far was she prepared to believe a man's charisma could reach.

More perplexing was the sexual urge she couldn't shake during office hours. Only when she left in the evening did it start to diminish. Only when she got home did she feel in any control of it. And only when she had thoroughly exhausted her fiancé could she sleep at all.

Now, with practically a full house, it had become clear she wasn't the only one suffering this energising malady. Christine's touchy behaviour made sense when viewed in this light. Offices with locked doors, pulled blinds and desperate grunting made sense. Dispatch riders who by-passed reception to deliver packages to clients, and who took half an hour to do so, made sense. Toilets engaged for too long made sense.

The only thing that didn't make sense was why. Again, she privately cited Dreave as the causative factor. And again, there was nothing solid to substantiate her theory. She had heard of Sick Building Syndrome, where the occupants were routinely ill, but what was happening here? Horny Building Syndrome? It would have been laughable had it not been so genuine and damned all-prevalent.

The last prospect for renting space was a businesswoman in her mid-forties. Suzy considered her demeanour to be uptight, haughty and severe on arrival. Within sixty seconds she was wilting and amenable, and eager to take up residence.

'Do you have two vacant offices, dear?' she asked Suzy.

'Just two, yes.'

'I want them.'

'I'll just show you them.'

'I want them.'

'Fine.'

Suzy received a pat on the bum as she led her client into the lift, and half-expected the woman to make a pass on the way up. When they emerged without incident onto the sixth floor, Suzy was shocked to feel more aggrieved than relieved that nothing had occurred. It seemed she was game for anything, though she had never thought that way about another woman before, and while she prayed not to be tested further, she craved the storm of spontaneous sex to break the sultry atmosphere.

The sixth floor was buzzing. Typically, a couple of doors were closed for private business. Of some sort. The other offices were open wide, and people were constantly emerging and disappearing, criss-crossing the corridor.

'What does this company do?' the woman inquired.

'It's three companies, actually. They just, uh . . . seem to get on rather well.'

The client halted briefly, breathing in the atmosphere. 'It's divine,' she said huskily, eyeing a young hotshot pacing around his office with a telephone to his ear.

'You're down here,' Suzy said, and proceeded with the guided tour.

THE SHORT CUT

At the end of the corridor, she unlocked a room. 'This is the larger o—' she began, but her client had vanished.

Along the way, the hotshot's door clicked shut.

12

It was a routine inguinal hernia operation. A 'cold' op. Negligible risk.

The patient was a twenty-four-year-old man named Karl. A budding body-builder who had lifted too much one day and had felt his groin pop. The following months he had ignored it, trying to push the rupture flat and hoping it would stay that way, but then it became irreducible and too painful to ignore. At which point he accepted he would have to be put under and put right.

He wasn't going quietly. With the exception of the ward sister, who could strangulate a hernia at a hundred yards, the female nursing staff had all been subjected to Karl's laddish tomfoolery, which took the form of sexual advances, both verbal and physical. It was only the approach and subsequent departure of a male nurse with talcum powder and razor blade that had taken the wind from his sails. A bald prick was a pitiful sight. Just knowing one was lurking beneath the bedsheets was bad enough, but knowing females knew about it could transform a lifelong Hyde into a meek-mannered Jekyll.

The op was scheduled for eleven a.m. Karl had been Nil by Mouth since the previous evening. With a grumbling tum and a bald prick, he had lain awake since five-thirty, feeling sorry for himself.

At nine a.m. the anaesthetist came by and asked him some questions. At nine-fifteen the consultant surgeon arrived, a Mr Ronald Lake, dressed in a horrendous combination of colours and textures. With him were two young doctors, who closed the curtains, then watched as the surgeon unceremoniously yanked down the bedsheets, yanked up Karl's bedshirt, had a cursory press around, uncapped what looked very much like an indelible marker pen, and drew a crude line across barren skin that only yesterday had been lush.

'OK?' was all the surgeon said to Karl, as though Karl, with his one GCSE in woodwork, was about to debate the incision.

'Uur, yeah. Uur . . . is it easy . . . you know . . . this what you got to do?'

'I'll have the manual open on your stomach. I don't lose many. I've had a good year this year.'

Karl's mouth fell open a little. He wanted to laugh, but the surgeon wasn't smiling.

'I'll see you later then,' said Ronald Lake. 'You, of course, won't see me, but that's the way we do things around here. Well done.'

The surgeon exited through the curtains, and one of the doctors indicated wordlessly that Karl could make himself decent again – whatever decent meant when his shaved crotch had just been written on – while the other doctor opened the curtains and exposed the patient's embarrassment to the surrounding beds.

The two doctors joined the surgeon, who was standing alone looking rather blank, and the three of them then swept out of the ward at speed, leaving Karl with the impression he had just been visited by Darth Vader and a couple of Storm Troopers.

'Well done?' Karl said under his breath, echoing the final words of the surgeon. 'Well done?' He shook his head. 'Fucking mad twat.'

Karl was wrong about his surgeon. But only by about two hours.

The interview was in South Kensington. It was set for eleven-fifteen a.m. Lake was to meet the casting director, director, producer and writer of the film. A daunting prospect.

The Underground rolled him into South Ken at ten-thirty. Always best to be early, in case they had a script to read. He made his way upwards. It was a miserable day. No sun, no rain, no snow. Just a bland, uniformly grey sky that seemed to extend all the way down to street level.

He was nervous even now, forty-five minutes ahead of time. This was the biggest part he had ever been up for. It was just a shame he didn't have much chance. Over the past two days, he had convinced himself he wasn't right for it. In truth, he didn't know why he'd bothered to show up. He didn't look like a doctor. Of course, in the real world, doctors were just human beings in white coats; they could be five foot short and ugly. But in the world of TV and film, they had to look as impressive as their death-defying skills.

Which was the nub of the problem. Lake was spike-haired and dark-eyed and stubbled. For casting purposes, he was a baddy; he didn't cure people, he killed them, and he had accepted typecasting years ago as a fact of his career. If they wanted your face, you were in. If not, forget it. It meant nothing that as an actor he believed he could *act* himself into practically any given role. It was a foreign concept.

Still, a slim chance was better than none at all. At least he was meeting important people.

TRIUNE PRODUCTIONS was the proud blue neon announcement above the main glass entrance. He tried to steel a bit of confidence into his expression, then went in. He picked up a script from reception and sat down in a vast, spongy sofa. Pot plants, hanging greenery and the less-than-sane prints of Gustav Klimt surrounded him.

What a waste of time.

'Will I have a scar?' Karl asked the porter who came to wheel him down to theatre.

'No, mate, it's all this keyhole surgery stuff nowadays. They'll go in through the end of your knob.'

'But they shaved—'

The porter's expression gave it away, and Karl managed a slight smile through the pre-medication morphia.

The corridor lights passed overhead in a bright blur. It was just like the cliché in American hospital dramas. Karl decided he preferred the TV version to the real thing. He had never known a feeling of helplessness like this. Imminent unconsciousness in the hands of strangers. He had relinquished his power. He wasn't Karl in this place, in this position. He had no points of reference by which to measure himself. This wasn't the gym or the pub or the nightclub. These sights and sounds and smells were different. Drab walls, linoleum floors, frightening machines tucked away in ward corners; sudden cries, bedpan clatters; disinfectant, the odour of mass food production.

He wanted out. Despite the calming morphia, he was scared. But he felt damaged as he was, with a ruptured groin, and it marred the image he had of himself, so he lay there trundling further into an alien world, but the only one which could return him to his own in a restored form.

They stopped at a lift. A sign above it read THEATRE USE ONLY. The porter called the lift. Karl was wheeled in and they descended. Karl would have felt better had they gone upwards. It was purely psychological. He didn't know what psychological meant; he just knew when something made him feel bad.

Straight out of the lift into a little room where he was greeted by the anaesthetist. Karl did know what anaesthetist meant; he just couldn't spell it.

'See you, mate,' the porter said as he left. 'Keep your pecker up.'

Karl smiled a pre-med smile. It disappeared when the syringe appeared. The sodium pentathol flowed into the back of his hand, and then everything disappeared.

It was a routine op.

Ronald Lake had lost track of the number of times he had performed it. He hardly had to think. His hands worked themselves. Which was good, because his mind was still wrestling with his bizarre reactions to his son's visit, three days earlier. First, preposterously overjoyed by Nathan's presence, then dejected beyond all measure by his departure. He had looked in the mirror later that evening and staring back was uncomprehending loss, like the face of a bereaved relative at hospital when told the ghastly news of a loved one's passing. His wife, Maureen, was equally baffled.

Dejection had soon turned to plain depression. He had been overcompensating for this, wisecracking to staff and patients alike, but as his face had failed to join in the deception, his dead-pan delivery had left his more cerebrally challenged patients clearly troubled and quite uncertain of their fate.

Ah, and speaking of cerebrally challenged patients, here was Karl being put in front of him like a Christmas turkey.

'I'll be Daddy, I'll carve,' he announced, holding up a scalpel. The theatre staff exchanged glances. Nobody laughed. Ronald Lake did not have the inclination or the expression to convince them he was only having a little jape.

He made a two-and-a-half-inch incision to open the skin, then went in deeper to reveal the problem.

* * *

86

Lake had foolishly accepted two coffees from the casting director's assistant, so now his heart was responding to events by trying to kill him.

His fears were confirmed with every candidate who filed in ahead of him, and queued up behind. Each one was a variation on the Richard Chamberlain School of Medicine.

Lake checked his watch: eleven-seventeen. At least they weren't running terribly late. He read his few pages of script twice more, then put them to one side and waited, and listened to his heart beat up on itself.

The theatre clock softly clicked to eleven-twenty-one.

They were behind schedule. Ronald Lake's preparation for the op had been unusually slow. He didn't want to operate that morning. He could have managed to work the theatre lift, but he suspected his concentration was woefully inadequate to perform a surgical operation. He felt thoroughly senile, totally confused, as though he had lost a dear friend an aeon ago and now felt the loss afresh, only couldn't think of the friend's name.

Despite this, he progressed, working from a saving memory of the procedure too engrained to be interrupted by wandering thought.

The clock advanced another sixty seconds.

Not that damned cut again.

Lake had noticed a wetness in his right palm. Sure enough, the cut was weeping. No blood. Just that white stuff. Pus or whatever it was. He'd have to see a doctor if it didn't heal soon.

The door to the interview room opened as Lake once more checked his watch. Eleven-twenty-two.

He wiped his palm on his coat.

This was it. Here goes nothing, he thought, and entered the room.

He took the director's hand first; a good, long, firm handshake.

Ronald Lake stopped what he was doing and pulled Karl's limp penis upright with his left hand. He gave a swipe of the scalpel, and Karl's pride and joy was sliced off at its base. Sharp spurts of blood like dual red urinations erupted from both severed ends.

The theatre staff gasped, eeked, screamed, froze, fainted.

Ronald Lake dropped the scalpel and pulled down his mask. His face became manic and his body hunched over. He brought the dripping stump up to his lips and put his other arm behind his back. He gave a bulge-eyed, grinning look to his audience, then took a brief suck on the dry end of the penis before waggling it about in front of his mouth in a way that seemed sickly familiar to the gawping staff around, at least those who were still upright. No one could speak.

Only Ronald Lake spoke, but he wasn't Ronald Lake any more.

'A man is as old as the woman he feels,' he said, backing the scrub nurse into the corner of the theatre and tweaking her right breast, making her yelp.

Then he turned and addressed the assistant surgeon. 'This woman said to me, if you were my husband I'd kill you. I said, if you were my wife I'd save you the trouble.'

He took another drag on his makeshift cigar and set off out of the theatre, waggling it as he went.

A moment later he popped his head back through the swing doors. 'Please accept my resignation. I don't want to belong to any club that will accept me as a member.'

Lake sat down after shaking hands with the panel.

They didn't ask him to read; they just all looked at him with wondrous eyes, and grinned at him, seeming to vie for the return favour of his own smiling face.

'Are you a doctor?' asked the producer, a rotund, middle-aged woman with a false tan.

What a frigging ridiculous question, Lake thought, and politely said, 'No.'

A certain twist in her smile revealed her utter astonishment.

'Well, I don't normally say such things in interview,' said the director, a grey-haired stick insect, 'but I cannot imagine anyone more suitable. I think I'm safe in saying that . . .' He sought agreement from the others and got it with nodding heads and eager grunts.

'Did you ever *consider* a career in medicine?' the producer needed to know.

'Never,' Lake said.

Her expression was incredulous. She turned to the writer, a bohemian type in his late thirties. 'Is Nathan what you had in mind, Tom?'

'Perfect,' Tom said. 'Perfect. He reeks medicine. Perfect.'

The others laughed.

'Um, well, I didn't mean *reeks* exactly. . .' The writer was lost for words.

And at that point, if called upon to talk, Lake himself would have been speechless; Dreave's method actually worked.

When Ronald Lake finally left the theatre to find a more appreciative audience, the assistant surgeon found the wit to attend to Karl and staunch the bleeding. He called the auxiliary nurse over to help him. 'Wake her up,' he told the scrub nurse, indicating the other auxiliary on the floor.

'What about . . . you know?' asked the operation department assistant, moving towards the door.

'I need you here!' the anaesthetist barked. The ODA came back.

'You!' shouted the assistant surgeon, looking directly at the student doctor, who was dithering uselessly at his appointed spot in the room. 'Go and get the prick!' Which could have meant two things.

'Ah, shit.'

'*Go!*'

The student ran. The natural order had tipped upside-down. He now had to chase a respected surgeon through the hospital to retrieve a patient's knob from his clutches, because Ronald Lake was not Ronald Lake any more, he was Groucho Marx, and Groucho Marx was evidently finding happiness in a cigar called Penis.

Emerging from the lift, it was clear from the audible commotion where Groucho had got to. The student rushed down the corridor and came to a sliding halt just inside the entrance to Ward One. He exchanged glances with the ward staff, who looked none to keen to intervene.

Groucho was passing along his whimpering, captive, bed-bound audience. 'I never forget a face,' he said to an elderly man with black eyes and bruises, 'but I'll make an exception in your case.'

And to a young man caught mid-chomp on a sandwich, 'You eat like a vulture. Unfortunately, the resemblance doesn't end there.'

Then Groucho sped out of the ward, hunched over, cigar waggling, and down the corridor. The student followed on.

'Sir!' he called. 'Mr Lake! Sir!' but there was no response, so he ran beyond him and turned to block the corridor. Groucho stopped dead.

'Sir . . . uuh . . . Mr Marx . . . I . . . I . . . I don't want to chase you, I want—'

'Many years ago I chased a woman for two years, only to discover her tastes were exactly like mine: we were both crazy about girls.'

'Fuck.'

Groucho set off again.

'Oh, fuck.' Short of felling the man with an oxygen cylinder, the student could see no way to stop his progress, and who was to say the surgeon would come off worst? Ronald Lake was on the wrong side of fifty, but he was a big man and clearly insane. The student had visions of being knocked unconscious with a playful swat and waking to wish he hadn't woken at all because his genitalia were wall-mounted at some secret location known only to an eminent consultant prize-loon.

Groucho was weaving through the corridors, causing people to hug walls. At the X-ray department he poked his head in the door and told the female radiographer, 'Anyone who says he can see through women is missing a lot.'

The Casualty department was next. Plenty of sad faces to entertain in there.

The uproar was instantaneous. Some who had barely hobbled in now sprinted out.

'They didn't like the play, but then they saw it under adverse conditions – the curtain was up.'

The student tried to collect his thoughts, but he had only one and that was *fuck*. He approached cautiously. 'Give me the . . . the cigar. Hand over the cigar,' he tried rather pathetically, unable to summon any authority.

Groucho regarded him with boundless relish.

'The cigar,' the student repeated. 'I want the cigar. Hand it over.'

'You've got a goal. I've got a goal. Now all we need is a football team.'

'Oh, Jesus,' the student groaned, as sudden desperation made him lunge for the prick.

Groucho retreated and hid the floppy red trophy behind his back. The student backed off to reassess the situation, though he had no idea how he would resolve it. The not terribly joyful solution was three seconds away.

Karl's penis was given a final suck, then it was held out temptingly, as if to say, you want it? But as the student slowly moved in, Groucho dropped it to the floor.

The student's eyes flared in horror, but he couldn't act in time.

Groucho brought the heel of his shoe hard down on his discarded cigar and squashed it flat, then stamped on it again and twisted it back and forth into the linoleum.

The student felt his face contort and nausea rise in him as he observed the bloody, fleshy mess spread out beneath the shoe.

At that point, the man in the green gown tootled off on to the street.

The student slumped in a red plastic chair. It was disgusting, repulsive, sickening, but he couldn't tear his eyes away from the ruin on the floor.

Man's most potent symbol of his power since the dawn of time.

Karl's cock. Crushed.

In the end, the interview was relatively short. No need to prolong a foregone conclusion.

'Can I ask,' Lake said finally, 'why you think I'm right?' It was a daring question, urging them to consider their gut reactions carefully.

The director spoke. 'This is an exceptional case in my experience. There's no question. I think we all sense your . . . genuineness for the role. I've certainly never openly discussed my feelings in front of an actor before.'

The others nodded their agreement.

'I don't think we need to know anything else,' said the producer.

Lake got up and extended his arm. Only then did he remember the weeping cut, but it was too late to pull back.

He shook hands with everyone.

'Thanks for coming,' said the casting director, giving him a wink.

'My pleasure.'

'Nice meeting you,' said the producer.

'And you.'

'Well done,' said the writer.

'Thank you.'

'See you soon,' said the director.

'Can't wait.'

* * *

Flash. Flash. Flash. Flash. Flash.

Lake hit the message button and listened.

Success had beaten him home. Lake was delighted with the news, but not at all surprised. Dreave had left his number. Lake had to call back.

First he needed to wash. On the return journey he had noticed his right palm was covered with smudged, dried blood. He wondered when it had taken over from the white pus. Was it during the interview or afterwards? Had he left the interview panel with blood on their hands?

Once clean, he checked his wound. Spotless. Gaping but spotless. So what was this display of intermittent infection? He wasn't a medical man but it didn't appear to be normal.

Then he burst out laughing. Of course he was a medical man. As of today.

Excitement swamped his concern. He didn't need a doctor. What had he got to show? Right now he had a small, inoffensive cut. He'd be given a Band-aid and the doctor would bite his tongue to avoid telling the paranoid hypochondriac to piss off.

He placed the call to his agent.

'Congratulations, Nathan,' Dreave said before Lake could speak.

Lake laughed. 'How did you know it was me?'

'You are my only client, remember?'

'Doesn't anyone else call?' Lake asked, still chuckling.

'Not if I don't want them to.'

Lake's amusement tailed off. 'Pardon?'

'Never mind. So now you see the wisdom of my advice?'

'Advice?'

'Regarding preparation and interview technique.'

'Oh, yes,' Lake said.

'Splendid. To business. They are offering fifteen thousand for the scheduled three months . . .'

Fifteen grand, Lake thought exultantly.

'Fear not,' Dreave continued nonchalantly, 'I will bump them up; double it for you. They will argue, they will plead poverty, as is standard practice, but they will accept my terms. They will not risk losing you. Filming begins in a fortnight. Always last minute with these people.'

'I can't thank you enough, Conrad.'

'You are right, of course, but there is no need. And now it is out of my hands. It is your turn to do what you do best. I will bank your cheques for you as they arrive but the production office will contact you direct with all the details, such as flight information, any injections you might require.'

'Hold on, hold on,' Lake said. 'Flight information?'

'Did they not say?' Dreave asked. 'You are to play an expatriate doctor working in the Maldives.'

'In the Indian Ocean?'

'The very place.'

'God, it's gorgeous there, isn't it?' Lake felt like the happiest man alive.

'It is paradise on earth, Nathan.'

'I can't believe it,' Lake squeaked.

'Why not? You have every right to your just deserts.'

Lake wasn't really listening. He had to tell his parents the good news.

Shortly, Dreave ended the call, and though Lake was itching to speak with his mother and father, he decided news of this calibre had to be relayed face-to-face to the people who loved him most.

'I hate him.'

Maureen Lake was in a state of shock across the table from her husband.

'I hate him,' Ronald Lake repeated viciously.

The uniformed police officer at the door of the interview room remained impassive. The detectives had left to discuss how to proceed.

'Who?' Maureen pleaded. 'Who?'

Ronald Lake just shook his head. The answer to that, if he aired it, and the reason for his thinking so, would only make his situation worse. There was no point letting on he had not emerged from the episode essentially intact. At some stage he would have to stop himself from saying 'I hate him' again and again, but at that moment it was something he had to release regardless of the continued appearance of lunacy.

'Who?' his wife asked again.

'N – No. No.'

He knew he would never practise medicine again. Fifteen minutes that morning had destroyed his career, wrecked his life. He had become lucid as he had tried, without cash, to purchase a cigar from a newsagent's when he didn't even smoke. The police had arrived in abundance shortly after. He couldn't remember his actions. His last recollection was of beginning the operation. All he possessed from the intervening blank time was a certainty that he had done something very bad, that one person was responsible, and that it wasn't him. When the police kindly filled in the gaps, he collapsed. It all made a kind of sick sense.

'I hate him,' he said again, softly this time.

'Darling, *who*?'

He looked down at the brown Formica of the table-top and began to heave as the tears of his private hatred made themselves felt.

Maureen took her husband home that afternoon. He had been released into her care pending further inquiries and psychiatric reports. If he launched into any more dodgy impressions, she was to call the police.

It was some consolation that Ronald Lake was unable to recall his butchery of young Karl, for at least he would be unable to relive it, but this was outweighed by the mere fact of the butchery and the knowledge that young Karl would never again be the cocky, spunky lad he once was.

He didn't speak as his wife drove him home. He had put a gag on his protestations of hatred for the unnamed individual. But if he couldn't speak that particular story, it seemed there was nothing about the rest of the world worth mentioning. An intelligent man, he realised he was more than likely hoarding the makings of real long-term lunacy some-where down the line, but how could he say what he knew in his heart to be the truth? The 'truth' would brand him a mental case. Either way, his madness that day would never be the brief episode it appeared to be. His only choice was whether to allow the truth to make him mad slowly by harbouring it within him or, by speaking out to ease the burden, have others very quickly label him a loon and lock him up for it.

The impossibility of his position made the evil done unto him even purer, for it could never be revealed without his suffering, and would not be believed anyway, and could not be proved, and thus the hated evil one would continue to prosper.

Ronald Lake did not eat that evening. Funnily, he had quite an appetite, but Maureen, in her fazed state, had not given much thought to the meal. Something easy, that was about all she could manage.

So out came the sausages. The ketchup she had dolloped beside them didn't help the picture.

Staring down at his dinner plate, Ronald Lake began to laugh and then cry. Maureen puzzled for a few seconds before she realised her mistake and took away the offending items. The doorbell rang as she scraped both plates of food into the bin.

'I'll get it,' she said, though her husband had not moved a muscle.

At the front door, her pale, drawn features managed a half-smile. On the doorstep was her son.

'What is it, Mum?' Lake asked.

'It's terrible. It's your father.'

From the dining room came a growl that did not sound human. It grew louder and drew nearer.

Ronald Lake flew out of the front door, knocking his wife into the lintel. He punched his son square in the face and fell on top of him, beating his head on the stone path. He was growling all the while, unable to give vent to the totality of his emotion through mere words.

Lake screamed, '*Dad! Dad! Don't!*' He thrust a knee upwards and caught his father where it hurt. Ronald Lake rolled off, moaning gutturally and still not at all like anything human.

Maureen dashed over and helped her son to his feet. Ronald Lake found his, and disappeared back into the house, to emerge some seconds later wielding a brass fire poker above his head.

'Nat, run!' Maureen cried. '*Run!*'

Lake didn't need to be told. At the pavement he felt the air an inch behind his head receive a swipe that would have split his skull. He outran his father, but only just, and he kept on running for twenty minutes, until he was thoroughly lost.

Sweat ran from every pore. His mind spun in confused turmoil. His lip was fat, his head sore and bumpy.

It hadn't happened. Couldn't have happened. It was a nightmare beyond the limits, an agony of hurt that almost made tears impossible. Almost.

He wept convulsively. He was in mourning, but it was worse than for a death. It was mourning for the end of a love he had thought endlessly inviolable, from father to son.

13

The first two weeks of the production did not involve Lake in front of the camera. He and several others of the acting crew had to work up their tans. In the script they had been *in situ* on the islands for years. Their pasty winter flesh was a dead giveaway.

Thus Lake was being paid to lie on a beach, but he would have preferred to work. His mind needed the occupation. Back home was a man sectioned in a secure psychiatric unit who hated his guts. Lake had no idea why this was so, and didn't think he would ever understand, so two weeks with nothing to do but mull it over didn't feel like much of a holiday.

Even when shooting eventually began he still found himself juggling elation and grief. Work of this nature was an actor's dream come true, but he couldn't shake the nightmare of his father's hatred, though it did help a little to conjure up an image of his next bank statement. Dreave had delivered on his promise to double the initial offer of fifteen thousand, and if the shoot overran into new contract territory, things would get really interesting.

Still, it wasn't the way he'd envisioned his big break. He had always thought that nothing could dampen those spirits which were elevated by success.

The memory of his seven-day sleep was woolly now. If it caught him at all, it didn't seem real any more. And his dream of Ben and RADA had lost much of its definition, as every dream is wont to fade. The question it had posed was academic now. He rarely brought it to mind. If he did, he considered he had found the answer in resolving to grin and bear the nine months of *Oedipus*. That it never came to pass confirmed he had guessed right.

Only Suzy stayed with him. She was in his heart, not his head. He wondered if she was happy with her policeman fiancé. In truth, he didn't want her to be, because if she wasn't happy, there was always a chance for someone else to make her so.

'Sue. Do you really want to marry me?'

Suzy traced her eyes around her fiancé's clean-cut, blandly handsome face, his regulation hair. 'Of course,' she said.

Philip Cage looked intently at his betrothed. 'Don't you want to know why I asked?'

'Good little place this, isn't it?' Suzy commented, looking around the intimate French restaurant at its tangerine walls and black and white photographs of Paris.

'Sue,' Phil persisted. 'Don't you want to know why I asked?'

'What?'

'Whether you really want to marry me.'

'No.'

'Why not?'

She blew gently on her spoonful of onion soup, then said, 'Because it's a stupid question.'

'Then why didn't it bother you that I asked it,' he reasoned, 'if it's a stupid question?'

She set her spoon down in the bowl. 'Because it *is* a stupid question. Would I have said yes if I didn't want to marry you?'

'You shouldn't have done, no.'

'Well, there you go.'

Phil regarded her uncertainly. 'Is there anything wrong? No second thoughts?'

Suzy heaved a sigh. 'There's . . . pressure at work. Things are a bit mad right now.'

'But we're OK?'

'We're OK,' she agreed.

Phil tried to make a joke. 'Because I don't want to find out in six months' time, when I'm standing at the altar.'

In response, Suzy closed her eyes and breathed deeply, out loud.

'Right,' Phil said. 'I hope the fish is good when it comes.'

'Yeah.'

'What is it?'

'Nothing,' Suzy snapped. 'I'm fine, I told you.'

'No,' Phil laughed. 'The fish. What is it?'

'Oh. Angel fish.' She grabbed the bottle of Sancerre and replenished her glass, leaving Phil's empty.

'Angel fish for my angel,' Phil cooed soppily.

Suzy made a noise as though she was about to vomit. She watched Phil go quiet, pour himself a fresh glass and sit there looking hurt.

They were a good half-way through their main course before either of them spoke.

'Is there someone else?' Phil asked, very calmly.

'No.'

Her reply had been immediate and, she realised, that was a mistake. She sounded guilty. As a question out of the blue, it should have taken her by surprise. It didn't. She had illegitimate sex on the brain. With Lake, with Dreave, with the entire clientele of Studio House in one big orgy.

Phil appeared to weigh it up for several moments, then said, 'Good. I wouldn't like it if you weren't faithful.'

The other clients had mostly all gone home for the evening.

Christine went downstairs. She had discovered sex. Dreave had introduced them. Christine, Sex; Sex, Christine. Delighted.

Dreave did not make any concessions to Christine's arrival in his basement, apart from the merest illumination of the ceiling spots. It was sufficient for her to distinguish basic shapes, saving her from effectual blindness.

He didn't shout for her, buzz her desk or appear in reception, but she knew when he had summoned her.

It was always the same. He was naked. Even his black glasses had been discarded. He stood in his office, proud and ready. He was no more than a ghostly white shape but she believed no other man could look so fine, and she had known no other to know for sure.

She undressed herself before him, like a ritual, like a sacrifice.

He laid her on the desk and climbed on top with the slick movements of a predatory beast.

99

She stared longingly into his eyes. The murk crowded in and stole their essential fire, but they were still so clear and bright. She could see no visible affliction; they looked normal. It was a tragedy they were forever shielded from the daylight world.

The sex began, though she believed they were making love.

God, the pleasure she had denied herself all these years. All that shit about saving herself for marriage.

'Let it go,' he urged her, taught her, and she did, physically, vocally.

She passed through pain and came out the other side in bliss.

Past a certain point she could escape from the darkness of the basement by closing her eyes. Colours exploded behind her eyelids, she was so connected to the current Dreave plugged into her.

If this wasn't good sex, she could not imagine what was, and if it didn't last long enough – as she had often heard girlfriends complain – then she could not imagine, when it was over, how she could have taken another moment.

She moaned, screamed, clawed at her own breasts until they bled.

She loved him, was devoted to him, would do anything to keep him inside her.

She believed she would even kill for Conrad Dreave.

The next day, Suzy woke with a hangover. She arrived late at Studio House and spent the morning idly swivelling her squeaking desk chair back and forth, trying to block out the now familiar noises permeating her walls from surrounding offices.

There was work to be done – rents were due – but her mind was not concerned with business affairs.

She was in turmoil over her private life.

It was silly, really. Nothing had changed since her engagement to Phil. Lake was in the past and Dreave was best kept as a sexual fantasy. It would be presumptuous even to consider that the man downstairs regarded her as anything more than a business associate. And whatever had been rampant throughout Studio House these past months was beginning to affect her less seriously. The atmosphere itself was no less pronounced; she was just handling it better. She still had storming sex with Phil as a result of it, but she was fairly confident that the idea of screwing her way through the building would remain simply that: an idea. Besides, with this level of promiscuity, if only one of the clients was HIV-positive, the whole bloody lot of them could be dead within ten years, and Suzy did not intend to be among the statistics.

So her future with Phil was a fact she had to accept. The rest was illusory and dangerous.

But the problem remained: in comparison, life with Phil seemed boring. She sometimes wished he would come home and tell her he'd blown a few scumbags away and enjoyed doing it.

She wanted some excitement, some fun. Was that too much to ask? Apparently.

Better forget it. Get back to work.

She pulled open the top drawer of her desk to retrieve her invoice pad.

A large manila envelope was the first thing she saw. It was bulging. On it was her name, in a familiar hand.

That wonderful man.

She unsealed the flap and pulled out the bank notes. Fifties. Plenty of them. Dreave had included a brief letter.

My dear Suzy,

I appreciate your commitment to me. This is for you. Forty thousand pounds sterling. Remittance of rent will be forthcoming.

Always,
Conrad

Suzy stifled a whoop. She totted up the backhanders thus far. Two lots of ten thousand, two of twenty, and now this. Total: one hundred thousand smackeroonies. And for what? Her 'commitment'? She had done little more than her job demanded. Granted, she didn't reveal to anyone the nature of his work, that it was something sensitive for the government, but how would he know if she did?

Instantly, that thought struck her as significant.

How would he know if I did?

She reviewed her dilemma: no excitement, no fun.

She thought of her small locked suitcase at the back of her bedroom wardrobe, full of cash for some serious shopping.

101

She recalled Dreave's admonition not to spend while he was in town. Then she asked herself again, *How would he know if I did?*

14

Nathan Lake had fallen in love.

He wasn't blind; he had seen from the very first day that his co-star, Brigit Kelly, was attractive, but his troubles had caused his heart to feel unloved and unloving.

The routine of work had proved a panacea. His zest for success was too buoyant. The weight of one sorry incident could not keep it submerged for long.

As the weeks passed by, he found that the regular evening beach parties became more enjoyable. Jokes became funnier, anecdotes more interesting, music more danceable. Their palm-fringed island was ever more like paradise, and Brigit Kelly had never been more lovable.

Lake thought she had the purest face he had ever seen. Her features were so fine and perfectly proportioned. Green eyes, lively and playful; auburn hair, boyishly short; a little wisp of a body he wanted to protect from harm. There was no one thing extraordinary about her, but the total picture was devastating.

Whether or not she felt similar emotions towards him was unclear. She responded well to his conversation, respected his skills as an actor, smiled when he glanced in her direction, and didn't shy away from his close physical presence. His intuitive side told him the signals were green, while his reserved side warned him she was only being nice. They did have to work together, after all.

One Saturday night, Lake was watching the embers die on the beach fire. It was late. The rest of the cast and crew had retired to their chalet complex behind the tall palms.

Lake was thinking of his father again. The loss. Of Suzy. The loss. He wanted to be loved again. Someone he could trust; who wouldn't leave him.

Suddenly, like an answered prayer, he saw the unmistakable figure of Brigit. She was at the far end of the beach, walking slowly through the moon-lit surf. She was weaving slightly, the sign of drink.

He waited for her to arrive. A short way off, she waved at him. He lifted his arm very casually. When she left the water and trudged through the soft sand towards him, he noticed her hair and dress were dripping wet.

'Hello, lover,' she called.

Lake hoped that was significant, but as she was playing his love interest in the film, he suspected that sadly it meant nothing.

'Hiya, Brigit. Been swimming?'

'Yep,' she said, dropping onto all fours in front of him. 'Every night, when you're all in bed. It feels so free.'

She was panting. He liked that. She was also giving him a great view down the front of her dress. He could see her small breasts swaying delicately.

'Want to go for a stroll before bed?' she asked.

Lake was on his feet before he said, 'Yes.'

They wandered into the night-shadow of the palms, where the trees met the white sand, then further into the darker clutches of the island's vegetation. Nature was fragrant around them, almost urging them to go with the flow. The sounds of the ocean grew distant, as a host of insect wings created that familiar tropical soundtrack. There was no conversation between them. Their footfalls were their only company. It seemed auspicious, the lack of words.

Slowly, as though it wasn't happening at all, their fingers touched, entwined, and they began holding hands.

After a minute, Brigit stopped walking. She came in front of Lake and looked up at him, taking hold of his other hand.

Dreamy and madly in love, Lake nearly sighed.

The perfect start to a love affair.

'Fuck me,' she whispered, rather dispelling his twee notion.

She grabbed the shoulder straps of her dress and peeled the clinging cotton from her body, rolling it down to slap against the dusty earth.

Lake was entranced by the sight of her naked form, petite and lithe.

She backed up against the trunk of a palm and yanked him towards her by the waistband of his Chinos. She unbuttoned his trousers, then took him out of his briefs. He groaned. Paradise on earth. He had fallen hard for her. The name Brigit Lake shot through his head and he gathered he was quite prepared to marry the girl.

He bent at the knees and she guided him in. They moaned together. His hands went to her bottom and lifted her up and she wrapped her legs around his lower back. She was light; he didn't need the support of a tree. He stood there, thrusting up and down inside her, thinking it was the most erotic sex of his entire life.

Brigit began breathlessly repeating, 'Oh, you're good, oh, you're good, oh, you're good, oh, you're good . . .' which gratified Lake no end. Her chant became a whisper after a couple of minutes and then faded into a long, undulating moan.

Lake was about to climax himself when Brigit sunk her teeth into his shoulder. Her bite cut through his shirt and skin. He yelped and his orgasm went away. He tried to prise her off but she was in the throes of her own shuddering climax, and she clung and bounced and bit, and Lake's pain was immaterial.

At last, she released his shoulder, unclamped her legs and pushed him away.

Lake watched as she picked up her filthy wet dress and struggled into it.

'Thank you,' she said, and pecked his cheek. 'That was nice.'

'But I didn't—'

'I did,' she said, and was off.

Another loss. Another person leaving him, spurning his love.

He couldn't take it. Wouldn't take it.

It reared up inside him like a tidal wave, carrying at its crest a red mist. The rising.

Losing himself, he stared at her departing form.

She stopped dead, turned back to him and ran.

Lake kicked his trousers and underpants from round his ankles and followed, chasing, no longer in control. He heard himself growling lowly, like a baited animal. The undergrowth whipped and thrashed at him.

He watched Brigit draw closer as he caught up. She veered towards the beach, hearing his onslaught. She wailed while she ran, then cried out as the sand stole her momentum.

Instinct drove him on. An alien instinct. He had been violated and had

105

to seek retribution. He had no say in the matter. He just scurried ahead, intent on his prey.

Ahead of him, Brigit got to the surf and picked up the pace.

Lake felt his feet and legs splashing down as he raced along the shoreline behind her. His penis slapped either thigh in quick succession. Salt water sprayed up and blinded him, but he was driven on by a clearer sense of vision.

Then Brigit stumbled and he was upon her.

She opened her mouth to scream but Lake pushed her face into the sodden sand. She flailed her fists out behind her to no effect.

Lake grabbed her hair and jerked her into the surf. Between sand and sea she let out a desperate shriek.

The warm water enveloped them. Lake ducked under and swam with both legs and one arm, dragging Brigit behind him with the other. He could feel her fight and twist but his strength was immense.

After a time, she ceased to struggle and her body became inert. But he didn't stop swimming. Across the coral reef he skimmed, into open water, then further and deeper, pulling her along by her short auburn locks, a reversal of the lifeguard's mission.

Out into the ocean and downwards, his one-night stand by his side, both of them held in suspension by pure blackness, too deep for the touch of moonlight.

On he went, never struck by the need to breathe or panicked by the sightless depths.

Time was meaningless. His crime was meaningless. He could swim forever. The liquid embrace of nature would always welcome him; always wash him clean.

Sometime later he released his lifeless cargo and headed up to the surface.

As he swam up, the rising sank down.

The island was a distant black lump on a moon-flecked dark ocean. Pin pricks of light flickered between the far-off, invisible palms.

He started for the shore.

15

Suzy had her shopping delivered on Saturday while Phil was working. He returned to their ground-floor flat in fashionable Parsons Green, south-west London, late that evening. Suzy saw he was tired and decided to wait until Sunday. It would be better in the light, anyway.

Just before he fell asleep, turned on his side with his eyes shut, Phil made a comment about the flat above them.

He said, 'Quiet upstairs tonight. Must be away for the weekend.'

Suzy's face cracked but she kept the giggles inside. She rolled over in bed so they were back to back and tried to imagine Phil's expression the next morning when he set eyes on her gifts.

She drifted off with a huge smile on her face.

The staccato beeps of their bedside alarm woke them at eight-thirty a.m. By the time Phil groaned reluctantly into life, Suzy was nearly dressed.

'Why d'you set the alarm?' he croaked complainingly.

'Get up!' she said, snuggling inside a thick pullover.

'It's Sunday.'

'Up!'

He pulled the duvet over his head.

She grabbed it and threw it off the bed.

'Shit, Sue,' he said, tightening himself into a foetus position. 'It's cold.'

'Then put some clothes on.'

'Why?'

'Because I've got a few things to show you,' she chirped. 'Presents for Philip and Suzy.'

107

Phil crawled off the bed and dressed himself. Jeans, T-shirt, sweatshirt, trainers. He moved to the window to open the curtains but Suzy stopped his tracks.

'Leave them shut!' she yelled.

He just shook his head and obeyed. His was not to question why, at least not on his day off. He checked his reflection in the bedroom mirror. His hair was typically swirled to one side by the pillow. It looked ridiculous but he often left it that way if he wasn't working.

He managed a bleary-eyed smile at his fiancée. 'This had better be good,' he said.

She led him down the hallway, past the kitchen and living room, to the front door of their flat. She unlocked it and went into the porch area, which contained the door to the upstairs flat.

'I don't want to go outside,' Phil said. 'Cold.' Through the small pane in the main front door, Phil could see blue skies. Early March blue skies. Early morning early March blue skies. 'Cold,' he repeated.

'Don't be such a wimp.' She turned the key and opened the door.

'Cold,' Phil said, as the outside air poured in, but he was smiling now. He followed her down the short path onto the pavement.

'Notice anything new?' she asked, bubbling with excitement.

He glanced up their tree-lined, car-infested road, all very quiet and twee on this idyllic Sunday morning. Nothing out of the ordinary. Then he turned and surveyed the exterior of their ground-floor flat. Nothing there. Out of curiosity, he peered at the upstairs windows of the two-storey, end-of-terrace property. The curtains were open. In fact, he couldn't see any curtains. Still, nothing to concern him.

'Maybe this way,' she said, beckoning him round the corner, left and down the side of the house.

Now he saw something new, but he didn't understand what it meant. The seven-foot brick wall which ran down the side of their little back garden, protecting it from the street, had a door in it. It always had, but now it was bigger, wider. He could see red brick dust on the pavement, and the lighter colour of the new masonry surrounding the lintels. He didn't have aspirations to become a detective for nothing.

Suzy used a big silver key to let them into the back garden.

On the patio behind their bedroom window was a large object covered with green canvas. Phil guessed what it was by the shape, but it still didn't make sense.

She ran over to it, giggling, and slowly drew the cover up from the ground at one end. A white-walled tyre was revealed. She tugged it higher and Phil saw a two-tone black and blue fender, two beefy front forks, a chrome headlight and wide bars. She pulled the cover to the back of the bike and dropped it on the paving. Two-tone tank, V-twin engine, twin chromed tail-pipes, saddlebags and dual seat.

'It's a Harley-Davidson Heritage Softail Special,' Suzy proudly announced. 'I had the door widened for the bars.'

Phil was mesmerised. 'It's beautiful,' he said.

'It's the one you wanted, isn't it?'

'In my dreams,' he said in an awed voice.

She ran a finger across the mirror paintwork of the tank. 'I knew you'd love it.'

'Did you win it?' Phil asked. 'Some competition?'

'Wait,' Suzy said. 'I haven't finished.'

She grabbed his arm and led him back onto the pavement, round to the front of the house and up the street a short way.

When she reached a cream-coloured Mercedes convertible, she stopped. Phil wasn't with it, until she dug in her front pocket and handed him a set of keys. On the fob was the Mercedes logo.

'This is for both of us,' she said, grinning broadly, then noticed a splat of bird crap on the bonnet. 'Bugger.'

Phil felt his face go slack and gormless. This wasn't possible.

'Just one last thing,' she said, producing some documents from her back pocket. 'The house is ours. All of it.' She handed him the papers. 'The couple renting upstairs, they've gone. I've bought the flat. The house is ours. All of it.'

'What?' Phil interrupted, dazed. 'What are you saying?'

'Well, I haven't bought it outright,' she said. 'Not yet. Though I'll be able to soon.'

'What's this?' Phil asked, indicating the papers. 'The lease to the upstairs flat?'

'Yeah. So we add that to the one for our place, take away the dividing door and we're in clover.' She held his hands and squeezed them. 'Phil? Isn't this brilliant?'

'Sue,' Phil said to his fiancée. 'Can I have a word with you inside?'

'What the fuck is your problem?'

109

'Where d'you get the money?' Phil asked placidly.

'I saved it.'

Phil hooted with laughter. 'Really? Well, let's see how much you collected in that little piggy-bank of yours. There's the Harley, which I know is over twelve grand—'

'I got a discount for cash,' Suzy cut in.

'*Cash!*' He began pacing the confines of their pine kitchen, two steps one way, two steps the other. 'Jesus, Sue.'

'Calm down,' Suzy said wearily, sitting on a wooden stool.

Phil held his hands up. 'All right,' he said, feeling anything but. 'We'll calmly calculate your sudden good housewifery, shall we? So we'll call the Harley an even ten.' He raised his eyebrows at her, requesting her approval of this amount.

Suzy shrugged.

'Fine,' he said. 'Now what was the Merc? Fifty?'

'If you say so.'

'And how much did you put down on the upstairs flat? Ten? Twenty?'

'Thirty,' Suzy said.

Phil rocked on his heels. 'And why were the couple upstairs so ready to leave?'

'They wanted to go.'

'No one walks out of decent accommodation in London just like that.'

Suzy shrugged again. 'I made it worth their while.'

'Shit. Go on, Miss Rothschild, how much?'

'Five.'

'I take it that's thousand,' Phil said sarcastically, 'as we don't seem to bother with lesser denominations in this household.'

Suzy leaned back against the fridge-freezer and stretched.

'OK,' Phil said, 'total bill, roughly ninety-five thousand pounds.'

'Give or take.'

'Sue, it's a bloody fortune.'

'Exactly. You ungrateful bastard.'

'You have to tell me where it came from.'

'I suppose,' she conceded. 'The other day this leprechaun—'

'This is no joke.'

'I stole it.'

'No, you didn't.'

'Then I saved it.'

Phil growled in frustration. 'Not three months ago you were about to join the ranks of the unemployed, and you were telling me how we'd have to tighten our belts in case that happened.'

'And now I'm rich and you're complaining.' She tutted. 'Such ingratitude.'

'Sue, I'm a police officer. How will it look if I turn up for work in a sodding Mercedes?'

'Don't go to work in it.'

'What if some vindictive bastard around here reports our new-found wealth to my superiors? Some folk don't like the police, you know.'

'I'm beginning to see why.'

Phil ignored her. 'You have to at least get rid of the bike and the car.'

'Bollocks to that.'

'I can't possibly use them.'

'So what? I can.'

Phil heard his voice become pleading. 'Sue, you can't. I'm a firearms officer. I have to be accountable.'

'I know,' Suzy said casually.

'It's going to look like I'm on the take, or that you're in the bleeding Mafia.'

'Your problem.'

'Yes, it bloody will be if you're into something dodgy. It'll end my career.'

Suzy stared him in the eyes. 'These toys make me happy,' she said. 'I want to be happy.'

'And I want to know where you got that money.'

'You're a copper,' she said. 'Find out.'

16

No one noticed Brigit was missing until shooting was about to begin on Monday morning.

Lake had spent Sunday sunbathing beside the pool. He didn't want to risk the beach; he didn't know what flotsam the surf might bring to the shore.

Saturday night was fuzzy in his mind. Not the sequence of events so much as the extent of his culpability. He had screwed and drowned his co-star; that was abundantly clear. At the same time, it could be argued, she had used and provoked him, making it a crime of passion. Legal terminology such as *mitigating circumstances* and *diminished responsibility* sprang to mind.

Equally, the word *possessed* seemed applicable.

None of this stopped Lake from inwardly panicking throughout Sunday, but his alarm only related to the legal repercussions of his guilt, not to the personal, moral implications.

He simply didn't want to get caught. If he got away with it, he thought he could square things with his conscience, though he was well aware that the passage of time might alter his view on this. His present justifications might be only a safety device against his breaking down and confessing while the magnitude of his crime was most immediately apparent. He still realised it could all return to haunt him at some later stage.

For now, though, he was coping. And as his acting teachers had been so fond of telling him, living in the moment was all that mattered.

So when Monday came, Lake casually hung around that morning's location, waiting for his co-star as though he really expected her to show.

Now *that* was acting.

They checked her chalet to see if she had overslept. The schedule was rearranged so they could film without her. By lunchtime they had decided she wasn't coming. Perhaps she had misread the call-sheet. Cast and crew who could be spared were sent to search the local village and have a general wander around. By dusk the stick-insect director ceased damning her to hell and began expressing concern. The island police were called in to help.

All the while, Lake was fighting a perverse desire to introduce the subject of Brigit's moonlight swims. He wanted them to establish accidental drowning as the most likely scenario, mourn her passing, come to terms with it and get on with the film.

Eventually, before they all retired for the night, someone did mention it. The cameraman told the assembled cast and crew that Brigit had perhaps gone for a little swim, that it probably meant nothing, but that Brigit did enjoy her little night-time swims.

Lake guessed how the cameraman might have come by that information. He wondered how many others were keeping quiet about their intimate knowledge of Brigit's nocturnal habits.

It was all fodder for Lake's process of justification.

The whole production descended into limbo for the following week. It seemed indecent to continue filming, but it was unthinkable to wrap on a partly completed shoot.

Then fate lent a hand. Or so it appeared to everyone but Lake, because Lake had no doubt that what happened next was the only logical step in the fulfilment of his prophecy.

Taking her vacation on a neighbouring island at that time was a young American actress, Sherry McCall, a rising star in Hollywood. She had heard about the film, then she heard of the gap in the cast list. She made contact, read the script and enjoyed it so much that she offered her services at the existing pay level should all else fail. All else wasn't even tried. The director was over the moon. Then he was reminded that Brigit was very likely dead, so he dropped just under the moon, at least publicly.

The added clout Miss McCall would bring to the film was obvious to everyone. Massive publicity and a Stateside release would now be virtually guaranteed.

At this point, Lake still had no inkling how significant was this particular turn of events. He recognised her name but could not picture her face.

Only when they were personally introduced did it hit home. He suspected he must have appeared totally starstruck.

The dream of Ben and RADA. The movie of the limousine, the red carpet, the photographers, the fans, the police, the actress on his arm.

The actress on his arm.

It was Sherry McCall.

Now he had the ultimate justification for killing Brigit.

It had set him on track to reach his promised future.

17

They were travelling north along Charing Cross Road in their big police Rover, approaching Tottenham Court Road. The traffic was slow-moving, a typical rush-hour London.

AFO Sergeant Philip Cage was up front in the passenger seat. Next to him, driving, was Constable Derek Green, and in the back was Constable John Temple.

Two months had passed since Cage's argument with Suzy over her spending spree and unaccountable wealth. His hopes for their forthcoming marriage were not high. He doubted they would make it to the church. Suzy hadn't even wanted sex these past few weeks, and that was the biggest turnaround in history. She still wouldn't say where the money had come from, besides maintaining her certain lie that she had managed to save it. If he pressed her on the subject, she breezed out of the house and roared off on the Harley. That was another problem. She hadn't passed a bike test; she had no insurance. Thankfully, she *was* legal to drive the Mercedes, but she wasn't doing that in a terribly lawful manner. She had picked up three speeding tickets and a wad of fines for parking violations. If he hadn't known better, he'd have thought she was trying to land him in it.

At the intersection with Oxford Street, Green stopped at a red light. The pavements were choked and bustling. Cage tried to keep his eyes peeled for potential wrong-doers, but his thoughts were poorly distracted.

The lights changed and they moved off.

A third of the way up Tottenham Court Road, passing Store Street,

117

Temple suddenly said, 'Derek, pull over. Back it up.'

Green checked behind and pulled into the kerb, then carefully reversed across the mouth of the side road.

'What is it, John?' asked Cage.

'Gun. Outside the pub up there.'

Cage checked. A hundred yards away, several patrons were drinking on the pavement, some standing, some sitting at white tables. He couldn't see a gun anywhere.

'Large-calibre revolver,' Temple specified.

Just then, a muffled shot erupted from inside the pub. The pavement drinkers reacted sharply and scattered.

There was no time to liaise with other armed response teams. Green was already squealing tyres, swinging the Rover into the street. Cage called it in, watching customers spill out of the pub door.

Green asked, 'See him, John?'

'No,' Temple replied as he opened the compartment in the rear seat. 'Male. Early twenties. Orange top, blue jeans.' Inside the gun box were two Heckler and Koch MP5 9mm semi-automatic carbines.

Cage patted his holstered Smith and Wesson Model 10. It offered little comfort. His mind wasn't on the job. Suzy. Bloody Suzy. The simple answer was to break off with her, but, fool that he was, he loved her too much.

Green stopped the car just short of the pub. They were out in an instant. Bullet-proof vests were distributed from the boot. Cage and Temple took a carbine each, pulled the bolts to chamber the first rounds, then switched to safety. Green was armed with his .38.

Though he was loath to, Cage entered the pub first, carbine up and ready, followed by Temple and Green. Safeties off. Fingers poised.

They sighted the target immediately. Orange top, blue jeans, gun in hand. His animated argument with the landlord was cut dead. Almost in slow motion, he turned round to face the officers, his face slack and white.

'Armed police!' Cage warned, in case he hadn't gathered. 'Put the gun down on the ground! Do it now!'

It was all a bit much. The ashen suspect found no meaning in the given order.

'Listen to what I say!' Cage said clearly, evenly, though the voice seemed to belong to someone else. Thoughts of Suzy smothered his professional instincts like a sodden mattress. 'Put the gun down! Do it!'

Understanding filtered through. 'But it's . . . it's not real,' the suspect squeaked, smiling idiotically at the unreality of it all. 'It's not real. Look.' He offered Cage the gun.

It would have been hard to construe it as a threatening action, but Cage panicked. His finger twitched on the trigger.

And nothing happened.

Temple shouted, 'Put the gun on the floor!'

'On the floor!' Green echoed.

Slowly, the gunman obeyed.

'Now move away from the bar,' Temple instructed.

The youth obeyed.

Cage was out of it by now. It was a miracle. Why had the bullet not flown?

'Lie down on the floor,' Temple said. 'Face down, arms out to the side.'

The youth spread-eagled himself on the grubby carpet, and Green collected the suspect's firearm.

It was all Cage could manage to keep his carbine trained at the suspect's head, though he made damn sure his trigger finger was now rigid outside the guard.

He had come so close to killing a man.

All because of Suzy.

The house was dark.

Phil lumbered in the front door and went for the drinks tray. He felt drained. He uncorked the brandy and poured a large measure into a stained coffee mug, unwashed from the night before. He took a swig, then put the living-room light on.

After another shot he let his throat recover, then bellowed, '*Sue!*'

The house was empty.

He finished his brandy, fixed another, put the light out and sat in the dark to wait for his beloved.

Suzy returned to Parsons Green at gone eleven o'clock. She had to leave the Merc in an adjacent road, the only parking slot she could find. She parked up crookedly, with the rear end jutting out.

She slammed the door but didn't lock it, and went around to the pavement side of the car. The ugly, jagged hollow in the front left wing made her grimace. Flakes of cream paint fluttered off under fingertip pressure.

'Oops,' she said to herself. 'Clumsy me.'

It wasn't her fault, though. There were too many parked cars, bunched together, edged right up to the end of each street. Difficult for a little girl to turn a big car through narrow gaps. Especially when she's had a few.

She made her way home, maintaining roughly a straight line.

Old Philly Willy had gone to bye-byes from the look of things. All dark windows.

She would sleep upstairs again tonight. She had installed a futon up there some weeks ago and was now making regular use of it. She didn't want Phil touching her. Not Phil.

Phil called her name as she rocked in the porch, trying to insert her key into the door of the upstairs flat. She had decided to leave the door where it was. Phil never ventured upstairs; it seemed to be his way of denying it belonged to them, and Suzy liked having a barrier between her territory and his. He had the ground floor and the cellar. She had the upstairs and the attic space.

'Sue,' Phil said evenly from the living room. 'In here.'

She hovered at the foot of the stairs, debating whether to ignore him, but he called again.

'Coming, sweetheart,' she said, and continued upstairs.

There was little more than the futon in her makeshift back bedroom. She hadn't bothered to hang curtains, the wall-paper was half-stripped, and underlay covered the floor.

She didn't put the light on, leaving the room in the pale clutches of the moon. As she kicked off her shoes, she heard Phil climbing the stairboards.

He appeared in the doorway and silently watched her change out of her business outfit, down to nothing, and into a bathrobe.

She tied the cord, folded her arms and slurred the word, 'Speak.'

'No,' Phil calmly replied. 'You speak. Tell me where you got the money.'

'Oh, not that again.'

Phil was across the room before she knew it. He practically punched her in the chest to make her sit down. She dropped backwards and fell heavily on the low futon.

'No bullshit,' he said. 'I nearly killed someone today because of you.'

'I'm touched,' she said, rubbing her right breast where he'd caught her.

He squatted down in front of her. 'I'm serious, I want to—' He sniffed, then put his nose up to her mouth. 'You absolutely stink of whisky.'

'So?'

'You didn't drive tonight?'

'I did,' she corrected him.

'Jesus,' he said, sounding deflated. In his squatting position, he swung his bum around and perched on the edge of the bed. 'Sue, what are you trying to do to me?'

She was starting to feel tired from the alcohol. 'You nearly shot someone?'

'Yeah.' Phil shook his head. 'Some prat with a replica firearm shot off a blank in a pub. Stupid bastard. Sue, what's the money for?'

'What d'you mean?'

'What I say. What's it for?'

She stacked the pillows against the wall and rested back on them. She stared through the darkness at his face. Even in her state, the thrust of his question was clear.

'You mean is it for *services rendered*?' she asked.

'You said that, not me.'

'Well, I suppose it's nice to know you think I'm worth forty grand a shag.'

'You've changed,' Phil announced sadly.

'And you never bloody do.'

Then Phil cocked his head and smiled slightly. 'So forty grand of it came in one go, did it?'

She kept quiet.

'And what about the rest?'

'Once a copper, always a copper.'

'Sue, you are not going to screw up my career.' He straightened his back and rolled his head on his shoulders, making his neck click and snap. 'We are going to sit here until you tell me the truth. All night if need be, and all next day. And if you fall asleep, I'm going to slap your face until you wake up.'

Suzy listened to the threat and believed it. There was an edge of steel

121

in his voice she had never heard before. And she so wanted to lie down, drift off, to be with Dreave and let him work his magic in her dreams until she came in her sleep.

But she really shouldn't tell the truth. She wasn't meant to spend the money. She had been a naughty girl. Dreave might find out. Phil might say something.

That clinched it. 'His name's Conrad Dreave,' she whispered groggily, closing her eyes. 'He rents in Studio House.'

'Why does he pay you?'

'To keep quiet,' she said. She wanted them to meet.

'About what?'

'His work.' She wanted the sparks to fly.

'Which is?'

'Government stuff.' She wanted to see Dreave in his true colours.

'You're lying,' Phil told her.

'Secret.' She giggled. 'Mum's the word.'

'You're lying.'

'Not.'

'Then you're being naïve. The government doesn't work that way.'

'Then *you're* being naïve.'

'Oh, you mean he's MI5 or something?'

'Something.'

'And he just gives you vast amounts of money.'

'He does.'

With accusing disbelief, Phil said, 'And you're not fucking him?'

Suzy pulled her feet up and slipped them under the duvet, then wriggled herself down into the bed.

'Enough,' she said. 'I've told you his name. Now let me dream.'

'Are you fucking him?'

'Dream,' she echoed softy, on the verge of unconsciousness.

'Are you?'

'Dreave,' she murmured breathlessly, and was away.

18

The entrance to the cellar was beneath the stairs. The stone steps that led down were narrow and extremely steep. The cellar itself was divided in two by a brick wall with a large gap in it. A bare light bulb lit each area. The only natural light to enter the cellar came through two small, grimy windows at ground level, one at either end of the house. The space smelt musty. The brickwork was always cold and damp to the touch. Cobwebs spanned from the low ceiling to the walls. An old bicycle rested in one corner, minus a wheel. Tea-chests and cardboard boxes sat empty, waiting to be filled in the next house move. Broken pieces of furniture lay neglected. A workbench was littered with tools. A depleted metal wine rack was crumbling into rust.

But there was something else down in the cellar. A secret. Philip Cage had a gun. No big deal for a firearms officer, but Suzy knew nothing about it. He'd thought she wouldn't approve of a gun in the house. From her recent behaviour, however, he suspected she may well have suggested they go out and see if they couldn't bag a few stray dogs.

It was all perfectly legitimate. Naturally he had a firearms certificate, and the gun was housed in an approved gun safe with a separate chamber for storage of ammunition. Neither did he consider himself gun-mad. He only had the one. He sneaked down to clean it occasionally, but he fired it very seldom.

There was actually little point in him having it at home at all. He knew unless a gun was loaded and immediately to hand, it was all but useless as a defensive aid. He could hardly ask a vicious burglar to hold on while he nipped down to the cellar and armed himself.

123

In fact, apart from the unlikely threat of massive and violent civil disorder, he had never really envisaged any practical need for it.

Until late last night.

Cage felt fully in control. His actions were going to be those of a sane man. OK, so they might not sit very well with his job as a police officer, but that didn't mean he was acting irrationally. In the circumstances, his actions were quite understandable. Not in a court of law, perhaps, but in the scheme of what any normal human being should be asked to tolerate.

He gave a brief nod to reassure himself, and eased out the three drawers in the old, abandoned bedside cabinet. The light bulb he had just knocked with his head swung on its wire, casting creepy shadows. He lay the drawers on the dusty concrete floor. The back of each had been hacked away to accommodate the gun safe. It was a larger version of the gun-in-the-Bible trick.

He reached inside the cabinet, inserted a key into the compact steel safe and opened it. He removed the pistol, wrapped in an oil-stained towel, and set it on top of the cabinet. Then he hesitated. Should he load it?

He was only going to warn the guy, right? More than likely, he wouldn't even reveal the gun. Guns were made to shoot bullets, not to frighten people. If he had no intention of firing it, he had no business producing it – unless he wanted to risk everything blowing out of control.

Even as he debated, he was unlocking the ammunition box and taking out a full clip, which he placed next to the pistol.

'Shit, what am I thinking?' he berated himself. He scrambled to his feet, knocking the bulb again. 'I'm a bloody police officer.'

Then he thought of the changes in Suzy. He thought of how Dreave's money could already have wrecked his career. He thought of a stranger buying sex from his fiancée. And he grabbed for the pistol.

He unwrapped it and shoved the magazine into the butt, then worked the slide, and satisfying metallic clicks spoke of a 9mm round being chambered. He smiled. Forget his police revolver. This was state-of-the-art machinery. A Glock semi-automatic. No external hammer. Never cocked until the trigger was pulled all the way back. Three safeties in the trigger mechanism, each one working sequentially. Beautiful.

He had been wrong earlier. He *was* gun-mad. It had just taken something like this to make him realise the fact.

* * *

The holiday would soon be over. It would be time to work again. He would have to cease banging the receptionist; his energies would be required elsewhere. His mind would go out to alight at mental doorways, poised to make contact on behalf of his bloodied client. Then his telephone would ring, and on the other end would be a casting director who felt uncharacteristically indebted to be conversing with Conrad Dreave.

Dreave had not yet decided on the next career move for his client. Lake certainly needed to establish his credentials. Perhaps some guest roles in popular TV dramas, maybe a series of his own; imprint his face in the public consciousness while they waited for Hollywood to bite after the release of his current film.

However, there was no rush to commit. Lake would not be back home for a couple of days yet, and a lot could happen in forty-eight hours.

Cage had never been inside Studio House. As he stood on the pavement in his civvies and surveyed the building, he realised he had never actually shown any real interest in Suzy's work. Perhaps that was how he'd lost her; too wrapped up in his own career. It wasn't surprising. Compared to his working day, Suzy's had to be unbelievably dull. The job of a firearms officer was important, exciting, dangerous. When did an office manager like Suzy ever come face to face with death?

He buzzed the street intercom.

'What?' came a testy female voice in response.

'Conrad Dreave,' Cage said.

'Yes?'

'I want to see him.'

'Good for you.'

'Pardon?'

'Do you have an appointment?'

'No. Is he busy?'

'He's an extremely busy man, yes.'

'Well, let me in and I'll make an appointment for some other time.'

'Phone,' said the voice, and the static of the intercom clicked off into silence.

How rude. How inconvenient. This was not going according to plan. Not that there was a plan, as such, but moving from the exterior of the building to the interior of the building had been a fairly critical part of the operation.

He buzzed again.

'Go on, what?' said the woman.

'I'm a police officer,' Cage said simply. Not the ideal solution. He hadn't wanted to announce his official status to anyone except Dreave.

'Sure you are.'

Cage tried not to get annoyed. 'I can show you my warrant card.'

An irritated sigh cut through the static and the intercom clicked off.

Cage waited and wondered whether he would have to try again, then a young blonde woman appeared round the corner at the end of the hallway and approached the door. He pulled out his warrant card and held it up to the glass.

She still looked wary, but she opened the door to him.

Cage stepped inside and surprised himself by saying, 'You're a very discourteous individual.'

'Up your bum,' Christine replied, and walked away.

Cage followed on, more shocked than angry. 'I know who runs this company,' he warned her.

'So do I,' Christine retorted, unimpressed, and sat down behind reception, eyeing him with open distaste.

'Where can I find Conrad Dreave?' he asked.

'Why?'

This was unreal. Did she know who he was? Was Suzy down there with Dreave right now? Was this woman covering for them?

He said, 'Because I'm a police officer and I want to know.'

'Mr Dreave. Downstairs.'

'Thank you,' Cage said without gratitude, and turned towards the basement steps, concluding he definitely was gun-mad; he suddenly had a hard-on with that Glock down the front of his trousers.

'Wait. I have to call down,' Christine told him. 'Mr Dreave might not want to see you.'

Cage swivelled round and leaned his head close to hers. 'If you insist on hampering my inquiries any further, I shall bloody well arrest you.'

She sneered at him. 'Pig.'

Cage felt his eyes blaze, his mouth tense. He pointed his finger at her and wagged it meaningfully, hoping some appropriate words would spring up to accompany the gesture.

He walked silently away, and the basement lights shone up to greet him as he descended into the world of Conrad Dreave.

'Oo dear,' said Dreave. 'Now there's a face that could sink a battleship.'

'Are you Conrad Dreave?' Cage asked, boldly entering the office.

'I am indeed.' Dreave did not get up, did not extend his hand, and he wasn't smiling.

Cage closed the door behind him. 'I'm going to ask you straight, Mr Dreave. What's between you and Sue Cooper?'

'My great long penis,' Dreave replied. 'Whenever I desire.'

Perversely, Cage felt a smile creep onto his face. He tried to shake it. He studied Dreave's deadpan expression, and his hand crept unconsciously towards the pistol in his waistband, beneath his zipped-up bomber jacket. His fingers drummed at the solid form of the butt. His mouth was parched of words.

'That is what you think, is it not, Sergeant Cage?'

Cage felt utterly undermined. His attack had been pre-empted and effectively wiped out. He said only, 'You know who I am?'

'Sue talks about you all the time,' Dreave said. 'She loves you very much.'

This was very confusing. 'Are you having an affair with my fiancée?'

'No. Sit down, Sergeant Cage.' Dreave indicated the client's chair opposite him across the desk.

'I'll stand.'

'As you wish.'

Cage no longer believed Dreave was screwing Suzy. He didn't quite know what to make of Dreave's initial comment, but he was sure it wasn't the truth. Would Dreave be that candid? Would anyone?

'Why did you say what you did?' Cage asked.

'To cut the crap,' Dreave replied. 'You see, I do so like your fiancée and I would hate any misunderstanding to arise between you and her as a result of my entirely innocent cash gifts.'

There it was again: complete candour, this time about the money. It made it difficult to believe he was hiding anything at all.

Then perhaps that was the ploy.

Dreave took a draught from a glass of milk on his desk.

Cage tried to see through Dreave's dark glasses. 'Why are you buying Sue?'

'I cannot buy what will not be bought,' Dreave said.

'Meaning?'

'Meaning, Sergeant Cage, that your fiancée accepts my gifts quite willingly and I do not believe that would be the case if she felt required to remunerate me with sexual favours.'

Cage remained puzzled and bemused by Dreave's strange, shifting accent.

Dreave explained, 'Do you think so little of your fiancée that you believe she would sell her body to a stranger?'

'Anyone can have an affair,' Cage told him.

'Of course. But selling sexual favours is not the same as having an affair. It is being a whore.'

'Sue's not a whore.'

'*Voilá*,' Dreave said, holding up his hands. 'And believe me, I am not the sort of person who either has to pay for sex or would settle for anything less than complete devotion if I did.'

'What?'

'I would hardly pay a woman one hundred thousand pounds for sex, then allow her to go to bed with you, now would I?'

'She doesn't go to bed with me,' Cage let slip.

Dreave spoke without insult. 'Then perhaps you should look to yourself, not to me.'

Cage pressed his palm against the Glock through the leather. He was beginning to feel impotent in the face of Dreave's clever put-downs. He tried to assert some authority and get onto a topic that Dreave could not defend.

He asked, 'So why d'you pay her?'

'I like her.'

'Doesn't wash.'

Dreave smiled and shrugged.

'You're not with the bloody government,' Cage said with certainty.

'Correct.'

'Oh.' Cage frowned. 'Sue said you were.'

'She may well have done, Sergeant Cage. I did not.'

'So what is your job?'

'That is confidential.'

'Who d'you work for?'

'Someone very powerful.'

'Anyone I might have heard of?'

'Most assuredly.'

'But you're not going to say.'

'Correct.'

'Fine. But it's got to stop.'

Dreave stood up and finished his milk. He walked slowly around his desk with the empty glass and halted four feet away from Cage.

Feeling a ripple of panic, Cage had to tilt his head back to look his adversary in the face. Dreave was taller by at least six inches.

'If you are referring to my gifts to your precious Sue, I am afraid I am unable to comply with your request.'

'I'm not asking you, I'm telling you. Her spending is going to land me in the shit.'

'Oh dear,' Dreave said. 'I did tell her not to go mad with it. But no matter. You cannot prevent me from giving your fiancée money, Sergeant Cage. There is no law against it.'

Cage advanced a pace towards Dreave, though in truth he felt distinctly unthreatening, even with the Glock. 'There's me,' he said. 'I'm the law. And I'm against it.'

'And how do you intend enforcing your rule, Sergeant Cage?' Dreave gave a dismissive chuckle. 'With *this*?' He shot out a hand and clamped Cage's palm over the concealed butt of the Glock.

Cage had never been more frightened in his life, either personally or professionally. He was frozen.

Then Dreave released his hand and began chortling quietly.

Cage backed up against the office wall, out of Dreave's reach. Damn it, Dreave had stolen his thunder again. But Dreave was right: force of arms was the only way to assert his wishes. It was just a tiny bit disconcerting that Dreave had left him with the option of doing so.

Still, he yanked up his jacket and whipped out the gun. 'You're too confident for your own good, Mr Dreave,' Cage said hoarsely, pointing the muzzle at Dreave's heart. 'Now, you are not going to give Sue any more money. You are going to say nothing to her about this. And I want you out of this building and out of our lives by the end of the week.'

Dreave shook his head. 'No.'

'If you don't leave, I'll shoot you.'

'I think not.'

'You think I won't pull this trigger?' Cage asked, almost tittering with fear. 'I'm trained to do it. It's second nature.'

'You have never shot anyone, Sergeant Cage. Don't kid.'

'But I will. You. You'll be the first. You want to fuck up my life with your stupid money, I'll *take* your life.'

Dreave smiled with supreme confidence. He began passing his empty glass from one hand to the other, back and forth. He spoke slowly, 'I say again, I think not.'

'I will.'

'Oh, I know you have the killer instinct. But you would never make it in time. Before the impulse became action, I would have this glass into your throat and through your carotid artery.'

Cage blinked and swallowed hard. Then he gave a wry glance at the expanse of blue carpet tiles between them and began laughing. 'Outpace my finger on this trigger?' he said. 'Course you would.' But at the back of his mind was a cautious voice insisting it would be deadly folly to think of challenging Dreave's outrageous claim.

'Leave me alone,' Dreave said. 'While I still allow you to.'

'This isn't over,' Cage warned, reaching for the door handle.

'Yes, I know that, Sergeant Cage. I know that very well indeed.'

'Conrad, is everything all right?'

'Everything is splendid, my dear.'

Christine stood in the doorway. She cracked her knuckles on each hand.

'Calm yourself,' Dreave soothed.

'Was he any trouble?' Christine asked. 'The pig?'

Dreave offered a reproving look. 'He was an officer of the law, Christine. Show some respect.'

She bowed her head; respect for Dreave, not for Cage.

'And he was no trouble at all,' Dreave told her. 'In fact, our meeting was immensely productive.'

'Because I can sort him out,' Christine said. 'Really. I want to help.'

Dreave smiled magnanimously. 'In time, you will.'

'Is there *anything* I can do for you?'

'Hmm,' Dreave considered. 'Now you come to mention it . . .'

And the light began to wane.

19

The end-of-shoot party was held back in London in a hotel near the production offices. It was a drunken affair. Hugs and kisses were compulsory.

Lake's American co-star, Sherry McCall, could not attend. Lake was disappointed but not gutted. He had developed a crush on her, but had learned enough to know that it was nothing more than that, and had made no romantic advances in her direction. A repeat of the Brigit fiasco was not a risk he could afford to take. Killing someone who was destined to figure prominently in his future would have been a monumental error. Indeed, since Brigit, his general spirit of celibacy had been quite remarkable, though not totally undinted.

As the evening progressed, Lake discovered that somewhere along the way he had acquired a bundle of interest from the opposite sex that he deemed wholly out of proportion to even his more vinous, optimistic assessments of his appeal. Females hankered after him all night, wanting him to kiss them goodbye, time after time and not with a wee peck on the cheek.

Finally he managed to peel his mouth away and slip out of the function room before he became seriously maudlin over the end of his spell of dream employment.

On the way back to the West End, he realised he was in a pretty sorry state. He was missing two people, and neither of them was a very good person to feel that way about. One of them was Suzy, and she was engaged, and the other was Dreave, and he was a man.

131

'Take me to Wardour Street, would you?' Lake heard himself say, correcting his initial instruction to the cab driver.

'Not Conway Street?'

'Wardour Street.'

So the cabby drove his fare to Soho and, at one-forty-five a.m., dropped him off outside the dark façade of Studio House.

Lake shivered as he peered up at the unlit windows. It wasn't cold, but he had grown used to a better climate. He giggled stupidly. Who on earth did he expect to find in at that time in the morning?

The answer to that was simple: Dreave. He was with Dreave now, and Dreave was for him.

He pushed at the glass door but it was locked. He tapped at a random sequence of numbers on the entry pad, to no avail. Then he simply tried knocking.

He jumped as Dreave's distinctive voice came through the intercom. 'Welcome, Nathan.'

The door buzzed and Lake gained entry. Several steps down the hall, the orange intrusion of the streetlamps was lost to a darkness that seemed positively laden. He went to the basement stairs and hovered nervously before taking the first steps very gingerly. As the basement lights heralded his arrival, his anxiety eased.

Dreave was in his office, putting the telephone back on its cradle, as Lake approached.

'Just talking you up with some American friends,' Dreave said. 'Come in.'

'Oh . . . great.'

Dreave let silence reign.

'Um . . .' Lake searched for some conversation. 'Are you working late or starting early?'

'Where does one end and the other begin?'

'Right.'

'Wonderful tan,' Dreave remarked. 'How was the shoot?'

Lake felt his face wince at the memory of Brigit. 'The odd glitch,' he said.

'Nothing disastrous, I trust?'

Lake wanted to tell Dreave about Brigit. He sensed only Dreave would understand. 'I . . . I . . . I had a good time,' he said. Brigit was the past, Dreave was the future, and Lake knew which direction mattered most.

Dreave smiled knowingly. 'So what do you want at this hour, Nathan?'

Truthfully, Lake replied, 'What I always want at any hour: to make it.'

'And you think I can work a miracle at this very moment?'

Lake shuffled on his feet and wobbled with the drink inside him. His face creased and tears began to well. 'You have to,' he moaned. 'I can't go back to unemployment. I can't. Not after this. I want more work.'

Dreave showed his flawless teeth in a grin. 'And you want it now. I know. And you will have it. All that you deserve.'

Those words were magic. Confidence filled Lake from head to toe. 'I do believe, Conrad, it's not that I—'

'If you lacked belief,' Dreave cut him short, 'I would lack the power to help.'

'It's just—'

'You cannot wait. I understand. I do like to see that in a client. I expect to see that in a client. We would not make such a splendid team if it were otherwise.'

'Do you have something in mind then? Another big part?'

'I believe I might,' Dreave said. 'For some peculiar reason, I can picture you in uniform.'

20

The call was not unexpected, except that it came at two in the afternoon and it woke him up. His hangover screamed its greeting the moment he became conscious. He scrambled out of bed and dashed for the phone.

'I have tracked down a wonderful role for you, Nathan,' Dreave told him. 'There is a new series just moved into pre-production. They have already begun lead-casting but I have managed to secure an interview for you in two days' time, on Thursday at two o'clock.'

'Thanks, Conrad,' said Lake, unable to pronounce his first fatigued words of the day properly. 'What's it about?'

'The police,' Dreave said. 'Hardly new, but tried and tested as a favourite staple of the box-watching masses. I know it will be a huge success, and I equally know that you will be brilliant in it.'

'I haven't got it yet.'

'No, but if you follow my instructions, the part is yours for the asking. Do you recall my instructions?'

Lake had to think. 'You mean the research?'

'I mean the research.'

'Is all that still necessary?'

Dreave's end fell quiet.

'Conrad?' Lake gathered he had somehow offended his agent. 'I just thought directors and producers might look more favourably on me now I've got a big feature under my belt.'

Dead silence. Lake twisted the loops of the coiled telephone flex around his left index finger and watched the skin underneath go white, and the tip red.

'Conrad?'

'Nathan,' Dreave said gravely. 'If you want to fade back into the obscurity from whence I plucked you, feel free to disregard my advice.'

'No, I don't want that.'

'No,' Dreave echoed. 'It would signal the end for you. You would fatally overdose or open your wrists inside six months.'

Lake's body was hit by a fierce judder at the thought. 'Jesus, that's a bit uncalled for.'

'Your options are limited, Nathan. You obey me or die.'

Lake let out a nervous laugh. 'Come on! Lighten up, Conrad.'

'It is you,' Dreave said sternly, 'who must *darken down*.'

Lake gulped to catch his breath. He wasn't enjoying this conversation. It was a bit depressing.

'Take nothing for granted,' Dreave said. 'As the expression has it, use it or lose it. Yes?'

'OK,' Lake conceded. 'OK.'

'Now how will you meet a policeman?'

Lake tutted, but quickly realised that it may have sounded bad. 'No, sorry,' he said, 'that wasn't . . . I didn't mean to sound . . . that noise, um . . . I just thought of something, a problem, but nothing I can't sort out.'

All friendly again, Dreave said, 'Stop squirming, Nathan. I am on your side, remember. Tell me your problem.'

'Well, there is a policeman I could talk to, but I'd need to speak to someone first, and I'm not sure if she'd want to speak to me.'

'Mmm, yes. That is difficult.'

'Never mind,' Lake said. 'Leave it with me. I'll arrange something.'

'No,' Dreave said. 'Perhaps you should pop in and discuss your difficulty. I may be able to help you resolve it. You never know.'

Lake wasn't keen on seeing Dreave that day, not after what had just been said, but he knew he had to accept the offer. Dreave was right: his options were limited.

Where could he go if not to Dreave?

There was a note pinned to Dreave's office door, and an envelope with Lake's name on it. The note read: *Nathan, business elsewhere. Had to fly. Envelope contains details of forthcoming interview. And* REMEMBER!

Curiously, there was no mention of the difficulty Dreave had promised to help solve, and no apology.

Lake untacked the envelope, folded it in half and shoved it in his back pocket. He began up the stairs towards reception but quickly stopped. He checked back over his shoulder. What was it with those lights? He trod the next step, still looking behind. Darker. He backtracked two steps. Lighter. He ran up four. Almost black. Turned and ran down into the basement again. Bright as day. He stayed where he was and stretched one leg out horizontally and placed the side of his foot on the fourth step. No change. He lowered his leg, walked up to the fourth step. Dimmer.

It wasn't the pressure on each step; it was his bodily proximity to the basement. Now how in hell did that work?

Christine's cheeks were flushed and burning. She had lost count of the times she had furtively made herself orgasm while sitting there behind reception, fielding telephone calls with the other hand.

Conrad had not summoned her to make love with him in over a day. A whole day. She wondered whether it would last; did he not love her any more? There was nothing to stop her venturing down to tempt him, but she instinctively knew that there would be no point. She sensed when he desired her, and she had not experienced that internal tug in over eighty-six thousand, four hundred seconds. She knew. She had worked it out, and it felt like a lifetime. She ached inside for the man, but she couldn't flee the building, run away from it, because without that pain she felt utterly soulless.

The telephone rang. She picked up. It was Dreave on the line. Her pulse quickened.

'Stop Mr Lake from leaving,' he said, 'then call upstairs and tell Suzy to come down to reception immediately. Do not say I asked for her. When she arrives, say nothing, simply point to Mr Lake. You will not have to explain further.'

As she hung up, Mr Lake appeared at the top of the stairs.

Christine said, 'Could you wait a moment, Mr Lake? Take a seat.'

Lake appeared to puzzle the request, but he sat down on the plush reception sofa. Then Christine phoned upstairs.

'Come down to reception now,' she ordered her boss.

'All right, Christine. What's so urgent?' Suzy asked impatiently, resting her forearms on the reception counter.

Christine jabbed a finger towards the sofa.

Suzy turned and her expression fell into a mirror image of the one staring back at her: gawping amazement.

'Nat?'

'Suzy Cooper. The very person.'

Seeing him, Suzy felt her old feelings blast through the changes of recent months.

'Come up to my office, Nat.'

Lake got up and followed her.

The wiggle of her bum going up the stairs caused a crotch enlargement Lake was wholly unable to control. He wanted her, he always had, but it was equally a symptom of something bigger, more subtle, that seemed alive in the very fabric of Studio House.

As if to prove the point, walking along the second-floor corridor, he noted there were some rather suspicious noises emanating from several closed offices.

Suzy wasn't smiling as she shut the door behind her and pulled the blinds at the doorside window to allow them some privacy. Lake prepared himself to face the wrath of the hurt he had caused her.

But in her eyes he saw only lustful desire. It was clear she didn't want any words. Not yet. Words would end it for them right there.

Two sets of crazy hormones went zinging off the walls, the floor, the ceiling, clashing and coupling, and the office was filled with the colours of their invisible collisions.

Lake had never felt so certain of acceptance. He shrugged his denim jacket onto the floor. Suzy locked the door and moved slinkily over to sit on the edge of the desk. She eased herself back on the desk-top, crunching under-bum papers, until her back was resting against the cork noticeboard on the wall. Then she pulled her feet up onto the desk, kicking off her shoes. She tugged her skirt up her thighs and splayed her legs for him. He knelt down. He didn't want to kiss her mouth and she seemed beyond that. This was not a romantic tryst. He placed his hands on her inner thighs and urged them wider. His finger slipped inside the white cotton of her knickers and pulled it aside. She purred softly. Her smell was strong, sweet, rich. He kissed her wetness and began to use his tongue. His eyes were open, hers were closed. He knew the spot, liked to see it, and he took her all the way until she juddered and screamed out loud and pushed him off. She smiled wickedly as he wiped his face. She got off the desk, brought him to standing and unzipped her skirt, letting it fall to the floor. Her knickers followed. Then she went down. He was straining. She unbuttoned his jeans and pulled them off, then his briefs. He throbbed in her hands. She ran her tongue around before she took him in her mouth in long strokes that made him growl and twist his hands in her hair. He stopped her while he could still stop himself. She lay back on the office floor. He joined her, slipping in easily. It was slow for a few minutes, but it soon became frantic. They built to a climax together. They knew each other's sounds, and timed it to perfection.

'That's it,' Suzy said as she zipped up her skirt.

'What?' Lake asked, having trouble folding himself into his briefs.

'That's an end to it. Don't come here again.' She sat down at her desk and began leafing through some papers, some of which were severely crumpled, and warm, and stained.

'Suzy . . .' It was only just beginning to dawn, and the realisation displaced the problem of her sudden coldness. 'Is this the place you run?'

'Of course,' she said. 'What would I be doing here otherwise?'

'Course.'

'You must have known that. Otherwise why did *you* come here?'

Lake swiftly reviewed his position. He didn't want Suzy to know he was with Dreave if she hadn't already guessed. It was quite possible that Mr Dreave was not everyone's cup of tea; he could be blunt to the point of frightening rudeness, and Lake was a recent ear-witness to that. She might not help if she disliked the man.

'I thought perhaps you had a different job now,' he explained himself. 'You'd mentioned the company was in difficulties a few months back. I thought this was a new job for you.'

Suzy squinted at him distrustfully. 'But presumably you used the work number I gave you before Christmas to trace me to this address. So when you saw me here, you must have known I was still in the same job.'

A genuinely flummoxed expression fell across his face. Proper little detective, wasn't she? 'Sorry,' he said. 'Yeah, I'm not thinking straight. I've been a bit feverish. I've been away. Could have picked up a bug.'

'Which I'll now have. Thank you very much.'

'Sorry.'

'Mmm. Anyway, why did you think to come and see me after all this time?'

'I missed you,' he said.

She didn't echo the sentiment but Lake wondered whether their being together might once again be on the cards. Were the fates lending a hand by installing his new agent in the very building run by his old girlfriend? He still loved her, and she seemed more attractive than ever. She was somehow stronger. And she evidently still had feelings towards him sexually, if not emotionally.

'Suze,' he said. 'Do you ever think that two people might be destined to be together?'

She smiled, as though she had brought some happy image to mind. 'Yes.'

'What about us?' he asked.

She snapped out of her reverie. 'Oh. Us. I don't think so'.

'So what was that?' He squatted down on his haunches beside her, and swivelled her round to face him. 'What just happened between us?'

'It was fun,' she said. 'We both enjoyed it. We used each other. You used me before Christmas. I can't do the same?'

'I didn't use you. I never have, never would. I want you, I love you, and you feel the same.'

'People move on, Nat. They change.'

'Not us, Suze. Not how we feel about each other.'

'Everyone.'

Lake thought of Brigit. Suzy was right, of course. People did change. One day an actor, the next a murderer.

'I haven't changed,' he said.

'What happened before Christmas? Tell me that.'

'Oh . . . shit.'

'Someone else?'

'What?'

'Another woman?'

'God, no . . . no, nothing like that.'

'OK. So what?'

He let his forehead fall on to her thigh. 'It's too insane.'

Lake was surprised when she merely said, 'Mmm, there's a lot of it about. How's the career going?'

'Very well,' he said, sounding quite the opposite.

'Really?'

'Yeah. You know I said I've been away. I was in the Maldives, doing a film.'

'Nice work if you can get it.'

'And I've got an interview on Thursday. A lead in a series.'

She smiled genuinely. 'I'm pleased for you.'

He rose to standing and moved over to the window. How could he ask about meeting her fiancé now, after lying about the purpose of his visit? Actually, he no longer wanted to mention it. He wanted to walk away very heroically and leave her with a pledge of his undying love.

But as he had been so pointedly informed, his options were limited. So staring down at the traffic in Wardour Street, he just came out with it: 'I need to speak to your boyfriend.' He balked at saying 'fiancé'.

She reacted calmly. 'This is not something you can sort out with him, you know. I'm not coming back to you, whatever happens.'

He turned to her. 'I don't mean that. I need to research a role.'

'And that's why you came by today.'

'*No!*' he objected, though he could see Suzy was not the slightest bit upset.

'I'd prefer it if it was for that,' she said.

'You mean you'll help?'

'Why exactly do you need to talk to him?'

So Lake told her. Naturally, he kept it all within the realms of accepted reality, which meant he had to lie a lot, but he conveyed the general gist of his need to meet her fiancé. She pointed out, quite correctly, that he had never been one for Method Acting, which this smacked of rather heavily. Lake agreed but said he was desperate for the part on Thursday – true enough – and anything that could help, like research into the role, might make the difference.

When he finished speaking, Suzy said, 'No, Nat. Sorry. I would ask if I thought he'd agree, but I know he wouldn't. You see, lately we've not been the best of friends.'

'This is so important to me, Suze.'

'I still don't see why.'

'Neither do I, I just know it works.'

141

She laughed. 'You've been reading too many wacko self-help manuals.'

He was hurt by her snidey remark. He gazed down at the carpet and the name Dreave began pounding in his chest like a heartbeat. His breathing became deep and steady. Why did he want to speak that name, like some magic charm to make things right?

'Suze, I haven't had my new agent for very long,' he said. 'He wants me to do this. I don't want to piss him off.'

'Sounds a bit iffy to me,' she ridiculed. 'Does he get you to do other things for him?' She winked. 'You know?'

Still the beat of Dreave's name in his heart.

He closed his eyes, then heard Suzy's squeaking chair swivel back to the desk. There was a rustle of papers being collected, smoothed out with the flat of a palm, stacked and boxed off.

Dreave's name beat away in his chest. He wanted to speak it out loud, but what difference would it make?

'Dreave?' Suzy said.

Lake looked up from the floor at her. She was staring at him sideways over her shoulder.

'Dreave?' he said.

'You said Dreave. How do you know Mr Dreave?'

'I didn't say Dreave.'

'You did.' She rotated to face him. 'You said Dreave.'

Lake frowned. 'I never said a word, I was thinking.'

'I heard you say Dreave,' she said, sounding riled.

He shook his head.

'Oh, I see, it's all in my head, is it? Don't fuck me about, Nathan.'

'I swear I di—'

'Fuck off.'

'Suzy, Dreave's my agent, but I did not s—'

'Agent?' Suzy pushed out of her chair and shot to the window, grabbing Lake's forearms tightly and standing almost nose to nose with him. 'Agent what way?'

Lake smirked. 'Theatrical. What else?'

'Of course. Silly of me. And Mr Dreave insists you do this, does he?'

'Well, it worked the last time.'

'Right, OK, I'll see what I can do.'

Lake gave a guarded, doubtful smile. 'You'll help?'

'I'll try,' she said. 'Go home and sit tight. I'll call.'

When Lake had gone, Suzy took the lift down to the basement.

'Good day, Suzy,' she was greeted by a cheerful voice as she stepped into Dreave's domain.

She did not respond, but hurried into his office and shut the door behind her.

'Conrad . . .'

'Yes, Suzy?'

'Conrad . . .'

'Yes, Suzy?'

'You're not a theatrical agent, are you?'

He smiled and tapped his nose with his forefinger. 'That all depends who is asking.'

'Sorry?'

'Mum's the word.'

Suzy felt herself blush. What a dumbo. 'I get it,' she said. 'It's a cover.'

'Precisely. Why do you ask?'

'It's just my . . . my, er . . . someone I know is actually on your books.'

Dreave opened his mouth in surprise. 'What a small world we live in.'

Suzy dithered and didn't know how to ask her question.

'Anything else?' Dreave said.

'Well . . .'

'Sit down.'

Suzy took a seat. 'If my . . . if the person I . . . if . . .'

'If Nathan requests your help, should you give it?'

'Uh . . . how d'you know he's . . . the one?'

'Nathan Lake is my only client. One is sufficient. I am new to the profession. I am building up my client base. Isn't that right, Suzy?' He tapped his nose again.

'Yes, you are, Conrad, you are indeed.'

'Splendid. So, do you help him?' Dreave asked rhetorically. 'Personally, I have grown rather fond of the boy. I should like to see him succeed. So if it is within your power to aid his ascent, I would be most grateful for your cooperation.'

143

'Mmm, thing is,' Suzy said, shifting on her chair, 'it'll be very difficult. Probably impossible.'

'So one hundred thousand pounds is not enough for a small favour?'

Instantly, Suzy felt like the most ungrateful bitch on the planet. 'No! I just meant that it might—'

'Ssshhh,' Dreave calmed her. 'You can only do your best. But always remember that nothing is impossible in this great universe of ours. We label as impossible only those matters we are too lazy or fearful to confront comprehensively.'

'You don't know the problem,' she defended herself.

'I don't need to,' he said. 'You are a resourceful girl. You can make an intelligent argument.'

'But what if someone's not prepared to listen?'

'Then attack the other senses. If you are not heard, make certain you are seen . . . and smelt . . . and touched . . . and tasted.'

Suzy felt her face redden, her groin ache. If Dreave had said the word, she would have surrendered her every particle of being to his will, but his desires seemed wholly separate from his intellectual acknowledgement of her physical gifts.

Though maybe that was all for the best, because a plan was already formulating in her head, and she might well need to employ some unrequited sexual tension later on that evening.

Suzy left the basement and went to pick up the Merc from the small private car park a few streets away. There was still a good hour before the local offices released their workers for the day, so the high-walled enclosure was packed solid with vehicles. The attendant had to carefully manoeuvre five of them on to the street before he could clear a passage to remove the Mercedes. He grumbled all the while until Suzy produced a crisp fifty for his troubles.

'If you'd been more obliging,' she informed him as she handed him the note, 'you could have had two of these.'

She slipped behind the wheel and pushed a button on the dashboard; the roof lifted up and back, folding itself away like a concertina.

Her destination was south-west London, she was heading home, cruising with the top down, but the Merc itself wasn't going the full distance.

In Fulham, she pulled up outside the exclusive dealership where she'd bought the car, cleared her belongings from the dash and glovebox, walked into the gleaming showroom, found the simpering senior salesman, agreed a deal and finished the remainder of her journey by double-decker bus.

Once at home, she telephoned the Harley-Davidson dealership, talked some numbers and arranged to have the bike picked up as soon as possible within the day.

After that, the estate agent.

An hour later, as the Harley was being loaded into the back of a van, a board was being erected in the front garden: FOR SALE — FIRST FLOOR FLAT.

Phil could hardly believe his ears. In fact, he couldn't believe his ears.

'I don't believe you,' he told her.

'I sold the Merc and the Harley, and the flat is up for sale,' she repeated, sitting on the kitchen fitments.

'Don't believe you.'

'Here,' she said, taking two banker's drafts from the top of the microwave. 'These are the dealers' cheques. And you can see the estate agent's board in the front garden. The paperwork'll be through in a few days.'

Phil didn't want to see the cheques. 'You'll forgive me if I don't crack the champagne just yet. For all I know, they're fakes, and that board could come down tomorrow.'

'What can I do to make you believe me?'

'You? Nothing.' He walked out of the kitchen. She hopped off the fitment and followed him into the living room.

'If the dealers confirm,' he said, 'then I'll believe you.' He picked up the telephone. 'Give me the numbers.'

'Er . . . Phil, it's ten-thirty at night. I think they might be shut.'

He narrowed his eyes suspiciously.

She smiled. 'Try if you like.'

The receiver went back on the cradle. 'I'm calling tomorrow,' he told her firmly. 'First thing.'

'Good. I want you to. If that's what it takes.'

He poured himself a large Canadian Club. 'Want one?' he asked.

She shook her head. 'No, thanks, darling.'

Phil's head jerked and he fixed her with a stare as she sat down.

'What?' she said.

Slowly, a hint of a smile softened his dubious expression.

She knew what she'd said; had planned it for this very reaction. 'What?' she asked again with a puzzled look.

'It's OK.'

She hit him again with it. 'Darling, what is it?'

He perched stiffly on a straight-backed wooden chair in the corner of the room and sipped his drink.

'What, darling?' she persisted, using the endearment a third time. She saw him struggle not to crack his defences; she had not called him anything other than Phil, or several less savoury names, for weeks now.

He studied her for a moment. She could see the relief in his eyes; the hard glint had vanished.

'Why the change of heart?' he asked, predictably.

'I've been a queen bitch,' she answered. 'I've no excuse.' But she knew she needed one to explain herself credibly. She made a vulnerable face. 'I suppose I got a bit scared. Marriage and all that.'

Phil responded in an ideally sympathetic fashion. 'Darling, you should have said something. Anyway, I thought it was my job to get cold feet.'

She tittered at his joke, but maintained her puppy-dog countenance. 'And it's been a bit hectic at work,' she said. 'You know.'

He became severe again. 'Yes, I do know. So is this the end of it?'

'Well, I'm coping better now,' she said, feigning ignorance of the real question.

'Dreave,' he said. 'I mean Dreave. His money.'

'Oh, yes,' she said obediently. 'I'll tell him he's got to stop.'

He nodded gratefully. 'Be careful, though,' he warned. 'He's dangerous.'

Suzy frowned and shifted forward on the settee. 'What do you mean? Have you met him?'

'Sue, he's dangerous.'

She knew Phil. He was hedging. Not the truth, not a lie, but she had her answer. Dreave now had to know she had flouted his instructions regarding the cash. She considered this. Why had he not given her a roasting?

'Did you hear?' Phil said. 'He's dangerous.'

She guessed their meeting had wound up as an exchange of threats and a macho stand-off.

'Don't be silly,' she said nicely.

'Sue . . .' He left a long pause. 'He threatened to kill me.'

She made an appropriately aghast face. Inside her stomach, delirious acrobatics made her want to moan.

Phil's face had gone grey at the memory. He finished his drink; his neck and head trembled violently and the glass chattered against his teeth. Suzy had never seen him more brightly spooked. She waited for him to speak, but he needed more alcohol. She watched him cross the room and replenish his glass. He shook his head before he knocked it back in one.

'Phil . . .' Suzy began. 'Sorry if I'm being stupid, but why couldn't you arrest him?'

He shook his head again. 'Reasons,' he mumbled.

'Such as?'

He shrugged. 'Circumstances.'

'Like what?'

'Forget it.'

'You can't let him threaten you like that and get away with it.'

'I'm not,' he said.

She got up, went over and slipped her arms around his waist. 'What's going on, darling?'

Phil's lips were tight, sealing it in. His eyes were creased in fierce debate. Then he said, 'You can't tell him.'

She smelt his breath, fragrant with whisky. 'What?' she asked.

'I'm making checks.'

'On Dreave?'

He nodded.

'You think he's a criminal?'

'I don't think, I know. The man's as bent as a three-quid note.'

She gasped for effect. 'Has he got a record?'

'No. I checked the PNC.'

'Is he under surveillance?'

He swallowed and his Adam's apple bobbed in his throat. 'This isn't official, darling. I'm using up a few favours. I've got an old pal, ex-job, now a private investigator. He's going to see what he can dig up.'

'What do you think he'll find?' she wanted to know, trying to sound concerned rather than aroused. At last, Phil was beginning to entertain her; he was almost fun to be with.

'I'm not sure,' he said. 'But I wouldn't be surprised if he was something big in the underworld.'

Sex was essential. She had accepted that. It would complete her volte-face. Physical communion to renew their bond. A literal and figurative coming together. She would give him a night to remember; something different. Then catch him unawares as he lay there, spent, grinning and gurgling like a demented Goofy.

They cuddled and petted on the settee, and bedtime loomed.

Suzy wriggled out of Phil's embrace and went to the door.

'Don't come into the bedroom,' she told him.

'Hey?'

'Fifteen minutes, then I'll come for you.'

'Sounds interesting.'

She winked and disappeared.

True to her word, she returned fifteen minutes later, and stood provocatively in the doorway in a pair of white knickers.

'Strip,' she instructed.

Phil got to his feet and quickly discarded his clothes.

Suzy stepped back into the hall. 'This way, officer.'

He came to her. She flicked the wall switch and plunged the living room into darkness, but the corridor was alive with soft, dancing lights. She led him down to the bedroom, between the candles she had placed along the length of the hall floor.

'Very romantic,' he said approvingly.

They entered the bedroom – a mass of tiny flames.

'You got religion?' he asked in jest.

'Something like that,' she responded. 'Lie on the bed.'

Phil obliged.

She pulled out the drawer of her bedside cabinet and removed four cream silk scarves. She pushed the drawer back in and draped the scarves across his bare torso. 'Spread 'em,' she said.

Phil splayed his arms and legs, but said, 'Darling, this is kinky.'

'Live a little.'

She tied his wrists, then his ankles, then secured each silk restraint to a leg of the bed.

When she was finished she looked at his erection. 'What a shame,' she remarked. 'I don't have another scarf to tie that down. How will I

148

ever deal with it?' She was already slipping off her knickers.

She climbed on the bed and sat on him.

Phil shuddered and sighed gruffly.

'Miss this?' she asked cheekily, as she began to move.

'Sue, Sue, *Sue.*'

'I thought so.'

Unlike her afternoon session with Lake, this was clearly not going to be a quickie. Phil's fortuitous input of booze had turned him into the Marathon Man. And as much as Suzy enjoyed her every sensation, she resented the fact that any of it was necessary.

When eventually it ended, Suzy was almost as keen as Phil to call it a night and get some well-earned sleep, but all this had been for a purpose, and she was not about to waste it. Especially as Phil's satisfied exhaustion meant he would never be more easily swayed than now.

She crawled off the bed and dried herself with a couple of Kleenex. Even in that short time, Phil, still tied up, began to snore sonorously.

'Oi!' She shook him awake and sat down on her side of the bed. 'Are you going to fall asleep like that?'

'Not bothered.'

'OK,' she said, then casually tutted. 'Oh, yes, I meant to tell you. The other day I bumped into an old friend on the tube. Got talking. Turns out he's writing a novel and needs some information on the police firearms unit to authenticate a couple of his chapters.'

'Mmm?'

'So I didn't think you'd help at the time,' she said. 'But –' She smiled and tickled his sleeping manhood, which remained resolutely dead to the world. 'Now we seem to be getting on a bit better, I thought you might be willing to meet him.'

'Do I have to?' he asked weakly, fighting sleep, his eyes half-closed.

'No, you don't have to.'

'But you want me to.'

'We were good friends at school.'

'I could do without it, darling.'

'You won't do it? For me?'

'I haven't got the time.'

'You're not on till two tomorrow.'

'Tomorrow?'

'He's not local. He said he's only in town until tomorrow evening.'

'I'd rather not.'

Suzy wanted to weep. She had failed herself; failed Dreave.

'I'd rather not,' Phil repeated. 'But for you, my love, I will do absolutely anything.'

'Darling, you're wonderful,' Suzy sang, hoping she didn't sound too overly happy. 'Thank you.'

She stood up and set about untying the scarves, and as she released his limbs and rolled up each length of silk, they arranged where and when he would meet her friend the next day.

21

For Lake, Tuesday afternoon and evening dragged. His telephone stayed silent. He wondered whether Suzy had been lying, winding him up. When he climbed into bed he was fully convinced she had made no effort to arrange the promised meeting. It was her revenge.

Sleep swiftly welcomed him. Dreams swept through his mind. Gradually, their content altered. Light faded, fear spread and Lake spiralled downwards to meet an old friend.

Ben was crying. Lake couldn't see him, but he recognised the sobbing. Lake's world was blackness. He groped his way around a house that was unfamiliar. The sobbing neither approached nor diminished. It wailed steadily just out of reach. A sorrowful noise and a fearful one. Lake could not decide whether it was for tragedies past or to come. After a while it became apparent to him that his blindness was caused by sunglasses. He took them off, only to reveal a house in total darkness. He could distinguish doorways and furniture, and those only vaguely. If there were any windows, it was black as pitch outside. And still Ben cried, always just through the next dark doorway. Lake fumbled his hand over a light switch. Click, click, click, and no light. In the next room his searching fingers found a standard lamp. He felt under the shade for the switch. Click, click, click, and no light. He moved through the room, arms outstretched, feet kicking ahead. Another light switch. Click, click, click. Click. Click. The darkness was a teasing claustrophobia. *You're not confined, just effectively blind.* Lake became frantic. He touched some hanging fabric – curtains. He yanked them apart and a moonless night burst upon him. A light switch, a table lamp. Click, click, click. Dead. Click. Dead. A fridge! Cold comfort from a tiny bulb. Please. But coffin black inside. He began to whine, a low animal plea for help.

A presence joined him, attracted by his fear, and the dark was its home. Behind him now and, unlike Ben, it wasn't keeping its distance. Lake moaned. Ben cried. The presence closed in. Click click click. Click click. Click. Where were the fucking *lights*?

The presence swept up to his face. A nude, waxen, hairless figure with black empty sockets for eyes and a toothless mouth that fumed the stench of Hell as it mocked Lake in its dry rasp. '*Lights? Down here? Lights?*' It screeched its laughter, then closed its mouth round Lake's in a stinking kiss.

Lake woke up with a strangled yell. 'Oh, *shit.*' His voice quivered to the erratic beat of his heart. 'Oh, Suzy, come back, *please!*' He cried wretchedly.

His pain had found an outlet in defenceless sleep. His mind was in overload, unable to compute the excess input: he had once again lost the great love of his life; Dreave had communicated some unpalatable home truths; his next job depended on the goodwill of one person who owed him nothing, and another who didn't even know him; and his last job had seen him commit murder.

All of this was bad, but it paled beside the location of his resultant nightmare.

The Dark Land.

Sudden questions quelled his sobbing.

Had he taken the Dark Path? Had he? Would he have known? Had he failed to learn the crucial lesson? If so, what was the lesson? Was losing Suzy a step along that Dark Path? Was killing Brigit? Was worse to come?

His bedside lamp sat beside him, the welcome banishment of night horrors. He reached a hand out to bring light into the room.

Click. And no light. Click click. Click click. Click click. Jesus. Oh, *Jesus* . . .

Lake slept on through his dream within a dream, whimpering loudly as the presence broke into the safety of his dream bedroom.

His slumber-terror lasted but a minute, and what was a minute in so many hours? A single stormy raindrop in a placid lake.

When he awoke in the morning, it was gone from his mind.

Suzy giggled in her sleep.

In her dream, Marcel Marceau was chasing Phil around a dark maze of corridors. Phil was armed to the teeth, but he was petrified, snivelling and weeping with fear. Marcel was grinning. His hands were empty, but he was miming a gun. When Phil loosed off a panic shot, Marcel appeared to catch it in his teeth. When Marcel pretended to shoot, the wall beside Phil exploded with the impact.

She was shaken out of it by Phil, gently rocking her shoulder.

'What's so funny, darling?' he asked.

For a moment, Suzy forgot herself and nearly told him to piss off and leave her alone. Then she remembered.

'Funny dream,' she said, struggling to sit up. 'Give me a kiss.'

He leant down and pecked her lips, then held up the banker's drafts for the bike and car.

'I called the dealers,' he told her apologetically.

'That's OK.'

'I had to be sure. I'm sorry.'

'It's OK.'

'They confirmed,' he said softly, clearly ashamed of himself. 'I'm sorry.'

She waved a hand at him. 'Sshh,' she went. 'It's over.'

He sat next to her on the bed. 'What about these?'

Without hesitation, she took the drafts and ripped them to bits. 'We don't need his money,' she said. She dropped the pieces on her bedside cabinet. 'And when the upstairs flat sells, I'll do the same again.'

'Thank you.' He gave her another kiss. 'And you're late for work.'

The digital read nine-thirty-three a.m.

'I'll let me off this time,' she said, crawling out of bed.

'Are you going to call your friend?'

She opened the wardrobe to choose her outfit for the day. 'His number's at the office. I'll call you here before lunch to confirm everything.'

'Right.'

She clicked unwanted garments along the rail, then unhooked a white shirt and yellow trouser-suit and lay them on the bed.

'Haven't seen those before,' Phil commented. 'They look expensive.'

'Ah. Shit.'

'Oh, I see. Well, you don't need to tear those into pieces.'

'Thanks.' She proceeded to get dressed and made up.

All the while, Phil just perched there on the edge of the bed, simpering blissfully.

22

The telephone chirped.

Lake was sitting transfixed by the banality of morning television. The question of researching for his job interview was temporarily retarded. Bright sofas, suits and smiles had dropped his IQ into a state of merciful shutdown.

It was all he could do to hit the mute button on the remote.

He clutched the phone to his ear. He didn't say hello.

'Nathan?'

Her voice animated him. His body stiffened to alert. 'Suze, what's going on?'

She gave him the details. She told him he wasn't an actor any more, he was a writer; he no longer lived in London, he lived in Brighton; and they weren't ex-lovers, they were old pals from school.

He assimilated all the information, at the same time racking his brain for a way to extend their brief reintroduction.

As a start he said, 'I'm very grateful.'

'Don't be,' she replied. 'I didn't do it for you.'

Then the line went dead.

The pub was old, in the centre of Covent Garden. The ceiling was tobacco brown, and genuinely so; it wasn't a shade by Dulux. The tables were small, round, unliftably heavy. The staff served drinks. They didn't pout or preen or juggle bottles. It wasn't Lake's idea of a decent boozer – it was unremittingly ugly – but it did have an appeal. It was a no-nonsense pub for no-nonsense people. Chosen by Cage.

155

Lake felt badly vindictive as he walked into the pub. It was jealousy. Cage had what he wanted. He wondered if he could wreck the copper's relationship with Suzy. A few words would be enough. Something along the lines of 'shag', 'office' and 'floor'.

At the bar he ordered a coffee. He felt alcohol would somehow spoil him; dull something essential within him that had to be kept honed.

A few minutes after he had claimed a seat by one of the huge frosted-glass windows, his coffee was delivered. He placed both his hands on the underside of his chair and jumped it forward, closer to the table.

As he did so, he yelped.

In his right palm, the small cut was open and bleeding. It had never properly closed, but it hadn't been any trouble for months. Now he'd snagged it again. He ran his fingertips carefully around the underside of the wrought-iron chair, but he could feel no imperfections in the casting.

He fished in his pockets for a tissue and found Dreave's handkerchief. He puzzled for a few seconds. What was it doing in his denim jacket? Hadn't it been in his winter overcoat? That was the last time he recalled . . .

Lake's thoughts stuttered to a halt.

The last time?

But for those three words, his mind had become a void.

The last time.

His brain huffed and puffed, but it was no good. Those three words stood alone. They were a stagnant pool beside a normally flowing stream of brain-chatter. They meant nothing to him, but he sensed they were far from meaningless.

Clenching the silk in his palm, he absently attempted to peel the lid from his plastic milk-pot, causing it to spurt all over the table.

'Bollocks,' he said, chucking the dripping container into the burdened, noxious ashtray. He had a slurp of black coffee and burnt his mouth. 'Shit.' Then the cup's ridiculous finger-hole handle slipped round his finger so the scalding pottery touched his skin. 'Bugger,' he muttered as a gloop of liquid spilled on his leg. 'Oh, fuck it.' He cracked the cup back on to the saucer and spilt some more as it landed unevenly on his sachet of unused sugar.

He forgot the cut and used the handkerchief to blot his stained leg.

At that moment a man about his own age stopped at the table. He was about five-eleven, slightly built, good-looking in a dull way, with dark, cropped hair in a side parting.

The man outstretched his hand and announced himself. 'I'm Philip Cage, Sue's fiancé. You must be Nathan.' His smile was an effort.

Lake stuffed the silk in his back pocket and stood up, already detesting Cage for his glib use of 'Sue's' and 'fiancé'.

'That's right. It's good to meet you,' Lake lied. 'Thanks for coming.' He took Cage's hand and shook it firmly. Both men squeezed hard.

Instantly, Cage's smile blossomed into a lively, boyish grin. 'No, it's my pleasure,' he said. 'Can I get you a drink?'

'I'm fine, thanks, but you have one.'

'No, I don't have much time, I'd rather talk.' His eyes were sparkling as though he'd met his Hollywood hero. 'What d'you want to know?'

Nothing was the answer to that. Lake needed only to shake his hand once more and the exercise was complete.

'Go on, ask me anything,' Cage urged. 'Anything.'

'Um . . . how did you know it was me, when you came in?'

'Sue said you'd be all in black,' Cage replied, with an obliging smile.

'You call her Sue?'

Cage nodded.

'Right.'

'Don't you?'

'No.'

'Oo. Maybe I won't then.'

Lake almost laughed. Was this guy for real?

'What else?' Cage asked.

Lake gave it some thought. 'What's the procedure when you get a call?' He supposed it was the type of question a bona-fide writer might ask.

With a glee verging on the positively puerile, Cage spewed forth detail upon detail.

It was most disconcerting. Cage was a likeable sort, but Lake felt a little perturbed that the public's safety rested with someone who probably still played fort in his back garden. He wondered whether Suzy had been attracted to the big kid in him.

The description of events lasted twenty-five minutes. Cage covered everything. Had Lake been a genuine novelist, he could not have wanted to know another single fact.

'What else? Go on.' Cage was grinning idiotically.

Lake held up his hands, as though to quell the antics of an exhausting child. 'No, you've . . . been great, very helpful.'

'What was that?'

'Sorry?'

'In your hand.'

'What?' Lake flipped his hands over to inspect his palms.

Cage pointed. 'That. What's that?'

Lake stared down at his right palm. The cut was dribbling a white fluid.

'What is it?' Cage persisted.

'Milk,' Lake answered. 'I had coffee.'

Cage made an exaggerated head movement to peer in Lake's cup at the leftover liquid. 'It's black,' he declared. 'You took it black.'

'Because I spilt the milk. See?' Lake indicated the outline of the dried milk stain on the table.

'Half an hour ago?'

'What?'

'You haven't had a drink in half an hour.'

'No.'

'Then why's that milk still wet?' Cage did not sound either doubtful or accusing, simply fascinated.

'No idea. Right, well, I'd better let you get to work,' Lake said, but could not imagine Philip Cage running around London with a live firearm.

Cage said, 'Yes, I have to protect people.'

Lake rose to his feet. Cage bobbed up with him, and his hand darted out. Lake wiped the white seepage on his coat, then gripped Cage's hand in a long, firm shake, as per instruction.

The change in Cage was instantaneous. His grin slipped away as his hand moved up and down in Lake's grasp.

As Lake took his leave, thanking Cage for his time, he noticed the policeman's new expression: thoroughly miserable, as though he couldn't bear to see Lake walk away.

But his eyes weren't focused on Lake. They seemed far off, his mind removed from external sights, inwardly searching, as though he'd forgotten where he'd put something very important, and understood he would never again have it back.

* * *

The one commodity Cage desperately needed when he returned home that evening was love. He felt thoroughly wretched, at the pit of a black depression. Something was very wrong. A dread sense of the terrible. There was an awful loss encompassing his whole being, but emanating from deep inside.

He wanted Suzy to reassure him, reaffirm her love, be the new, improved fiancée today that she had been last night and this morning.

But Suzy wasn't home, and it was past nine p.m.

His first action was to fill the house with light. As much as possible. He stormed through each room, flicking switches. Ceiling lights, standard lamps, bedside lamps. In the kitchen, he punched the door button of the microwave to illuminate the interior, and yanked the fridge door back on its hinges. He shot upstairs and lit the bare bulbs hanging in the first-floor flat. Suzy's futon had disappeared. At least that was a good sign. The only place he left in darkness was the cellar. It felt right to leave below ground in its natural state.

His heart was creating havoc, palpitating and stealing the breath from his lungs. He didn't want alcohol. He didn't want to watch the TV. He didn't want to do anything but hold his fiancée and hear her whisper sweet somethings in his ear. Failing that, he wanted to hold his Glock, put it in his mouth and take the back of his skull off with a hollow-point.

He slumped down in the kitchen, on the cool tiles next to the back door.

An hour passed. It felt like a year.

Another hour. He felt ancient, ready to die.

His heart hammered away, shortening his breath. He shook and sweated.

It was no good; he needed fresh air. He undid the floor bolt of the back door, scrambled to his feet and slid the top bolt. Grabbing the key from the window ledge, he unlocked the mortice. He pulled open the door and practically leapt into the back garden.

Then his heart really went crazy. He swayed in a circle on his feet, unable to catch his breath at all now. Light-headed, shivering and sweltering all at once.

He stared agog at the green apparition. The canvas cover cloaking a familiar shape.

He staggered over to it and tore the material up from the paving.

159

Light splashed out from the back door and down from the uncurtained upstairs windows. Low-light gleams bounced off the Harley's chrome bits and lustrous cream paintwork.

A whining filled his mouth, then seemed to fill his whole head. Tears welled up but he was too shocked and livid to cry.

Hold on . . .

Cream paintwork?

It was black and blue before.

Wasn't it? Was he mistaken? Was it a respray? Was it a new bike?

He didn't know. Nothing was certain any more. He launched a kick at the bike and knocked it on its side with a metallic crunch.

The front garden. He knew what to expect but he had to check. He pelted into the house, through the kitchen, down the hall and opened the front door.

The estate agent's board was gone. He hadn't noticed earlier.

His head swung left and right, eyes searching for the Mercedes. It wasn't there, but he knew damn well it would not be at the showroom either. It was obvious. She had returned in the afternoon, bought back the car and driven it to work. And her tearing up the cheques? Nothing more than the dealers would have done had she handed them back intact.

Now he did venture into the cellar. He needed the Glock, and not for his own head. He was going to shove that icy muzzle against her temple and scare the truth out of her. If that didn't work, he would lie in wait for Dreave, stalk him on his way home and kill him. No questions, no confrontation, just pull the trigger. Once, twice, three times, four times. Four shots into the kill-zone. Three chest, one head. Make sure.

At the foot of the cellar steps he stopped dead. A space had been cleared among the clutter. In the centre was Suzy's futon bed. Not dumped in its component pieces, but laid out flat with a fresh duvet and plumped pillows. Beside it on the concrete floor was her digital alarm clock, its wire snaking away between two cardboard boxes into the cellar's single power point. The red digits glowed eerily at eleven-twenty-seven p.m.

An unnamed fear filled him, wiped him utterly clean of anger, relegated his black depression to a minor inconvenience. There was evidently something terribly wrong with his fiancée and he sensed he had just walked into the evil midst of it. He no longer wanted answers from her, or revenge against her weirdo benefactor – they were welcome to each other. He simply wanted out of the entire situation. Having waited over two hours for Suzy's return, he now prayed she would stay away long enough for him to pack the essentials and scarper.

He trod across her bed and knelt down at the old cabinet, housing his gun safe. Out came the drawers, out came his key and into the lock it went. He twisted the key and pulled open the door.

'Jesus fucking Christ.' His hand patted the flat, empty lump of oily towelling. 'What the *fuck*?' He removed the key and jittered it into the ammunition compartment, twisted and opened. 'Oh, shit. No, no . . .'

He stepped back and sat heavily on the bed.

It had to be Suzy. There was no one else. It wasn't hard to work out. Somehow she had discovered his secret; spied him from the top of the steps when he was cleaning it perhaps. Then borrowed his keys, probably this morning, and tried the two or three on his fob she knew didn't relate to the house doors.

That really did put the seal on his decision. He had to clear out and fast. She was the one with the gun now, and he was beginning to suspect that she was quite sick in the head.

As he dashed up the steps, he was already mentally packing, picturing which belongings he would grab and where they were located.

In the bedroom, he reached on top of the wardrobe and brought down a suitcase which he laid open on the bed. Clothes and personal knick-knacks and documents were carelessly chucked in, some items ending up on the floor. He zipped up the case and fled his home.

Speeding up the road in his Vauxhall Carlton, Cage was dazzled by an approaching vehicle with headlights on full beam. He screeched to a halt and was passed by a weaving cream Mercedes lightly bumping parked cars. He wound down his window and stuck his head out. The Merc stopped fifty yards behind him. Suzy got out and wobbled in the road, laughing and gesticulating at him.

'*You warped fucking bitch!*' he screamed at her. He didn't wait for her reply; she had a gun.

He drove off with her hysterical cackling ringing in his ears and was sobbing his heart out by the end of the road.

23

Thursday was relentlessly wet. The sky was disturbed, off-colour; grey, with a tint of orange, a hint of green. Its unearthly disquiet found an echo within the police Rover.

Cage felt awful. He should not have been in charge of a school crossing, let alone on patrol with a firearms unit.

His shift had begun at midday. Green and Temple had asked after his health. He guessed they meant his mental health. The normal chat as they cruised central London was noticeably absent.

Cage had stayed the night with a civilian friend. He wanted nothing of his troubles filtering back to his superiors. Of course, he was under no illusions; they would find out soon enough, but he would tell them himself when his head was a little clearer, when he could talk about it calmly and rationally, without this macabre dread darkening every inch of his mind. They would revoke his firearms authorisation, but he would welcome the decision. He wasn't fit to handle a weapon. He wasn't stable.

He decided: at the end of this shift he would confess the entire story. If he was dismissed from the force altogether as a final outcome, then so be it.

He just needed these few hours to straighten his thoughts. When he turned his fiancée in, he did not intend to be the mental wreck he was at that moment. And he most certainly did have to turn her in. She had stolen his gun to his certain knowledge, and if his suspicions were accurate concerning Dreave, then she was involved in something far more serious.

163

The irony was, he truly believed he could have handled all this if only he hadn't already been inexplicably and totally depressed. Ever since yesterday lunchtime, meeting that writer. It didn't make sense. He should have been happy, at least until the revelations of last night. Suzy, so it appeared, had mended her ways and returned to his bed. But he had actually been almost suicidal, such was his feeling of loss.

Green interrupted his thoughts. 'Sarge, you all right?'

The question had to sink in. 'Um . . . oh . . . yeah.'

Cage sensed their natural concern. He assessed he could still hack it if they had to do the business, and he almost craved a request for help to come over the radio so he could at least take his mind off the aching void within, but his desire to pull out of his nameless misery was so intense, and futile, it felt like the very verge of madness.

Lake's job interview was scheduled for two p.m. He entered the room nearly ten minutes past the hour.

As Temple would have to confirm to the investigation later, the incident began at nine minutes past two. He knew this because he checked his watch the second before Sergeant Cage yelled, 'Hey, asshole! Stop the car!'

It was clear from the outset that Cage was several rounds short of a full clip.

'Stop the car, ya goddamn asshole!' he shouted like a hay-seed cop from the American Deep South, before he did the job himself by yanking on the handbrake. The Rover slewed sideways in the wet and came to a halt. The car behind bumped them, and a series of collisions filled the street with metal hammer-blows and breaking glass.

The ARV was in the Charing Cross Road, adjacent to Leicester Square.

Green had barely recovered from their impromptu halt when Cage reached a hand down and unclipped his seat belt, then grabbed him by the back of his head and rammed it twice against the steering wheel. Just short of unconscious, Green moaned and lolled. In the back, Temple's natural calm worked against him. Not prone to panic, he sought a sensible explanation. Torrential rain on the roof only helped to confuse.

Before Temple could discern the true danger from his comrade-in-arms, Cage was already out of the car, pulling open the back door and climbing in. The dripping fringe of his cropped hair flew forward at the younger officer, and the forehead under it broke Temple's nose. Temple went saggy, and Cage opened the opposite back door and tumbled him out onto the road.

'I swore to Boss Hogg I'd git those goddamn Duke boys, and I will,' Cage mumbled to himself as he opened the gun box. From it he took one of the carbines and snatched the clip from the second.

He backed himself out from the rear seat, muttering, 'Shoot! Can't get deputies worth shit!' and marched away towards Leicester Square.

The man who used to be Philip Cage arrived outside the Empire cinema.

At the sight of the armed policeman, people scurried into the cinema foyer to join those queueing for a film and escaping the downpour.

All eyes were to their blue protector. Puzzled, half-smiling faces jabbered to each other, friend to friend, stranger to stranger, out of the corners of their mouths.

He was dripping wet. His Metropolitan Police pullover steamed, as though the rain had permeated through to some internal workings which were about to short.

He slid the bolt on the carbine and chambered the first round.

Still the faces looked on. Guns in the wrong hands were frightening. In the right hands they were intriguing.

With his gun at waist level he began to shoot.

The first bullet holed a massive pane in the cinema's black-glass façade. The window stayed in its frame. Somewhere at the rear of the foyer, an attendant wearing a striped waistcoat fell to the carpet, mortally wounded.

His trigger finger made the same steady, repeated movement, making the carbine crack at half-second intervals. Figures in the cinema dived for cover; some just collapsed and died. The windows shattered open to the elements under the lead onslaught.

'*You Duke boys are dead meat!*' he bellowed, beneath the repeated cracking of the carbine until the first clip was spent. '*Dead meat!*' he yelled into the sudden, rain-soaked lull.

The empty magazine clattered on the concrete, and he loaded the spare from his trouser pocket. Bolt back. Ready to go.

He walked now, loosing off bullets as he screamed his insanity at fictional men. '*Shouldn'a crossed Boss Hogg, boys! No, sirree!*'

The window of a poster shop shattered and dropped. Bodies behind it did the same. One solitary figure, a woman, made a break out of the doorway.

He stopped walking. With gleeful, shining eyes he watched her go and shouted after her. *'You can't run, boy!'* Taking a wide stance, he hefted the carbine up to his jaw, jammed the stock firmly into his shoulder, leaned his head in for his eye to sight the target and fired.

The target's momentum took her another four steps, then she fell and splashed down, splayed out in a huge puddle.

'I gotcha, Bo!' he shrieked. *'I gotcha!'*

The woman didn't move. Another two shots thumped into her back and made sure she never would.

Screams and moans began to filter out of the blown-open cinema and gaping shop fronts.

The indiscriminate firing ended. He kept the gun up and targeted individuals.

'Luke!' he called, laughing and firing. *'Luke! I shot your kin! Bo's dead! Luke!'*

First on the scene was Derek Green, still nursing a groggy head. He had donned an armoured vest and was clutching his .38.

The sarge was killing folk. Before his very eyes. Picking them off, one by one. Shouting like a madman. Aptly enough.

Green took position in the cinema entrance. Cage was shooting the opposite direction. Green raised his revolver, but something caused him to shout not shoot.

'Sarge!'

Cage swivelled round and loosed four shots in quick succession. One caught Green in the left arm.

Adrenalin, fear, rain, pain, blood. It was too much, and Green went faint. He tried to aim, but he was dangerously unsteady.

A hand came over his shoulder and gently lowered his gun for him. It was Temple, with the bloody, squashed nose.

Some sixty feet away, Cage dry-fired on an empty chamber.

It was another success. Lake had believed it when he first shook their hands on entering the room. Now, leaving them all with his firm grasp, he somehow knew it as a fact.

* * *

Cage unholstered his sidearm and cocked the hammer.

'*Luke! I'm a-comin' to git you! I just . . . shot . . .*' The rambling loony-tune monologue died in his mouth.

Sergeant Philip Cage whipped his head from side to side.

. . . *Oh, Jesus Christ, what have I done? What the fuck have I DONE?* Carnage, everywhere.

With the .38 in his hand, Temple dashed across the puddles, through the downpour, towards a litter bin. Nearer to the target. Further from the citizens. He had a few precious seconds to prevent more deaths by causing one.

He knelt down behind the bin, wiped the rain from his eyes.

Cage saw Temple approach, but his brain was a white-out. A blinding flare of comprehension had illuminated his return to sanity.

The loss. Since yesterday. It was his *mind*! His *SOUL*!

From a deeply disturbed sky, a billion tears were shed.

That fucking writer stole—

Three shots.

'Lights out, sarge.'

24

Sirens wailed through the rain-slashed sky. Fast tone, slow tone, English style, American style.

Lake stopped on Regent Street outside the casting director's offices. He had never heard such a din.

An ambulance streaked by. A paramedic truck. A police car. Another ambulance.

Something had occurred close by, Lake could tell. The sirens were not tailing off into the distance. Those that weren't approaching and growing louder seemed to be steady and centred not too far away from his current spot.

Still, it wasn't wise to dwell on such matters. To take every tragic event to heart would be too depressing. It was better to think, *There but for the grace of God go I,* and get on with the job of living.

He tilted his head up at the sky. The warm rain pattered his face. He loved the sky as it was today; grey, normally so miserable, but enlivened now by a subtle wash of green and orange. He could not see the two colours together, but if he looked for one and then the other, both were there. In any one year there were only a couple of days with skies like this. They were ominous, portentous.

He turned and walked away from the hubbub, through the continuing deluge, towards home.

There was the good news, and then there was the bad news.

Lake received the good news via the telephone.

His message light was flashing. Dreave's voice confirmed what he

169

already knew. He was back in work again. A seven-month shoot beginning in three weeks. Fifty thousand pounds, including a buy-out for the second UK showing. Dreave had agreed the contract on Lake's behalf. Lake gave an almighty whoop.

He received the bad news via the television.

Had he waited, it would have found him sooner or later, but he was chasing it, searching for a news flash to satisfy his morbid curiosity; keen for an explanation of the sirens in the West End.

He got exactly what he wanted.

It had begun at approximately two-ten p.m. No names were being released until next of kin had been informed, but initial reports put the number of dead as high as twelve, with seventeen wounded, some critically. Among the dead was the perpetrator of the massacre, apparently a member of a police Armed Response Unit. No further information was available as yet.

Lake sat rigid on his sofa. He stared at the pictures in front of him as they returned to their innocuous afternoon shapes and noises.

No names were being released.

He didn't need to hear any.

It had begun at approximately two-ten p.m.; spot on.

And the perpetrator of the massacre was apparently a member of a police Armed Response Unit.

Of course.

He needed no outside confirmation of the name Sergeant Philip Cage. The conviction was within him.

In the past months there had been so many questions unanswered. Some he couldn't answer, some he didn't wish to. So many odd happenings. All of which he had opted at some level of mind to ignore, or, if possible, forget.

This he could never hope to ignore.

He glanced down his arm at his right hand, clenched white on the sofa cushion beside him. It was as though some alien creature lay dormant but deadly at his side.

The first time it didn't add up: the cut, the blood, the white fluid, his father's unusual behaviour, then his father's insanity, then his father's hatred of his only son. Lake's mind had chosen to sever the obvious connection between the man who gave him the cut and the consequences of its unhealing nature. Thus it was simply a cut.

A little odd perhaps, but harmless enough.

Not any more.

He remembered being bothered about the cut yesterday, just before Cage walked into the pub. Those three words in his head, *the last time*; unable to develop his thoughts any further. Then Cage baffling him with his openness.

Now Lake understood. Sergeant Philip Cage had probably not acted that way since junior school. It was a part of the same process suffered by his father, the end result being madness, the effect of which was defined by the tools to hand. His father had a small blade; Cage had a big gun.

The dream of Ben and RADA returned as a vivid memory, though still somehow older than it was, like a crystal-clear childhood recollection. So much had happened since then. His life had changed. He had changed the lives around him. Some he had even destroyed. Brigit was not the only death on his conscience now.

He smiled, then laughed.

Jesus, he was getting carried away. What a fertile imagination. This wasn't the twilight zone, this was planet earth. And he was Nathan Lake, essentially a good man, give or take the odd lapse into a homicidal frenzy.

No names had been released. So it could have been any deranged firearms officer.

But the timing was right. Exactly when his job interview commenced.

Pure coincidence.

But did he really believe in the concept of random chance? Had he not seen too much to negate the theory?

Twilight zone again, Nathan. Pack it in.

But what about the Dark Path? The Dark Land?

The fanciful imaginings of a bad dream. Anyway, hadn't he managed to learn the lesson in time to keep him on the Light Path? Hadn't he accepted it was his lot to endure nine months of *Oedipus?* Wasn't that the answer? Suffer the shit, and grin and bear it? It even rhymed, and wise saws often rhymed.

Of course, he could swing his belief one way or the another with a single phone call.

He looked at the telephone.

No. Not yet. No need if it turned out Philip Cage was not the dead police officer.

He settled back on the sofa for the hours of viewing that stretched ahead.

The candle flame flickered in the dark cellar. Shadows shifted and bobbed against the brick walls like nervous criminals about to make a break for it.

Suzy lay naked on top of her duvet, her eyes following the twitching shadow of the unlit light bulb on the ceiling. It was hypnotic, relaxing.

Those frigging policemen had wound her up. Offering their tea and sympathy at the office, offering to leave a WPC to drive her home and share her grief.

Didn't they understand? No one could share her grief. They couldn't share what she didn't have.

Then coming to her home. More tea, more sympathy, and the start of the questions; their true concern in all this mess. Why had one of their precision instruments malfunctioned? Question after question, softly spoken, delicately put, but an interrogation in all but style.

She told them nothing to aid their comprehension. After fifteen minutes she rose to her feet, picked up the inspector's peaked cap and left the room. In a moment of intense human understanding, they allowed her thirty seconds before following.

In that time Suzy had opened the front door and thrown the cap out onto the road, where it was promptly squashed flat by a passing car.

The inspector and the WPC emerged from the sitting room, walked past her and stepped outside, then turned to face her.

'You would like us to leave,' the inspector said with great solemnity. 'I quite understand. I appreciate the enormity of your distress. If I could just have my hat, please, Miss Cooper.'

Suzy pointed over his shoulder at the black pancake in the road. He swung round and kept his face to the street for several seconds. Suzy guessed he was trying to calm down, not shout at the bereaved.

'Never mind,' he said to her through gritted teeth. 'When may we call again?'

'The next time I'm burgled.'

'I'm sorry?'

'He's dead,' she said. 'And I didn't kill him. So you and I have nothing to say to each other.'

The inspector frowned heavily. 'But don't you want to know *why*?'

'Shit happens,' she told him, and shut the door.

Now, lying in the cellar thinking about it, she began to cackle. That was funny with the hat. She wished she'd laughed at the time. A burp cut through her amusement and an aftertaste of champagne filled her mouth. She kicked her leg to the side and knocked over the empty bottle and cackled some more.

With her private income from Dreave, and the forthcoming proceeds of Phil's life insurance, things were really looking up.

An uneasy sleep had claimed Lake about an hour before he suddenly jolted wide awake.

He had been dreaming of a five-year-old Philip Cage scampering around a school playground in a massively oversized police uniform. His playmates giggled each time he tripped over the trailing material of his trouser legs. Until, with hate pouring from his innocent eyes, he picked himself up, magically produced a machine-gun from the folds of his voluminous blue jumper and shot his little buddies full of holes.

On the television was a late-night news summary. Lake wondered whether the mention of a familiar name had seeped into his subconscious and woken him. He grabbed the remote and whacked up the volume.

'_. . . went berserk in Leicester Square today. With the deaths in hospital this evening of another two victims, the number of dead rises to fourteen. A police spokesman said earlier that a full investigation was already under way, but no explanation has yet been offered for why the officer, who was later shot dead by a police marksman, carried out this apparently motiveless attack in the heart of the West End._'

'Who was it?' Lake pleaded with the newscaster. 'What's his name?'

'_It is believed that only the torrential rain prevented the casualties from being even heavier by keeping many people off the streets._'

'The name—'

'_Sergeant Cage had served as a firearms officer for five years._'

'Fuck.'

'_Now other news—_'

Lake switched off the television. He waited for the inevitable surge of emotion. Would he scream, sob, head-butt the wall, throw himself out of the window?

He stood up and made himself a cup of tea. For the next ten minutes he sat in silence and drank it. It was true about tea; it was a real comfort in times of woe. It could not erase the fact that he was responsible for the deaths of fourteen people – fifteen including Cage, sixteen including Brigit, not forgetting the ruin of his father's life, and therefore his mother's – but it was certainly to be recommended as a heart-warming beverage.

With his mother in mind, he decided to make the call he had put off making in the afternoon. If it was all true, all he now believed, she was the person to provide the final damning proof of his guilt.

He went to the phone and called. It was late but his question wouldn't wait until morning.

Maureen Lake picked up after five rings. 'Hello,' she said, and reeled off her number. She sounded weary, tired, but not as though she'd been asleep.

'Hi, Mum,' Lake said with forced good humour.

'Oh, hello, dear.'

'You're still up?'

'I don't sleep much these days,' she told him. 'Can't.'

Tears pricked in his eyes. 'I'm sorry, Mum.'

'So am I, dear, but it's hardly your fault.'

Lake was choked by the simple lilt of his mother's voice. He wished he could be beside her again that instant as her little boy, return to the wall the vanished calendars of two decades. Even if it put the bad years ahead of him once more, it didn't matter; he just wanted the three of them together as a family again.

'How's Dad?' he asked.

'Let them out,' she said.

'What?'

'Your tears, I can hear them.'

Lake's chin wobbled.

'It's OK, dear,' she said. 'You can cry.'

'I can't,' he told her, closing his eyes, fighting the urge.

'Come on, this is your mum. Why not?'

He breathed deeply. The storm had passed. He said, 'Because I'd never stop. Mum . . .'

'Yes, dear?'

'When did it happen? With Dad?'

'The day?'

'The time. I know the day.'

'Why are you asking at this hour?'

'Because . . . because I need to know.'

'Yes,' she said. 'I have times like that. Questions that won't go away. Silly things sometimes. But there's no one to answer them. About eleven-fifteen.'

'What?'

'When it happened. About eleven-fifteen.'

Clunk. The final piece of evidence fell into place. The time of his job interview that day: eleven-fifteen. Verdict: guilty as sin.

'Right,' he said quietly. 'Thanks.'

'Nathan?'

'Yes, Mum.'

'Feel free to come and visit.'

'I'm sorry. I know I've been bad.'

'No, only if you can spare the time.'

'I'm sorry. I will make the effort.'

'I love you, Nathan.'

Lake felt winded. He couldn't recall his mum ever saying the words.

'And I love you, Mum.' A first on both sides.

'Do you want to talk?' she asked.

'I don't know that there's much to say. Do you want to talk?'

'No, dear. You should get to bed.'

'Mmm.' He debated whether to tell her his career news. Did he even want the work now? He could barely see past the end of this phone call, let alone seven months hence. 'I got a job,' he said.

'That's wonderful. Terrible about that policeman in Leicester Square.'

'Uh . . .'

He realised it was simply her exhausted, flaky mind hopping subjects, but it was still eerie to hear another person place the two things side by side.

'Puts it all in perspective,' she said.

'Mmm.'

'Well, I'd better say night-night, dear.'

'Yeah . . . Mum?'

'Yes, dear?'

'Give Dad my love.'

There was a long pause. Then, 'Better not, dear. You know . . .'

'OK, 'night, Mum,' he said quickly, and his tears very nearly beat the receiver to the cradle.

25

The sun came up over Regent's Park. Lake welcomed its golden warmth, though his heart was ice.

The damp night scents were still fresh in his nostrils. The recent rain had stirred the grass and greenery. Their nature floated about him, invisible but wonderfully tangible. Through the dark hours into the dawn, he had been able to smell the approach of summer in the air. Now he could see it in the sky. So blue this morning. So much better than the heavy, doom-laden hues of yesterday.

He hadn't slept all night. His wooden bench was not conducive to sleep. His mind was positively averse to it.

After talking to his mum, the flat had become claustrophobic. He had to find a place where bad news couldn't reach him, crowd him, suffocate him.

It still seemed incredible that his presence on this planet had been the catalyst for so much pain in people he had never met. Even less conceivable was the effect of his life on the people he was meant to love. But he knew it was not his mere existence that caused the damage; it was his hateful ambition, his choice to move in a specific direction, regardless of the odds against his reaching his destination.

Sixteen dead.

It was unreal. He felt removed from it. Was that the human mind springing its defences to protect the organism? Had to be. If not, he would have gone cuckoo last night.

He was a killer. Nathan Lake, essentially a good man, was a mass murderer by proxy. Except he didn't feel any different. At least, not in

177

any sense of crossing an unseen divide between good and evil. He had changed, of course. He was a successful actor now, and was on his way to becoming an international star. It was all still there for him, if he wanted it. No one was about to arrest him and put him away for the rest of his life. He could damn himself all the way to hell and back, but he was the only one who could. Apart from Dreave, no one else knew the facts. His future was assured. It was his, bought and paid for. It was not a price he would have paid willingly had he known the currency – blood spilled from innocent veins – but the deal was well and truly struck, and the goods were non-returnable.

The big question: should he carry on?

A female jogger plodded past, apparently half-asleep. Lake watched her bright figure shrink away along the path.

And he thought again, what about his own Path?

It was Dark; it had to be. He still couldn't work out how he had failed to learn the lesson and correctly solve Ben's riddle, but clearly he *had* flunked it, and disastrously so.

As far as he could tell, he had two choices. He could stick with Dreave and continue with his proven Method, or he could find a new agent and take his chances with the rest of the acting profession.

For Lake, essentially a good man, the choice was easy. He would break with Dreave and seek employment on his own merits. His CV now included a major feature film; that would help his cause. And he could blitz casting directors with a massive mail-shot during his forthcoming television series. Those two things combined had to make him an impressive bet for further work.

He looked at the small, detestable, gaping cut in his right palm. Even without his 'research', would it be safe? He wondered whether the solution was as simple as covering it with a plaster. The thought flashed through his mind to cut his hand clean off with an axe. He shivered. Bad idea. That might rather limit casting possibilities. And it might hurt.

He resolved that from this day on he would endeavour to live a blameless life. There was no question of making amends: there was little he could do to cancel his past sins. He couldn't bring back the dead. He couldn't take away his mother's pain or make his father sane.

It was within his power to help just one person. Suzy offered his only chance for an ounce of redemption. Not by stepping into the shoes of a dead man, as her new lover. That was a sick notion, especially in view of the circumstances of her fiancé's death. It was also unlikely that she would accept it; she had changed, hardened, and that was precisely the reason he had to help. He believed she had fallen under Dreave's charismatic spell. He could warn her, open her eyes to the treacherous influence of the man. Catch her before she fell too far. It wasn't too late. He was certain of that.

Like him, she was essentially a good person at heart.

Suzy was woken at seven a.m. by an insistent knocking on the front door. She had slept wonderfully, a refreshing dip into a dreamless black pool. The cellar was the best room in the house. She felt so at home there.

As the caller pounded the wood, Suzy pretended she wasn't at home at all. She lay still and waited for whoever it was to give up and go away. It couldn't be anyone she wanted to speak to. The police should have known not to call again; she had abandoned her few friends over the past months; and if the press had discovered her address, then no way did she want those vulturine arseholes picking away at the remains of her old life.

A pattern soon emerged. Ten seconds' knocking, five seconds' silence, followed by the same. It lasted three minutes before ceasing altogether.

She settled for another couple of hours' sleep. If she was late for work, so what? If it weren't for Dreave's continued presence there, Studio House would have already lost its manager. Her job meant nothing. No job meant anything. Set against the big picture, the human need for gainful employment had become an abhorrence to her. It was petty; just an older version of children squabbling over an unfair toy-swap. Its only point was financial reward, and that was pitiful for the majority of the population. But still people convinced themselves how terribly important it was that they meet quotas, increase output, maximise potential, beat deadlines. The very things they derided at school were now the centre of their adult universe. Kids knew the score: life wasn't about work, it was about enjoyment, making mischief, staying out late and spending pocket money as soon as it came. Grown-ups weren't these great mature individuals, they were simply children gone dull and pubic. The only deadline worth beating was the one on the hospital monitor; the one that *proved* kids had it right.

The front door received another bout of hammering. She listened, and could hear the same pattern. She let it continue for two minutes before accepting that the persistent little bastard had earned an audience with the mistress of the house.

She rolled off the bed and started up the cellar steps, then stopped and thought she'd better put some clothes on. Then thought, fuck it, why should she?

The man on the doorstep went scarlet and lost the power of speech. Suzy could see him trying desperately to keep his goggling eyes on her face. She thought this was the most freeing experience of her entire life. The dawn sun filled the hall, warming her skin. A slight breeze wafted in and raised goose bumps and nipples.

'Aaahh,' he went, and that was it.

She had immediately assessed him to be a policeman. He was casually dressed, with long and tangled fair hair, scruffy red stubble, carrying a bit of excess weight in the cheeks; a pleasant enough face, if understandably gormless at that moment in time. He actually looked nothing like a copper, and she had no idea what sense had told her he was.

'Yes?' she said. 'What can I do for you?'

She saw him struggle with the phrasing of her question.

'I . . . aahh . . . Miss Susan Cooper?'

'Guilty.'

'Ah. I'm . . . uuhh . . . you . . . aahh . . .'

'Come in, why don't you?' she said. She stepped back and pulled the door wide open. He shot nervous glances up and down the road, then crept into the hallway. She closed the door.

'I'm . . . uuhh . . . listen . . . aahh,' he stammered.

'Talk,' she said. 'I'm sure this is nothing you haven't seen before.'

'Well, no, but . . . uuhh . . . listen, could you . . . uuhh . . . thing is, I never thought I'd say this to . . . uumm . . . a beautiful naked young woman, but . . . could you put some clothes on, please?'

'Having a hard time?' she asked.

Fresh colour flooded his cheeks. 'Uumm . . . please.'

She shrugged. 'I don't know who you are, but you're a dismal loss to the male species. Make the most of my arse as I walk away.' She turned and padded down the hall into the bedroom she used to share with her dead fiancé. From the wardrobe she picked out one of Phil's white shirts

180

and put it on. It fell to her thighs, but she selected a pair of panties from the drawer too and pulled those on.

'Right,' she said as she returned to her caller. 'In here.' She disappeared into the lounge and sat cross-legged on the sofa. The man entered the room. 'Don't get comfortable,' she said, pointing to the straight-backed wooden chair in the corner of the room. 'Sit there, talk fast. I'm easily bored.'

The man took his seat. 'First of all, I want to extend my deepest sym—'

'Yeah, yeah,' she said. 'Move on.'

He looked shocked. He crossed his legs one way, wasn't comfortable, crossed them the other, uncrossed them and leant forward, elbows on knees. 'My name's Martin Simms,' he said. 'Philip and I were friends. We were probationaries together.'

So her hunch had been right. 'And?'

'And now I'm a private investigator, and Philip asked me to check into something before his death.'

'Conrad Dreave.'

Simms sat up straight. 'You know?'

'Apparently.'

He crossed his legs, right over left, then left over right. 'Can I stand up?' he asked.

She waved a hand to indicate her indifference. He got up and began shifting his weight from leg to leg.

'Chill,' she said.

'I'm fine.' His expression spoke of huge internal confusion. 'Where was I? Yes . . . the problem is that although I told Philip I'd do it as a favour, I've incurred a few out-of-pocket expenses. Back handers, you know.'

'Which you want me to reimburse.'

He sat down again, bum perched on the very edge of the seat. 'I was hoping you would.'

'How much?'

He hesitated a split second and she knew he was going to lie.

'Five hundred pounds.' He made an apologetic face.

'I see,' she said. 'Then your real problem is that you need to speak with Phil about it, and as I don't possess a Ouija board, you're out of luck.'

'You mean you don't have the money?'

181

'I mean I don't take on other people's debts.'

'He was your fiancé,' Simms said, clearly aghast at her attitude.

She considered. She had to admit she was keen to know about Dreave. 'I'll give you the money if you tell me what you found out.'

He screwed up his face. 'I don't know,' he said. 'That's privileged client information.'

'Fine. Then burn your notes and pop them in with Phil's ashes.'

Simms winced.

'I'm not paying for nothing,' she told him.

'OK,' he relented. 'What I've got for you is absolutely zilch. According to all records I've checked – and I've been thorough, I pride myself on it – Conrad Dreave does not exist. Of course, he *does*, but I've not been able to trace him.'

'And you think that's worth five hundred quid? Bye-bye.'

'Wait,' he said, standing up anyway. 'What you *can* pay me for is what I'm about to do.'

'Which is?'

'Philip said that if anything happened to him, I was to give my information to his superiors.'

'But you don't have any information.'

He held up a hand. 'No, but I think it's significant that Philip feared for his life, and then he was killed.'

'I take it you didn't advance too far up the ranks during your time with the police.'

'Beg your pardon?'

'It's fairly common knowledge that Phil was shot by another police officer, not Conrad Dreave.'

'That's as may be, Susan, but—'

'Miss Cooper,' she corrected him.

He nodded slowly. 'That's as may be, Miss Cooper, but I'm still curious about our Mr Dreave, and even if Philip's superiors don't wish to mount an investigation, I still have contacts.' He winked at her, and swaggered. 'If Dreave's not kosher, I'll know about it.'

'Yes, I believe you will.'

'My friend's dead,' he announced dramatically, like an aggrieved cowboy. 'If there's a connection, I'll find it.'

She conjured a suddenly grateful expression. 'Thank you, Martin. How very thorough.'

'I pride myself on it.'

'You said.' She smiled sweetly. 'So you're going to give Mr Dreave a rough ride?'

'Count on it, Miss Cooper.'

'Suzy, please.'

'Suzy,' he repeated, allowing his eyes to wander obviously over her bare legs.

'Well,' she said, rising straight up from cross-legged to stand on the sofa. 'I've decided you do deserve paying off, after all.' She hopped off onto the carpet. 'If you'll follow me . . .'

'My pleasure.'

'I keep a small safe in the cellar.'

The receptionist of Studio House looked completely mental. She was staring directly at Lake as he approached her desk. Her eyes were round and sunken, cupped by exhausted purple. Her blonde hair was wild and greasy, a stranger to brush and comb. Her skin possessed an anaemic pallor. The application of cosmetics had become an alien art form. Garish red lipstick adhered to the general mouth area, but in no correlation to the contours of her lips. Her cheeks were rouged to an almost clown-like degree. Blue eyeshadow and black mascara were layered thickly, compounding the natural, sick hues of her eyes to make her appear recently beaten up. She resembled a six-year-old after a furtive dip into her mother's make-up bag, or a sad old woman with sharp memories and poor eyesight.

It was another symptom of Dreave; Lake had no doubt.

Christine's eyeline did not alter as he stopped before her. She stared straight over the top of the counter at his chest.

Then Lake noticed the glazing of her eyes; she wasn't looking at his chest, she was looking through it at some fixed point in space. He stepped to the side. Her mad eyes never wavered from dead ahead. He wondered whether she even knew he was there. She appeared lost to the world.

But she was not entirely motionless. Her right hand was dipped beneath the desk, working rhythmically, causing her right arm to jerk slightly, as though in spasm. He couldn't see exactly what she was doing, but he could guess. Her skirt was hitched up, bunched around her upper thighs.

Shit, if he'd wanted a Soho sex show, he could have nipped in a few doors down the road.

'Excuse me,' he said, feeling reluctantly aroused.

Christine groaned, whether in response to him or some other stimulus, he couldn't tell. Her far-off expression never flickered.

'Oi,' he said, rapping the top of the counter with his knuckles.

'Yes,' she replied breathlessly, and Lake still wasn't sure.

'I need Suzy's home address,' he told her, waving a hand in front of her face.

'Mmm,' she said.

He briefly debated his next action, but did it anyway.

Christine did not react to her lightly slapped cheek.

Lake tutted, debated some more, shouted, 'Oi', then belted her.

Christine's head flew to the side and stayed there for a moment. Her hand stopped. An intense frown creased her face. Then it vanished and she gazed at him.

'Hello, Mr Lake,' she said, as though he had just that second arrived.

'Morning,' he replied with a smile, as though he hadn't laid a finger on her. 'I wonder, could I have Suzy's home address?'

She reached down to the floor and picked up her handbag. She sat it on her knees and clattered through its contents, removing a small address book. At the appropriate section she opened it, tore a page out and handed it up to him.

'I could have written it down,' he said.

She shrugged and passed him a pad and pen.

He jotted down the address and thanked her, but he could see she was already slipping back into the state he had found her in.

Then off he went to Parsons Green, to offer his sincere condolences and stern misgivings.

An hour later he was back in Studio House.

He slapped the receptionist back into conversation.

'Suzy's not at home,' he told her. 'Do you know where she might have gone? Is she staying with friends or relatives?'

'She's upstairs.'

'Sorry?'

'She's upstairs.'

Lake felt extremely pissed off. 'Upstairs?'

184

'Upstairs.'

'Why didn't you tell me that when I came in earlier?'

'You didn't ask.'

'I wanted her address because I wanted to talk to her.'

'You didn't say.'

'I thought she'd be at home. Compassionate leave or whatever.'

'You should have said.'

Lake regarded her severely and wanted to hit her again, this time so she'd know about it. 'Right,' he said, and turned away towards the stairs.

Nearing the first floor, he was greeted by strange noises. Their origins were not unknown to him, but they were odd in the context of an office building. There had been similar sounds last time he visited, but they were not so pronounced and widespread, and he and Suzy had been causing a rumpus themselves.

He stood at the end of the first-floor corridor and listened. There wasn't a whole lot of work being done in those offices.

It was Dreave. He was screwing up the whole building, and he had the whole building screwing. Lake felt horny himself, but he wasn't sure if it was a primary urge or a secondary reaction.

He carried on to the next floor. Suzy's office was at the end of the corridor. His walk along that corridor was quite an eye-opener. Every door was closed, but there was a narrow window beside each door, and he could see through the slatted blinds the carnal activities inside each office. It was happening on the desks, on the carpet, against the filing cabinets, on the filing cabinets; two people, three people, four, five. All of them stripped off. A couple of people noticed him peeking in and beckoned for him to join them. Despite his aroused state, Lake found the idea repulsive. It would be bad enough swapping spit and all sorts with complete strangers, but it would mean more than that. It would mean further succumbing to Dreave's sordid influence.

He went along to Suzy's office, tapped on the door and entered.

Suzy continued to scrawl doodles on the back of an envelope for several seconds before swivelling her chair to look at him.

'Hello, Nathan.'

'You're working in a knocking shop, Suze.'

'I'm not actually.'

'You are.'

'I mean I'm not working.'

185

'Oh,' he said, and bowed his head. 'Yes. Sorry. It must be difficult to concentrate with . . . recent events.'

She met his eyes with a puzzled expression.

He returned the look. Did he really have to explain his comment?

'What are you on about?' she asked.

'Your fiancé,' he said incredulously, and came over to her.

'Huh?'

He leaned his hands on the desk and peered at her. 'Your fiancé . . . Philip Cage. *Remember?*'

'It's in the past,' she coldly announced.

'It's a *day* in the past. Doesn't it bother you?'

She began doodling again. He preferred to think she was just in shock, reacting so casually, but her apathy was too clinical.

'It bothers *me*,' he said.

'Oh? You two became bosom pals in your fifteen minutes yesterday?'

Lake walked over to the open window and sat on the sill. 'We, er . . . shared some moments.'

Suzy rotated to face him again. Her chair squeaked. She let her weight slump down in the seat, making her skirt rise up. 'So you came here to take over from him?' she asked. 'Fill his shoes, and –' she parted her legs suggestively '– whatever else you might fancy filling?'

With some effort he managed to ignore the invitation, though he gathered it was merely a cruel tease.

'I don't want that,' he said. 'I want to protect you. I feel responsible.'

'For me? How touching.'

'For you and . . . for what happened.'

'Oh? How?'

'I – ' he began, and faltered. 'Dreave killed your fiancé, Suzy.'

'My fiancée Suzy?' she said. 'Surely you mean my fiancé Phil.'

'You know what I mean.'

'You're screw-loose.' She shook her head. 'You're talking out of your arse.'

He stood up from the sill, turned and looked out of the window. 'I know what it sounds like,' he said. 'But he is responsible.'

There was a pause before he heard her quiet response: 'I thought you said *you* were responsible.'

He wondered how much he could say, how much she might believe. 'Dreave killed Philip Cage and all those other people . . . through me.'

186

On a credibility scale of one to ten, he knew he had just started off with a big fat zero.

He jumped as he felt a hand on his shoulder. He hadn't heard her rise and walk over. All he heard was the continuing sex next door, opposite, down the corridor, from the floor above and the floor below. She pulled him round so they were standing head to head, inches from each other.

'Honestly,' he added. 'As good as pull the trigger, Conrad Dreave killed Philip Cage.'

'Through you,' she said.

He nodded.

'You know what I think?' she asked, jabbing a finger hard at his chest. 'I think you are responsible. Just you.'

He stuttered at the start of a denial, but she cut him off.

'I think you told Phil about us, the sex before Christmas and the other day.'

'No,' he protested. 'It's Dreave, he's—'

She pushed him and the back of his head cracked the open window frame. He sat down on the sill, feeling the street air envelop him.

Her voice was harsh, implacable. 'You told Phil about us and you made him insane with jealousy and the next day he went out and shot all those people because of you, what you said—'

'No!'

She clutched the material of his T-shirt, twisting it in her fists. 'You made him do it. You killed those people, Nathan, not Dreave.'

'No!'

'You're jealous of Dreave.'

'No!'

'He's a man like you'll never be.'

'Dreave's evil!' Lake yelled at her. '*Evil!*'

He pleaded hopefully, frantically with his eyes, and his position dawned on him. The front of his T-shirt was balled tightly in her fists. He could feel the individual pressure of her knuckles, pressed against his sternum. All it needed was a gentle shove and he would tumble out into Wardour Street, two storeys down.

'Go on,' he said.

'What?'

'Push me out.'

She laughed. 'Kill you?'

187

'Yes.'

Her face became stony and he thought she'd do it. Then she offered an ironic smirk and released him. 'You're the evil one, Nathan, not me. And not Dreave. I won't commit murder to absolve you of your sins in this life.'

'Then forgive me.'

She smiled; a corrupted mouth shape. 'Forgive you? I won't even fuck you.'

Once Suzy had bundled Lake out into the corridor, she shut the door and leant back against it. She closed her eyes and listened. The air was frantic with sex.

Forgetting her expedient romp with Phil and her slight misdemeanour with Lake, she had resisted all temptations. It had been a pure effort of the will. Any day she could have weakened. There were attractive men in the building. Attractive women, come to that. Her own desires were no less than theirs. There was no question of non-acceptance. Pre-mating rituals were non-existent. No one received formal introductions, had dinner together, flirted. Compatibility tests had been abandoned. Marital status was not an issue. If she stepped into another office, she became an instant player.

Against all this, she had maintained her resolve. She had saved herself for Dreave. Endured the worst deprivation. Now she was free to be with him. A single woman again.

She removed a small mirror from her handbag and set it on top of the filing cabinet. She brushed her hair and applied some rich and vampish make-up. Blood-red lipstick, dark and moody eyes. She blew a kiss at her reflection. Good enough to eat, she thought; hoped.

The telephone chirped. She went and picked up the receiver.

'Come down,' Dreave said.

It was her time.

The atmosphere in the basement smouldered. The lights blazed overhead. From the foot of the basement steps, she could see Dreave. He was sitting alert at his desk. He looked immaculate as always: blond, cream and white. Only his wrap-arounds marred the beauty of his perfect face, dividing it with its curve of sinister black glass. His mouth broke apart in a grin as she entered the room.

'I think I have something you want,' he said to her, rising to his feet and moving around the desk.

She rippled with anticipation, and was pleasantly shocked to see the crotch of his trousers bulging magnificently. She stopped in front of him, and he towered above her. Her heart fluttered crazily, her breathing felt erratic. Her palms were moist, her hands twitched, impatient to claim her reward. She was ready. In every department.

Dreave's left hand moved from his side and began to unzip his fly.

Suzy stood mesmerised.

The zip inched down all the way. He pulled the gaping cloth apart, and his other hand slipped inside. There was a lot of fiddling, trying to extricate himself. Then he had it. He smiled at her and brought it out.

'For you,' he said, handing her a rolled-up wad of fifties. 'Sorry if it's a tad warm.'

Bewildered, she took the money and stared at him.

He zipped up and dipped his hands into either jacket pocket, bringing out two more rolls. 'More than one in each pocket,' he said, retrieving a fourth from his breast pocket, 'and they do so spoil the cut of my jacket.'

Suzy limply accepted the proffered cash.

'Twenty thousand,' he told her. 'Buy yourself a nice black outfit.'

'Huh?'

'When is the funeral?'

'What? Phil's?'

'Yes. What have you plumped for? Burning is good, very space-efficient, but then there is the ozone layer to consider. I think the biodegradable option is preferable. Give something back to the earth.'

Suzy's head spun. Why the facetious comments? Why no condolences? She didn't mind the first or want the second, but he wasn't giving much quarter to the possible wreck of her emotions.

Then again, she sensed he knew her inside-out.

'I'm going to freeze him,' she said. 'Then when science advances, I can bring him back and find out what made him snap.'

'Touché.'

'What d'you think he'd tell me, Conrad?'

Dreave appeared to ponder seriously.

She was testing him with her inquiry. Did he really know her that intimately? That it was she who had driven her fiancé to murder. Because, in truth, though guilt remained a stranger, she held herself to be accountable. Her wicked behaviour had taken its toll. The accusation she had levelled against Lake, that he had spilt the beans on her infidelity, had been voiced only to kill their relationship. She put little store by it.

'I suspect,' Dreave said, 'that Philip would first blame your ex-lover, Nathan Lake, then his thawing digit would point in my direction.'

Suzy felt herself go cold. Dreave's words echoed Lake's own rationale. Whatever else she might have believed, she certainly hadn't given any credence to *his* wild explanation of events.

She squeezed the rolls of cash against her stomach. Her insides were flipping. Curiously, she felt elated more than confused and scared. She was in the presence of an immense power, even greater than she had imagined. Either Dreave had been able to convince a reasonably sane man that he was responsible for mass murder – a neat trick – or, a real mind-fuck, Dreave and Lake had jointly and genuinely manufactured a massacre.

'Are you serious?' she said.

'Deadly. You know I am.'

'Are you saying you killed my fiancé?'

'Are you saying it bothers you?'

She was thrilled at such elemental talk; quite carried away. 'Who are you?'

He sat down. 'I am the person you have long awaited.'

She knelt before him, hugging her money. 'I don't understand.'

'Ssshhh,' he went. 'It takes time.'

'But I need to understand.'

He smiled kindly. 'Have you heard it said, Suzy, that money is the root of all evil?'

She nodded.

'Do you know where that comes from?'

'The Bible.'

'And do you realise I have misquoted?'

Puzzled, she cocked her head to one side. 'Pardon?'

'Money is inanimate,' he said. 'It can be neither good nor evil. Only man can make it this way or that. He invests it with his own intentions. The same money can purchase medicine or machine-gun. Correctly quoted, we learn that the *love* of money is the root of all evil. And, Suzy –' he chuckled lightly '– you do love my money, don't you.'

She cast her eyes down to the cash cradled in her arms like a baby. She lifted a roll to her mouth and kissed it.

'But I don't want the spoils,' she told him. 'I want the battle.'

'In time,' he soothed.

'I want –' She couldn't think straight.

'You want me,' he said, easing down his zipper once again.

She let the cash fall to the floor, reached out a hand and slipped her fingers inside his fly. She could feel him growing.

Dreave growled.

Suddenly, Suzy stopped the seduction and regarded him with passionless eyes. 'No,' she said. 'I don't want you.'

Without a word, Dreave zipped himself up.

Suzy struggled with her thoughts for a moment. Then crystal understanding lit up in her eyes. 'It's not you I want. It's what you have. I want your power.'

'Is that all? Would you like the shirt off my back as well?'

'I want everything. You can't bring me this far and then dump me. You have to give me everything.'

'Not possible, I'm afraid.' Dreave swivelled his chair towards his desk.

Suzy got to her feet in sharp, peeved movements. 'I mean it, Conrad. I can't turn back now.'

'Now you're just being plain melodramatic.'

'Don't make fun of me, you bastard.'

Dreave swung to face her. He pouted his lips, considering. 'What makes you think you're so ready?'

'Because I killed a man today.'

'And why would you want to do a nasty thing like that?'

'To protect you, that's why.'

Dreave sat in silence.

'Do you see now?' she asked.

'Yes. As I said: you are not ready.'

With a frustrated whine, Suzy spun on her heels away from him. '*Why can't you just give it to me?*' she shouted at the wall.

Seconds passed, then, very softly, Dreave spoke. 'What you want, Suzy, cannot be given. It must be taken. And even then, if it is not meant for you, you will never own it.'

Suzy turned to him. 'I don't understand,' she said mournfully. 'How do I take it from you?'

191

'Work it out.'

She lost her temper again. 'Fuck, I could really hate you.'

'That's good,' Dreave said. 'Hate is good. Very useful.'

'You mean . . . ? How d'you mean?'

'Work it out.'

Suzy began to snigger. 'I think I just did.'

'We'll see.'

26

The task of dumping his agent was not one Lake relished. In fact, it scared him half to death. After Suzy had seen him off, he traipsed the length of Wardour Street so many times he lost count. He was plucking up courage. But even when he steeled himself to carry it through, he still had no courage, he had just become tired of pacing.

He had briefly entertained the possibility of walking away from the entire business of acting. Dreave could object to his finding a new agent on the dubious grounds of loyalty, but surely not to his quitting the profession altogether.

The prospect of his forthcoming employment put paid to that noble, if somewhat feeble, idea. Lake enjoyed the work too much. Added to that, if at some time in the future he did decide to quit, then he might need his earnings from the series to tide him over into another career.

Damn. Even at this momentous point in his life he was making excuses, selling out to his cursed ambition.

He barged through the entrance of Studio House. The nutty woman was still there, not all there, behind reception. He hurried past her and down the basement steps.

Turning the bend in the stairs, he nearly had a coronary and fell the rest of the way. Dreave was waiting at the foot of the stairs, his head tilted up, facing him.

Lake halted mid-step. 'Hi, Conrad,' he tried not to squeak.

Three seconds elapsed before Dreave replied, 'Good afternoon, Nathan,' in very sombre tones.

Lake waited for Dreave to back off, which he did, before going down the rest of the way. He sensed his agent knew this visit was special. Dreave was now standing beside the closed lift door. There was no invitation to join him in an office. All the office doors were shut. They stood looking at each other for several seconds. Lake kept attempting conciliatory grins, but they made him feel like an imbecile because Dreave never cracked his face in response.

The bronze lift door suddenly opened.

Dreave said, 'Would you get in, please, Nathan?'

Timidly, Lake asked, 'Why?'

'We have to go somewhere.' He opened his palm towards the bright compartment.

Lake overcame his futile desire to question Dreave any further. He entered the lift and Dreave followed in behind. The door closed to seal them in.

Dreave poked a slender finger at the button marked 6. Seconds passed before the lift jerked an inch. Then a delay, then another sharp movement.

'Shit,' Lake said, and reached for the alarm button, but Dreave caught his arm and lowered it for him.

'Sit down, Nathan. Make yourself comfortable.'

Lake remained on his feet. Several minutes passed before he again felt the lift jump and stop.

'Really, Nathan, sit down,' Dreave urged. 'Better still, lie down. Sleep a while.'

Lake's mouth dropped open. '*Sleep?* This is a frigging lift, not a transatlantic flight.'

'Suit yourself.'

'Oh, this is ridiculous,' Lake said, and tried again for the alarm button.

Dreave grabbed his finger before it struck. 'If you do that once more,' he said, 'I will bite it off.'

Lake shrank away into a corner and thrust his hands deep into his pockets. Dreave folded his arms and stood bolt upright in front of the control panel. Lake eyed the alarm button.

'But why can't I . . .' he started to say, then fell silent.

Of course. How stupid of him. The infamous slow-lift routine.

He slid his back down the rear wall and sat on the floor.

Thirty minutes later the lift lurched minutely, then was

still. Lake checked his watch: one p.m.

'I know what's going on,' he announced.

'Not so,' Dreave replied.

'I do. I dreamt this.'

'If you truly understood, I would not be presently wasting my time with you and your armpits in this confined space. This is not my idea of fun either, Nathan.'

'I know what's going on,' Lake repeated. 'I don't know what you're bothering with all this crap for. I know exactly what you're all about, Conrad.'

'Quiet,' Dreave said, and put his back to Lake.

'Fine by me. I'll just sit here. Quiet as a mouse. Not a word. Silent as the grave.'

'Shut up, Nathan.'

'Okie-doke.' Fear was causing him to be dangerously flippant.

It had turned one-thirty before the lift moved again; the briefest hop. Lake calculated they had made it about six inches up the shaft. He let his head loll to one side and closed his eyes. Surprisingly, he drifted off almost instantly.

When he woke, his watch read three-twenty-two. Dreave was standing in the exact same position.

'Where are we now?' Lake asked.

Dreave did not turn round. 'Nearly there.'

'Thank God.'

'Ground floor coming up in seven minutes.'

Lake groaned. 'Bollocks.' He shifted his numb bum and closed his eyes again, but he had slept his fill for the time being.

He sat for the next hour, biting his lips, peeling the skin from them with his teeth until they were raw and bleeding.

'OK!' he yelled. 'Enough! I admit it! I don't know what's going on. All right?'

'Quiet.'

'No. I've had enough.'

'Quiet.'

Lake pushed himself to his feet. His legs felt like jelly. 'No. I've really had enough.'

'Ssshhh.'

'Fuck you. I want to get off.'

Dreave slowly turned to face him. 'But, Nathan . . . we are between floors.'

'I don't mean that.'

'I know.'

'Huh?'

'I know what you mean.'

'I want to get off my Path.'

'I know.'

Lake went faint. His own morbid assumptions he could stomach. Just. But hearing them confirmed made him want to throw up. He sank to the floor.

'I'm on the Dark Path,' he said weakly. 'Aren't I?'

'Of course you are, you stupid turd. I took it for granted you knew that much.'

'Right. So I know. So let me out of this frigging lift.'

Dreave sighed. 'I am afraid you have yet to learn the lesson, Nathan. Purely academic now, but it may help you come to terms with your predicament. We carry on until you understand.'

Five p.m. came and went.

'You've got to let me out,' Lake said, getting panicked. 'I think I'm developing claustrophobia.'

'Don't be such a luvvie.'

'I *mean it*!' he screamed. 'I can't *stand it*!'

'What can't you stand, Nathan?'

'This . . . this . . . this interminable fucking *waiting*!'

'Oh dear,' Dreave mocked. 'Do you have a problem with that?'

'I fucking *hate it!*'

'What?'

'*Waiting*, you dumbfuck. *Wai*—'

Lake gawped up at Dreave with ghastly comprehension in his eyes.

In a horrified whisper, he said, 'I couldn't wait. The lesson. Ben's riddle. Going up took ages. I hated it. It was the same future both ways, but it was quicker going down. Awful, but quicker.'

'Finally,' Dreave said with relief, and hit the stop button.

'But I accepted it,' Lake said suddenly, with hope. 'The nine months of *Oedipus*. I knew I'd have to wait. I accepted it. I learned the lesson.' He thought Dreave looked almost sorry for him. 'Didn't I?'

'It is not the waiting, Nathan. It is the manner in which you bide the time.'

'Huh?'

'Forgive me preaching the ways of the Light Path,' Dreave said, 'but your salvation would have lain in your waiting with *good grace.*'

'Good grace?'

'Smiling through and all that happy shit.'

'I don't get.'

'*Patience,* Nathan.'

'Patience? Is that it?'

Dreave nodded. 'The irony is, had you found the answer, you would not have played *Oedipus* anyway. Your reward for understanding was just waiting for you.'

'All those lost interviews,' Lake mused sadly. 'In the second week.'

'Indeed. Naturally, none would have proved the monumental career moves you have enjoyed under my tutelage, but it would have been the beginning of a slow but definite upturn in your fortunes.'

'Shit.'

'Indeed.'

'And Suzy?' Lake asked. 'Why did I have to lose her?'

Dreave scowled slightly. 'You chose the Dark Path, Nathan. Love never survives a trek along the Dark Path.'

Lake felt sick to his heart. 'Patience,' he whispered to himself.

'A simple answer,' Dreave said, 'though far from easy. You are not the first to miss it.'

'I'm not the first?'

'Nathan, you would be surprised just how many of your Hollywood idols have risen up on the back of evil. You have joined an illustrious constellation. The brightest stars necessarily burn with unearthly light.'

'But not heavenly,' Lake suggested.

Dreave bowed his head and said nothing.

'This is all my fault, isn't it?'

No reply.

'I wanted to blame you, but I asked for all this. Didn't I?'

'You called, I answered.'

Lake squinted at Dreave, studying him. 'What are you?'

'I am a man, like you.'

'You're not like me.'

'No. I have gifts. But gifts you now share. So how different can we be?'

'Are you human? Honestly?'

'That is my form: flesh and blood. Like you.'

'Yes,' Lake said. 'But it's not the form that matters, is it? It's the essence within. You told me that once in a roundabout way. You said you weren't what you seemed. That there was a deeper meaning to everything. But I suppose that's just another lesson I've learned too late.'

'Too late, my boy? Nonsense. You are just starting out on life.'

'I've killed people.'

'Well, boo-hoo for Nathan.'

'You don't get it, do you?'

'You are the one who doesn't get it, Nathan. Nathan, people die every day. This is life. No one's getting out of it alive. Look at the big picture. The creation of a single life of magnificence is easily worth the sacrifice of a thousand wastrels.'

Lake stiffened. 'My father wasn't a wastrel, you arsehole.'

'Nathan, one thing it is too late for is name-calling.'

'Conrad, find yourself another protégé.'

'Stubborn boy,' Dreave said. 'I had hoped the lesson learned might make you more amenable to continuing along your chosen Path.'

'Why would it?'

'Because you now know what you successfully avoided. All that *interminable fucking waiting*, to quote your eloquent good self. And don't try to tell me you could have coped. You were at your very wits' end.'

Lake stood up. Dreave was still taller, but getting off the floor made him feel better.

'I'm at the end now,' Lake said. 'It's over. Our contract has expired and I don't want to renew. I'll find another agent and take my chances.'

'Then don't expect to work again. Ever.'

Lake scoffed at Dreave's words. 'Come on, Conrad, if I go for enough interviews, odds are—'

'*Odds?*' Dreave echoed with contempt. 'I removed all the odds when I took you on. I made you a dead cert, Nathan. And without me you will remain a dead cert. For lifelong obscurity.'

Lake believed it was the truth. 'Then I'll get out of it altogether; forget the acting. I'll live a blameless life from now on. Work for charity.'

Dreave huffed disdainfully, and Lake realised it was a fairly naïve proposition.

He tried again. 'Then I'll kill myself.'

'Ah, yes,' Dreave said. 'And what about afterwards?'

'My day of judgement? I'll take my chances.'

'Your chances of avoiding eternal damnation, Nathan, are roughly equivalent to your odds of worldly success without my Method.'

'I'll risk it.'

'Then your mind is made up and I will respect your brave decision.'

Lake watched Dreave hit the button marked -1. The lift responded normally, descending the short way into the basement.

The door slid open and Lake took a step forward. But only one.

Outside was darkness. Not the murk of unlit bulbs, but a pure black void. No floor, no walls, no ceiling, nothing.

Lake retreated, stumbling against the lift's rear wall, recalling the repulsive floating corpse from his dream.

Dreave turned on him and whipped off his black glasses.

For a split second, his eyes appeared a normal blue, before the effect of the lift lights narrowed his pupils into vertical slivers.

Lake stared petrified at Dreave's almost completely white eyeballs.

Sniggering, Dreave said, 'My grave affliction. Like the play on words?'

'Put them on,' Lake moaned. 'The glasses, put them on.'

'No, no,' Dreave said, pinching the bridge of his nose between thumb and forefinger. 'Isn't it ironic? I put them on, I am a spectacle-wearer; I take them off, I am a spectacle. You can get out any time, Nathan.'

'*What?*'

'This is your stop. Death Central. I am saving you the trouble of committing suicide. Don't thank me. I know, I am too kind. Out you get.'

'Like hell.'

'It is, isn't it? Very like hell. Identical, in fact. Bye-bye.'

'No way.'

Outside the lift, a nude, waxen, hairless corpse with pure black pupils floated up to the doorway and bobbed about.

Lake uttered a high-pitched whine.

Dreave looked over his shoulder at the figure, then turned to it. He reached a hand out to its jaw and began waggling it up and down. In a silly voice out of a motionless mouth, Dreave said, 'Is Nathan coming out to play?' He continued speaking normally, leaving the corpse's mouth shut. 'In a bit.' Then the ventriloquist routine again, waggling the jaw. 'Please, Mr Dreave, we'll have so much fun.' Then Dreave's voice again, 'All right, but I want him back on the dot of eternity.'

He let go and the corpse drifted upwards, out of sight.

'Nathan, come on,' Dreave chivvied. 'Your friends are waiting.'

Lake shook his head in short, frantic movements.

Dreave's voice changed; became hard, insistent. 'Out, Nathan.'

'Wha—'

'Out.'

'This . . . this was . . . this was just a warning, right?'

Dreave drew a breath, making it hiss reproachfully through pursed lips. 'Is that what you think?'

'Conrad, you've made your point.'

'I made my point a while back. But you knew better. Now get out.'

'No, I won't, no,' Lake said, testing stubborn refusal as a ploy.

'You will.'

'I won't.' Lake sidled into the rear left corner of the lift, diagonally opposite Dreave, as though the extra couple of feet between them would make a crucial difference. 'And you can't make me,' he added, knowing instantly what a foolish thing he'd said.

Dreave faced him squarely. 'Can too,' he said.

'You know, you are such a fucking *wanker.*' Lake had retreated into the last flimsy bastion of the defeated man: coarse insults. He was in serious bother. In the next second, Dreave would effortlessly reach across to him, grab a handful of throat and casually fling him into the black beyond.

Lake adopted a fighting stance, something he thought might look vaguely martial-arty. 'Come on, then,' he said, attempting to dredge some aggression from beneath all the fear.

Dreave folded his arms. 'I never indulge in fisticuffs, Nathan.'

'Big ponce underneath it all, eh?'

'I don't need to,' Dreave clarified.

Lake's insides turned to ice. He waited for a host of demons to swarm in from the Dark Land and drag him back out with them.

It didn't happen.

But Lake soon understood.

The lift was beginning to tip forward, inch by inch. Lake could feel his balance shift, his body-weight being urged away from the rear wall of the compartment. He shuffled his feet in front of him and leant back to oppose the movement, but it was clear such tactics could work for only so long. Gravity would inevitably pitch him towards the open door.

As this realisation sank in, Lake noticed something that, perversely, made him almost smile.

Dreave was still standing perpendicular to the lift floor.

Like a marvellous stage illusion, it just looked such a neat trick that Lake wanted to smile. Then he caught Dreave's expression – perfect indifference – and it cured the twitch. There was no hope in indifference. It said, the world turns, so what? End of story.

Lake's world was turning quite badly now. Any moment, he would have to give up his position in the rear left corner of the lift and skid down to the front left corner. His hope was to claim the small area of wall beside the lift door as his new floor.

Just as he prepared to move, the lift rotated slightly to the right as it continued to tip forward. It was a cruelly calculated adjustment on Dreave's part. If Lake went now, he would be straight out of the door.

He had to do something, fast. The lift was tilting through forty-five degrees. His trainers wouldn't keep their grip much longer. His floor was on its way to becoming wall, and if he couldn't replant his feet quickly, he would be out, never to touch another surface as long as he lived . . . existed . . . died.

He looked at Dreave, his body at an impossible angle in the confined space of the lift. The man was rooted firm by his defiance of gravity.

Lake decided to jump for him, grapple him and never let go of the bastard. If Dreave had been telling the truth, he wouldn't fight, and perhaps he would respect Lake's tenacity for life and Lake might be saved.

And if, as Lake expected, they both fell out into damnation, at least he wouldn't be alone.

As Lake's muscles tensed for the leap, Dreave walked two quick steps up the incline into the opposite rear corner of the lift. Out of harm's way.

'Wanker,' Lake said feebly, hearing his rubber soles begin to screech and feeling his spine lose touch with the wall.

The black hole of the lift door gaped ravenously below him.

'God help me,' Lake said.

Then gravity won the day.

*   *   *

There was no vision to be blurred by his tears, no skin to feel them run down, no mouth to taste their pitiful tang. Even the tears didn't exist. He only felt them inside his new being, filling out every millimetre of a form no longer defined by skin and muscle and bone. But, real or not, his tears were invested with an unknown level of sorrow that made those shed over his father's madness seem joyful. This pain was immense, immeasurable, unfathomable, complete. It wasn't inside him. It *was* him. It was all he was and all he ever could be.

Now Lake knew: hell was nothingness. It wasn't fire and brimstone and the meting out of gross physical punishments. It gave nothing, contained nothing. It didn't accommodate. It wasn't a space or a place. There was no one else involved, no floating ghouls for company. It didn't work on fear, not any more.

It was guilt and regret and self-blame and unbearable self-loathing. It was forever drowning in the endless Sea of Universal Mind, where each man's sin is every man's suffering. It was a dreadful knowledge of missed signposts and bad turns and false detours. It was a final destination and the start of another journey that had no end.

He had lost all concept of time. Had a day passed? A week? A year? It felt like a millennium but why count? It made no difference when the sentence was eternity.

He was pure essence. A damned spirit, a lost soul. He existed as a sentient mind and nothing more, and all he felt was racking sorrow. He saw nothing, heard nothing, touched nothing, smelt nothing, tasted nothing. Even his mind's eye was blind. In the upper world he had used his senses poorly. Down here they were justly forfeit.

With his emotional torture, cogent thought was nearly impossible. He knew only that he was already sick of silently weeping his invisible tears for a burden of ills that weren't all his but he couldn't help accepting as his own. And the more he suffered, the more he would suffer; to think his tears would grow old but his torments be always fresh and plentiful. It was pain upon pain.

And on it went. And all the interminable fucking waiting in the entire fucking world could not compare with this perpetual stretch of hurting.

He wanted his old life back; would even embrace the new life Dreave had given him, if only all this could be taken from now to another time. If he could only have a few years' respite, some time to prepare. If that was possible.

He hadn't known. He really hadn't known.

Lake was engulfed by light and crashed hard against a metallic wall. He squeezed his eyes tight shut. The light. His pupils would never cope.

Then the glorious realisation: he was back. His senses were restored. He felt the floor beneath him; heard Dreave's laughter; saw the brightness through his closed eyelids; smelt his own body odour; tasted his saliva, stale with fear.

He began to cry, and just as quickly he began to laugh, because his tears felt so innocuous, so painless. At last. An end to the sorrow.

'Did you miss me?' Dreave asked as Lake struggled to open his leaking eyes. 'I missed you. I felt quite alone for the ten seconds you were away.'

Lake looked up. His widening eyes instantly dried. 'What?' he said, and climbed to his feet – so good to have feet again. 'Ten seconds?'

'Yes, not wise to risk any longer. Don't want you going insane, do we? Might spoil the career.'

'*Ten seconds?*' Lake could only repeat in high-toned disbelief.

'I know. Doesn't time fly when you're having fun?'

Lake groaned.

Dreave's slivered, light-shy pupils fixed Lake meaningfully as he spoke. 'So I take it we are agreed; little Nathan remains a thespian.'

Lake groaned and nodded.

'And I don't have to hide the kitchen knives or check the medicine cabinet?'

Lake groaned and shook his head.

'Splendid. Now you are quite sure about that? You don't want to die?'

Lake wilted against the back wall of the lift. 'Get me back to the light. *Please.*'

Dreave pressed 1. The door slid shut, then immediately open. They were in the basement. Dreave indicated that Lake should leave the lift.

'After you,' Lake said, understandably wary.

His agent stepped out and the lift door began to close. Lake grabbed it, making it withdraw, then hurried out.

'You know,' Dreave said, donning his wrap-arounds, 'that last bit was actually quite unnecessary.'

Lake couldn't speak, he was so angry.

'There is really only one thing to prevent you giving up now, Nathan, and that thing lies within you.'

Lake grunted.

'Your ambition,' Dreave told him. 'It would never allow you to fail. Not at this late stage, when your career is all set to sky-rocket. You are thirty years old. You may live to ninety. Could you endure another period of twice your current years, rotting in poverty and obscurity? No. You will make the utmost use of your remaining time, Nathan, living a famous life of luxury, because your entire existence has been dedicated to that goal. And if you ever again have thoughts of abandoning my ways, think on what awaits you at the end of it all, when you are dead. You are going to suffer horribly anyway, Nathan, so make it worthwhile.'

Lake was empty of argument. It was all true, every word Dreave said. In a low, distant voice, he quoted one of the few snippets he remembered from Shakespeare: 'For mine own good, all causes shall give way. I am in blood stepped in so far that, should I wade no more, returning were as tedious as go o'er.'

'Bravo,' Dreave said. 'The Scottish play.'

'*Macbeth*,' Lake said.

Dreave opened his mouth in phoney horror. 'You said it, you said the M-word. Oh, woe. Bad things will befall the House of Lake.'

In spite of himself, Lake smiled.

'That's the ticket,' Dreave said. 'The world is yours. Enjoy it.'

Lake looked at his agent, briefly nodded and headed up the stairs out of the basement.

'Let's do lunch!' Dreave called after him.

Leaving Studio House, Lake checked his watch: six-oh-four p.m. Christ, he'd spent five and a half hours in that bloody lift.

He made his way up a busy Wardour Street towards home. Phew, it certainly was warm for the time of day. He removed his denim jacket, then noticed a clock above a tobacconist's. Its liquid crystal display indicated thirteen-ten. Obviously broken.

Half-way up the road, he was already sweating with the heat. It was ridiculous.

He carried on a bit, then stopped dead. This wasn't right. It was too hot.

Something was wrong.

He turned around and walked back to the tobacconist's.

The clock now read thirteen-twelve. He pondered. OK, not broken. But slow. Very slow.

Or . . .

Simmer down, Nathan. Don't jump to conclusions.

He collared a passer-by. 'Excuse me, have you got the right time?'

The young woman pulled her left sleeve back an inch. 'Ten past one,' she said.

'Uh . . . thanks.'

The woman nodded and walked away.

Shit. Lying bastard, Dreave.

How long had he really spent in the Dark Land? Days? Months? Years? Lake stopped another pedestrian, a grizzled workman in overalls.

'Sorry, have you got the, uh . . . the right date?'

'The right *date*?' the workman questioned, lightly amused.

'Humour me,' Lake said.

'Today's the twelfth.'

'Month?'

'No, December's colder than this.'

'What?'

'It's not the twelfth month.'

'No, I mean, what is the month?'

'May.'

'It's the twelfth of May?'

'All day.'

'Good. That's just as it should be.'

'I'm pleased for you.'

'Er . . . just one more thing—'

'Nineteen-ninety-five.'

'Thank you, thank you so much.'

'No, it's been fun,' said the workman, who walked away laughing.

Lake heaved a sigh. So at least that was all right: he hadn't been time-warped again, like during his seven-day sleep.

And then he realised: yes, he had.

He had set foot in the lift at twelve-thirty p.m. He had spent five and a half hours in there. He had come out at one p.m.

Some time he'd have to tell Dreave to stop messing with his head.

27

The afternoon was a bizarre experience. Lake felt disorientated, mildly jet-lagged. He was starving hungry for dinner at lunchtime and ready for bed when dinnertime arrived.

He sat in front of his television the whole afternoon, with the volume set too loud. It was difficult to think straight, and that was the idea. Being damned to hell for eternity was not the happiest prospect to mull over. One conclusion did come clear to him: his real test of faith would happen only after filming his new series, when he would be called upon to employ Dreave's Method to gain further employment. Thus far, his role was confined to that of the unwitting fool. Even Brigit's murder had been committed under the influence of the Rising. But now he knew the ruinous power that lay in the palm of his hand, what part would he choose to play the next time he presented himself for interview: martyr or monster?

He changed channels and further increased the volume; he had no desire to answer that question until it became absolutely necessary.

At seven-fifteen p.m. someone buzzed his flat from the street door. He jolted.

'Piss off,' he said, looking at the intercom box on the wall.

It sounded again.

'I'm not interested.'

An extended buzz followed.

He switched the TV off and went to the window. Carefully, quietly, he eased it up, sufficient to poke his head out.

It was Suzy. He recognised her from just the top of her head; it had been a familiar view in the past.

'Hold on!' he shouted down. Suzy tipped her head back and nodded up at him. He went to the intercom and buzzed the front door, then opened his flat door to welcome her.

In the thirty seconds it took for her to reach him, he could think of no reason why she should want to visit. After this morning's little set-to what else was there left to say?

Just as she appeared in the doorway, he did think of something: she had not come to talk, she had come to murder him. Believing him to have caused the death of her fiancé, she had decided to take a biblical stance and claim an eye for an eye. Had he thought of this five seconds sooner, he would have slammed the door and bolted it and called the police. He stood by his earlier decision: considering his afterlife, a premature death was to be earnestly avoided.

Suzy closed the door behind her. She looked serious. Lake noticed she was wearing gloves. At the end of a lovely warm day.

'Hi,' he said, trotting across the living room to the kitchen-in-the-wall. He needed a weapon: a meat cleaver, a carving knife.

The drainer was bare. In the sink was a teaspoon. He wasn't convinced it was possible to spoon a person to death, but he'd give it a damn good go.

'I've got something for you,' she said. She dumped her shoulder bag on the back of the sofa, thrust a hand inside and produced a gun.

Lake felt the impulse to lunge at her, but the pathetic nature of his weapon suddenly overwhelmed him. He took an almost Pythonesque leap sideways down the short corridor that led to his bedroom and locked himself in the toilet.

There was no sound for a moment, then he heard her right outside the door.

'Nat?'

'I didn't do it. You're wrong, I didn't do it,' he said.

'Nat.'

'Go away. It's not my fault.'

'Come out.'

'You don't understand. I don't want to die. I can't die. Not yet. I'm not ready.'

'Nathan, I haven't come to kill you.'

Did he believe her? Could he allow himself to?

'Nat?'

'How do I know you're not lying?'

'Because if I wanted you dead, I'd have shot you through the door.'

Made sense. 'All right,' he said, and let himself out of the toilet.

Suzy wasn't in the corridor. He popped his head into the living room and saw her perched stiffly on the sofa, her face downturned to her lap. He couldn't see the gun.

'Hi,' he said.

'Hi.'

He went and sat next to her.

'Sorry,' he said. 'I, er . . . I have rather a heightened aversion to death these days.'

She didn't seem to hear.

'Suze? Are you OK?'

'Yes,' she said, unconvincingly.

Then a more important question struck him. 'Suzy, what is the gun for?'

'It's for you. To protect yourself.'

'But why do I need protecting?'

'Because you were right about Dreave. I think he's evil.'

'Why?'

'Because . . .'

'What?'

'I don't blame you, Nat. About Phil. I don't believe you had anything to do with it. I was angry. I'm sorry.'

'I understand.'

'I do love you,' she said softly. 'I don't want Dreave to hurt you.'

'He won't.' Then he smiled as her words registered. 'You love me?'

'I always have. Always will.'

'Then . . .' He twisted his body to face her. 'D'you think we might get back . . .'

She gave him a wonderful smile. 'In time. So much has happened recently.'

'Of course,' he said with great compassion. 'But . . . why the gun? What's happened with Dreave?'

'He . . . I just think you ought to have it.'

'Suze?'

'Take it. Just in case.'

'In case of what?'

'I don't know,' she said. 'Anything. I think he's capable of anything.'

'Why?'

'He . . . he . . . please take it.'

'I will. But why?'

'I'd better go,' she said, rising to her feet.

He caught her hand and gently made her sit down again. 'Suze, what's happened?'

She looked at him sadly. 'Let me go,' she said. 'I don't want you doing anything stupid.'

He was beginning to feel exasperated, panicked. 'You're not making sense.'

'I don't want you using it on my account.'

'The gun?'

She nodded.

'Why would I?'

'I hope you never have to use it.'

He shook her. '*Suze.*'

Her dark eyes, large and desperate, filled with tears.

'Dreave raped me.'

'You weren't going to tell me, were you?'

'No.'

Lake hugged her tightly. Her head was nestled under his chin.

'God, Suze, I'm sorry. When did it happen?'

'This afternoon. He called me down to the basement.'

Lake's primary emotion was sorrow, but he could sense something else beneath the surface: an intense, unprecedented hatred. And he fully expected, when the first eased for Suzy, the second would take over towards his agent in a violent act of retribution.

But had Dreave been telling the truth? Was his form really human? Corruptible flesh and blood?

'Don't do anything silly,' Suzy said, interrupting his thoughts.

'No,' he replied. 'Nothing silly.'

It wasn't a lie. For sure, he would try and kill Dreave, but he didn't consider that a silly thing to do. Under the circumstances, taking all he knew into account, it would be the sanest, most sensible decision he had ever made. It would be payback for Suzy, for his mother and father, for Cage and his victims, for Lake himself, and for the poor unfortunates who would die in the future if Lake chose the gutless way out and stuck to his Path.

Lake no longer needed Dreave for his career. Any agent would do. Even the worst agent could arrange at least one interview, and provided he continued with Dreave's Method, one interview would be all he required.

He kissed Suzy's forehead and asked, 'Would you like to stay tonight? No strings.'

'Thanks, but no,' she said. 'I need to stand on my own two feet for a while.'

'OK. You know where I am.'

She broke the hug and stood up. 'I'll leave the gun here,' she said, pointing to the sideboard. She removed it from her bag and placed it on top of a *Yellow Pages.* 'Will you say anything to Dreave?'

'Don't know.' He went to the door and opened it for her. 'But don't worry.'

Suzy kissed his cheek. 'I'll call soon.'

'Do. And take good care.'

She stepped onto the landing. 'Nothing silly,' she reminded him.

'I promise.'

Lake picked up the pistol and hefted it from hand to hand. Its weight felt right. He put it to his nose and enjoyed the smell: carbon steel and gun oil. The name Glock was stamped into the metal. He spoke the word out loud and liked the sound of it.

He didn't know much about guns, but this one didn't have a hammer. He'd just have to pull the trigger and hope for the best.

He tucked it down the front of his waistband. It was heavy, uncomfortable, cold through his thin shirt, but immensely reassuring.

When would he do it?

Not right now. He was too tired. He had been awake five and a half hours longer than anyone else. He had to be sharp, alert when it happened. There would be no second chances. Any hesitation and Dreave would send him to hell in the blink of an eye. Not tomorrow day either. There should be no witnesses. He decided he would sleep until ten-thirty, then do it. He didn't doubt he would find Dreave in at that time. He seemed to reside permanently in the basement of Studio House; it was closer to the world he came from, and Lake had been able to catch him there once before after office hours.

It crossed his mind that the disposal of Dreave's corpse might be troublesome whatever time it was done, but that was not his imminent concern. He first had to make sure Dreave turned into a corpse, and if the first Dreave knew of his arrival was a bullet in the back, so much the better. He wasn't a hero. He was a coward and he didn't want a showdown.

In the bedroom, Lake programmed his radio-alarm, placed the gun on the floor beside the bed, lay down in his jeans and T-shirt on top of the duvet, closed his eyes and, amazingly, managed to rest in peace.

Eight-fifteen p.m. Time to wind up the toys.

Dreave picked up the telephone and called reception. He knew Christine would not have gone home. Some nights she stayed until midnight, hoping she would again be summoned into the basement.

She answered.

'Come down,' he said to her.

It took Christine just over five seconds to reach him.

Dreave watched her dash towards him. She caught her blouse on the door handle and jarred to a halt. She tugged a moment, then walked another two paces into the office, leaving her arms trailing behind her. The blouse peeled off her shoulders, down her arms, turning inside-out, and hung there on the handle.

Her distress was obvious. He was immune to it. Her body squirmed with unrequited lust. Her head made staccato poultry movements. Her face twitched with muscular tics while her hectic eyes were welling up, expectant, but without real hope; the basement was light, and he had used the telephone to call, not more ethereal means.

He gave her a concerned, caring look. 'Sit, my dear.'

Christine obeyed, taking the client's chair. His desk was a block between them.

'Naughty Conrad,' he said. 'Have I been neglecting you?'

She nodded forlornly and began sobbing.

'Should I explain?' he asked.

She nodded again.

He sighed deeply. 'There have been several complications in both my personal and my business affairs. I will spare you the nitty-gritty, but the upshot of it all is that your boss, Miss Susan Cooper, is making my life a misery.'

Christine gasped.

'Yes,' he said. 'A misery.'

Her sad face twisted grotesquely; sadder still.

He put a hand to his mouth. 'No, this is wrong of me. I should not burden you with my problems. Please return to your desk and forget I mentioned it.'

'No,' she said, and her tears began to ease. 'I mean, I will if you want me to. I don't want to disobey you. But I want to help. If you want. I do. I will. Let me. Please. If you want. Or I'll go. If you really want. But I'd rather help.'

'You are sweet,' Dreave said. 'It *was* my intention to ask for your advice.'

'Anything, anything. Really, anything.'

'If you insist. Thank you.'

He leant forward and beckoned her closer with a finger. She wiped her eyes and shot to the edge of her chair, inclining her upper body almost flat across the surface of the desk.

'Well, my dear,' he said. 'I hope you know how I feel about you . . .'

Her tear-tracked face lit up.

'But you have had a rival for my affections.'

A black cloud settled above her. With venom, she said, 'Cooper?'

He nodded. 'For a time, I must confess, my devotion to you was sorely tested. But I was strong and I denied her for the sake of our love.'

Christine crowed sickeningly.

Dreave raised his head to peek over her, out of the doorway. She checked behind, over either shoulder, confirming the coast was clear.

He lowered his head and lowered his voice. 'But she has a hold over me. She has stolen a highly classified document from me. I can tell you because I trust you. You see, I work for a covert government department, and the tasks I perform are sometimes ever so slightly illegal. They are, of course, always in the interests of national security, but I am not above the law. And Suzy has threatened that if I do not leave you to be with her, she will take this document to the police and destroy me. Destroy us, my dear. Our cherished future together.'

'Shitting bitch,' Christine hissed.

'Indeed. So what should I do?'

Christine fumed.

He asked, 'What would you do in my position?'

'Kill her.'

Dreave gasped. 'Really? Is that not a little drastic?'

'It's our future.'

'Hmm,' Dreave mused. 'Yes. Yes, I think you should then. That would be best all round.'

'What?'

'If you killed her.'

'Me?'

'Oh. I thought you wanted to help.'

'I do.'

'But it is a lot to ask, I realise that.' He stood up and offered his hand. 'Well, goodbye, Christine. No hard feelings.'

'What?'

'She has won. Your boss has won. I suppose I should nip upstairs and tell her the news. She will no doubt force me to indulge in some wild sex with her—'

'I'll kill her.'

'—but I have no option. Pardon?'

'I'll kill her.'

'Oh, would you? How splendid.'

The telephone rang just as Suzy was all set to head into town and raise some hell.

'What?' she said testily into the receiver, without polite preamble.

'You have to go to Studio House,' she was curtly informed.

'Oh, it's you, Christine. Why?'

'The police want you.'

Suzy smiled; Dreave dead already. Good old Nathan. Gullible twat. Odd though; she didn't feel any different.

'Anything serious?' Suzy tested.

'Don't know,' Christine replied. 'I'm at home. They couldn't find your number so they called me.'

'How'd they get your number?'

There was a pause. 'Don't know.'

'And it can't wait till tomorrow?'

'I'm just the messenger, Suzy, but it sounded urgent.'

Suzy wondered whether she'd get a glimpse of Dreave's body, holed and bloody. She didn't want to miss that. She'd have to get a move on or the coroner would beat her to it.

'I'm on my way,' she said, and cut the connection.

214

* * *

Suzy's first view of Studio House, shortly after she turned left off Shaftesbury Avenue into Wardour Street, led her to one conclusion: Christine had been lying. If that was a crime scene up ahead, it should have been swarming with police vehicles, uniformed officers, detectives, forensic examiners.

None of that.

She pulled up outside the darkened building in her Mercedes.

There wasn't even a length of blue and white tape strung across the glass doors.

She drove away, but turned off into an alley a short way up the street.

It was disappointing to think Christine had tricked her. It put a slight dent in her pride, but she was more disturbed that it meant Dreave was probably still alive.

Never mind. The night was still young and Christine had aroused her curiosity with this little ploy of hers.

She locked the car and walked back towards Studio House.

The shitting bitch had gone. Driven off down the road. Had not even set foot on the pavement.

Christine ran back to reception with her murder weapon. She put the scissors down, switched on her desk spot, rooted through her handbag in the pool of light and found her address book.

She had wanted to avoid doing it at Cooper's house. Her presence there might later be easily detected: hairs and fibres. At her place of work, trace evidence from her person would be commonplace, non-incriminating. In effect, she would have been an invisible assailant.

But the shitting bitch had gone, and needs must . . .

Double damn. The relevant page was torn out. Now why was that? When had she done that? She couldn't remember. Things were all a bit of a blur recently.

Tomorrow then. Have to be. First thing. Go straight up to her office and do it. The clients would be too busy fucking each other stupid to see anything, and she imagined a death scream and a sex scream were pretty similar sounds.

She froze. The front door of Studio House had unlocked itself with a click. Someone had input the entry code.

Christine killed the light and hunched down out of sight. She tried not to breathe too loudly, and waited for the person to come round the corner into reception.

Behind her, the door swung shut by itself and locked.

Suzy shouted, 'Hey! Christine! What's the big idea?'

The streetlamps threw a sloping block of orange light through the glass entrance into the hallway. For ten feet ahead of her, the marble floor glowed warmly. Further down, towards the lift and the stairs, darkness ruled.

She stood perfectly still and listened. The street sent her fading cars, distant voices. The shadows of Studio House were deathly quiet.

She walked on. At the lift she called again, 'Hey! You dizzy tart! Show yourself!' To her right was the reception area. She wandered casually in.

Fear did not infect her mind. With or without Dreave's power, she felt bold and strong. Why Christine had lied to get her there was a mystery, but if it came down to it, Suzy was more than ready to rumble. Christine was weak; she looked drained of energy. At large, alive in the building, was an unnatural force. As it had boosted Suzy, so it had sapped Christine.

There was no one around at reception.

Besides, if danger had been lying in wait, she believed she would have sensed it by now.

She turned to leave.

The noise and the impact seemed to register all at once. A scuffling behind her and a metallic, clanging thud against the rear of her skull.

Her legs wobbled and she felt her mind swim away as the marble floor rose up to break her fall.

When it swam back to her, consciousness was indeed a wet experience.

Suzy squirmed on the ground as her attacker streamed water onto her face. Her hands flailed, trying to deflect its path from her eyes, before it moved away down her neck, onto her chest, soaking her designer dress to her skin.

'I'm awake!' she screamed, and some water trickled into her mouth.

She tasted it, almost choked, and spat.

Once upon a time it may have been water, but not now.

She shrieked, kicked her legs blindly and tried to scurry away on her backside. The pattering torrent moved across her stomach, down her right leg and continued splashing on the marble.

Suzy had already guessed it was Christine, but a familiar laugh confirmed it before she could wipe her eyes to see.

'You filthy bastard!' Suzy shouted, watching her receptionist stand legs apart.

Christine drew her legs together and the pleats of her skirt closed up tight again. She was holding a pair of long, thin scissors in her right hand.

'Get up,' she said. 'We're going upstairs.'

Suzy climbed to her feet. She touched the back of her head, and winced when her fingers skimmed a painful bump. On the floor, on its side, was the reception's metal litter bin.

'What d'you think I've done?' Suzy asked calmly.

'Start stepping,' Christine ordered.

Suzy did as she was told.

'I'm right behind you, Cooper. You try anything, I'll cut your ugly fucking head off.'

'I hear you,' Suzy said, and began up the stairs. Her dress was horribly uncomfortable: pungent and clinging. The skin of her face was taut and tacky. She badly wanted a shower. From a showerhead. Rounding the second floor, she began her defence, though her crime against the receptionist remained unclear.

'I've never hurt you, Christine.'

'No talk.'

'What have I done?'

'Nothing yet. And I'm going to make certain you don't.'

'What d'you think I was *about* to do?'

A sharp point jabbed her bottom and made her jump and squeak.

'*Shit!* Christine, if you're going to kill me, I'd like to know why I'm dying.'

'Sure, you really don't know.'

'I have no idea.'

'Just climb.'

'Where are we going?'

'Where we won't be disturbed.'

They left the third floor behind. Only a faint orange phosphorescence lit the way. The streetlight poured in through the office windows, crept through the open office doors, faded across the corridors and was all but lost in the stairwell.

Suzy debated whether to launch a backward kick. She didn't do it because, presumably, in the ensuing fight one of them would die. For obvious reasons, she didn't want it to be her, and if it were Christine, she would never know what this was all about. It was a potentially fatal curiosity.

'On the next floor, Christine, I'm going to stop walking and face you.'

'I'll kill you.'

'Then I'll die, but it's going to happen.'

'I will kill you.'

'Then do it now, because I'm about to stop walking.'

Suzy waited for the scissors to breach her skin.

'OK, stop,' Christine said as they reached the fourth-floor landing.

Suzy slowly turned around. She could hear the sound of sex in a nearby office. Christine kept her distance. Out of range, but in control.

'Is this about Dreave?' Suzy asked.

Christine's eyes flared. She pointed the scissors at Suzy. 'You do know. You know damn well.'

'I *don't* know,' Suzy quickly countered. 'I only ask because everything in this building is about Dreave. Can't you feel it? He's taken over.'

'We're getting married,' Christine said flatly.

Suzy thought to mock, then decided better of it.

'And you're not going to stop us with your stinking blackmail,' Christine continued. 'Trying to fuck him, or destroy him, send him to prison, take my only happiness away from me.'

Suzy was shaking her head. 'I didn't even know about you and Dreave. But now I do, I'm very happy for you.'

A contemptuous snort showed what Christine thought of that.

Suzy tried again. 'There's something in this building, Christine, like a virus. Do you really think it's normal for every office to be full of writhing sex? Do you think other places are like that? Was it like that before Dreave arrived?'

Christine narrowed her eyes and looked askance. Suzy could tell something had got through. She tried to build on it.

'Have you seen yourself in the mirror lately? Christine, you're exhausted. You're not thinking straight. You need to get away from Studio House.'

'Oh, I see—'

'No,' Suzy cut her off. 'Take Dreave with you. I don't care if I never see him again. Christine, I've just lost my fiancé. Why would I want another man so soon?'

'Because he's perfect and he's mine and you're jealous. Now *walk*.'

She closed on Suzy with the scissors, and Suzy gathered she would die there and then if she didn't move.

They trekked upwards past the fifth floor and on to the sixth. Above them was the roof. Christine ushered Suzy towards the fire-escape door.

'Push the bar,' she said. 'Then up.'

Suzy released the door and stepped out onto the metal walkway. For the first time, apprehension slinked along beside her. Fear and fresh air raised goose bumps. Over the edge, six floors down, was a deep, dark, beckoning well, its four vertical sides filled with black windows. Her pulse quickened. She negotiated the steep metal steps up onto the roof, clenching the rail with both hands.

It was relatively light up top. The black tar surface shone dully under the gaze of a full moon. Suddenly, Suzy felt death drape around her like a fug. She could smell it. Bittersweet, more scent than odour. She waited at the top of the steps to kick Christine to her death. Forget any unanswered questions.

'Back away,' she was told, her plan foiled.

Christine gained the roof, scissors leading the way. Suzy whipped her head left and right and behind, searching for a makeshift weapon. Apart from a large square structure housing the lift mechanism, there was nothing up there. A simple two-foot-high wall ran around the edge of the building, a token bar to prevent an accidental fall, but useless against a deliberate push. Along the street edge, a fuzzy orange halo hovered up into the midnight blue of the sky.

'Any last requests?' Christine quipped melodramatically.

Suzy faced her and backed to the centre of the roof, the safest place, stalked by a menacing underling.

'Christine, what could I do to put Dreave in prison?'

'That document.'

'Huh?'

They began to circle each other.

Christine's eyes glittered with moonlight. 'Those secret papers. Conrad's a government agent and you know it.'

Suzy had to think fast. 'Oh, Christine, of course he's not, he's a theatrical agent.'

'Crap.'

'My ex, Nathan Lake, he's an actor. You've seen him at reception.'

'So?'

The circle tightened. Suzy suddenly stopped and pulled back from the scissors. Christine closed in, and Suzy further retreated, drawing perilously close to the rear plummet.

The moment of truth loomed.

'Nathan Lake is Dreave's client,' Suzy appealed. 'Dreave is a theatrical agent.'

Christine gave no reply.

'Well, have you ever seen anyone more sinister than him go down into the basement?'

'There was a policeman once.'

'That was my fiancé,' Suzy pounced, sensing Christine might have handed her the convincing argument. 'You know why he was there? To stop Dreave giving me money. How do you think I got the Mercedes? Dreave's been trying to get me into bed since day one. He used that government-agent shit to impress me until Nathan put me straight on things.'

Christine looked at once furious and beaten. 'No,' she said, with scant conviction.

'That's why Dreave's turned you against me,' Suzy said, 'because he's bitter; angry I wouldn't sleep with him.'

'It's not true,' Christine cried, but the scissors fell slowly to her side.

'Come back down with me,' Suzy implored. 'We can talk about this over a coffee. I'll send Dreave packing, then everything can get back to normal. You can take a long holiday. A paid holiday. I'll pay for it myself. You've had a terrible time, my girl. I'm afraid Conrad Dreave has lied to you.'

A sad, tearful expression stole every ounce of threat from the defeated receptionist.

Suzy said, 'Come on, darling, it's been a crazy night.'

Christine nodded, sobbing steadily. Suzy carefully approached and lay a comforting hand on her shoulder.

'You know,' Suzy said with a smile, 'this sort of thing could come between some people.'

Christine giggled through her tears.

'There,' Suzy said. 'Nothing's so bad that we can't laugh at it, eh?'

'I'm sorry,' Christine whispered. 'I don't think I'm very well.'

'I know, don't worry. We can forget this ever happened.'

'Thank you. You're so good to me.'

Suzy shook her head. 'No, I'm not. Not really. Now do you want to give me those nasty scissors?'

Christine looked down to her side. She nodded and handed over her weapon.

'Now I should put these where they belong,' Suzy said. 'Don't you think?'

Christine nodded.

So Suzy inserted them into Christine's belly.

Christine gasped hoarsely, her mouth and eyes wide.

Suzy said, 'That's for lying to me.'

She pulled them out and stabbed her again.

'That's for hitting me.'

And again.

'That's for pissing on me.'

And again, blades open, a double puncture.

'That's for screwing Dreave behind my back.'

Christine inhaled a long rattling stream of night air and staggered around a little.

Blades open, another thrust, and this time Suzy used a cutting action when they were still inside.

'And that's for making me shitty coffee all these years.'

Christine squealed, and Suzy left the scissors sticking out of her.

Sudden applause spun Suzy round on her heels.

Dreave was standing on top of the housing of the lift mechanism. He finished clapping.

'Bravo,' he said. 'You killed a man to protect me. But this was pointless, gratuitous. Pure hatred. Pure evil.'

Suzy understood and recognised her achievement.

Her glory lasted but a brief second.

In her final moments of life, Christine lurched at her killer.

The near-dead weight knocked Suzy tottering backwards. Heavy arms clung limply round her shoulders in a mortal embrace. She tried to stop the momentum, but Christine had hit her like a sack of spuds, and back they went.

One heel struck the retaining wall, then the other, and the inevitability of death washed over her in a nauseous wave. She grabbed a handful of Christine's hair, then felt herself tip from the vertical to the horizontal as the scenery behind Christine's horrified face rolled up ninety degrees from cityscape to stars.

* * *

Dreave heard Suzy's scream, then the dull dual whump as his girls hit the concrete six floors down.

He jumped off his perch, trotted to the edge and peered over. 'I just can't seem to keep a girlfriend these days.'

The manhole cover eased out and slid back. It scraped across the concrete, its noise echoing around the high-sided well of buildings. Dreave straightened up and clapped his hands together, and a cloud of dust puffed into the air.

Christine first.

He grabbed her hair, matted with blood, and dragged her body over to the round black hole.

'For as much as it has pleased Almi – Oh, the hell with it.'

He bundled her down through the gap in the ground and listened to the thud she made in the trickling sewer. With his foot, he pushed the cover back into place, then turned his attention to Suzy.

Suzy deserved respect. He knelt down beside her and swept her into his arms. He kissed her cut and swollen forehead, then carried her indoors and down to his black lair.

Outside the lift, he pressed the call button.

The door opened instantly. He entered the compartment and lay Suzy's body on the floor with great care. To the unfamiliar eye, she would have appeared essentially undamaged. A little blood, that was all. But Dreave knew. Her bones were smashed, her internal organs a mush.

And it was what lay within that mattered. Indeed it was.

He rose from his haunches and pressed 1, then stepped back into the basement.

But before the door could close, he removed his black wrap-arounds and threw them into the lift.

He didn't need them any more. His job was done.

Then he watched as the bronze door slid shut and sealed her fate.

Shortly afterwards he called the lift again.

The door opened. The compartment was empty.

28

What a wonderful dream.

Lake was annoyed by the interruption of Capital Radio. He had been dreaming of failure and depression and unemployment and empty bank accounts and useless agents. Ah, those were the days.

Ten-thirty p.m. He switched on his overhead light, rolled to the edge of the bed and looked down at the pistol.

The spoils of success. Spiffing.

He got up, turned the radio off, yawned, lay down again, forced himself to get up and meandered sleepily to the wardrobe. From inside he unhooked a khaki combat jacket he hadn't worn in years, and put it on over his black T-shirt. He slipped into his trainers and laced them up, then took a black woollen skull cap from a drawer and pulled it down around his ears.

Finally, he shoved the Glock down the waistband of his jeans and buttoned up his jacket.

He felt so weary doing all of this. He wanted to sleep. Sleep and never wake up. Not die, mind. Just sleep.

Feeling quite pathetic, he marched out of his flat, determined to complete a successful mission.

Designated target: Conrad Dreave. Special instructions: terminate with extreme prejudice.

Locked.

First phase of operation a resounding dud.

Studio House was locked. So much for the subtle approach.

Lake went to press the intercom, but the door buzzed before he could touch the button. Evidently, he was expected.

He pushed the door and went inside. On with the mission. He strode down the hallway and round to the basement stairs.

The lights below were already full on. He descended.

'The Deer Hunter as I live and breathe,' Dreave said as Lake drew to attention in the office doorway. 'What can I do for you, Bob?'

Lake had no idea how these things were meant to happen. Was he supposed to hit Dreave with the accusation, then they could shout at each other for a while, up the ante to the point where violence was the only solution?

Dreave leant back in his chair and dumped his feet on the desk-top. His laces were undone. He wasn't wearing his dark glasses. His demon eyes unnerved Lake; it was almost reason enough to shoot him without further ado.

'You said you were human,' Lake challenged.

'As you see me now, yes.'

'So you have human failings.'

'Failings? No. Evil is always a conscious choice for me.'

Lake nonchalantly unbuttoned his jacket, leaving only one button fastened.

'So you never have any . . . urges?' he asked.

'Nothing I cannot control.'

'So you'd have no excuses if you did something bad.'

Dreave raised his eyebrows. 'I think you forget where I come from.'

'No,' Lake said. 'That's one thing I'd never forget.'

Dreave ran a hand through his blond hair, mussing it. Several long strands flopped over his forehead. Lake had never seen him anything less than immaculate. Strangely, it saddened him.

'Are you all right, Conrad?'

Dreave closed, then opened his eyes. Lake just caught the narrowing of his pupils, like a cat's.

'I've had a busy day,' Dreave said. 'It's time for me to rest.'

Lake was simultaneously heartened and upset by the revelation of this human trait.

Dreave's head lolled forward and he seemed to notice something. He wet the tip of his finger on his tongue and rubbed half-heartedly at a tiny reddish-brown smudge on his sleeve.

'What's that?' Lake asked suspiciously.

'Blood,' Dreave told him, still engrossed in his stain-removal.

'Whose?'

'Not sure.'

Lake unfastened the last button on his combat jacket. 'You don't understand,' he said. 'I know whose it is, I just want to hear you say it.'

Dreave shrugged and worried away at the sleeve.

'Whose is it, Conrad?'

'Not sure.' He lifted his head, appeared to think. 'Can't remember.'

Lake pulled the gun out from his waistband and pointed it at his agent.

Dreave was unimpressed. 'Woe is me. Nathan has a gun.'

'You don't seem too surprised.'

'When you've lived as long as I have, my boy, surprises are few and far between.'

'Whose blood, Conrad?' Lake asked evenly.

'Not sure. Could be Suzy's, could be——'

There was a deafening explosion and Dreave slammed back in his chair, then fell on the floor. It was a moment before Lake understood he had pulled the trigger.

Dreave made no sound as he rolled himself onto all fours, then clambered to his feet.

'I shot you,' Lake said stupidly.

A black hole in the centre of Dreave's stomach was leaking crimson down his white turtleneck sweater.

Dreave glanced down at his wound, then to the insignificant stain on his sleeve, then back to his wound. He pointed to the blood on his sweater. 'I'll never get this out,' he said. He touched his fingers into the dark stream and suddenly flicked a spray of droplets at Lake's face.

Lake flinched as they struck; Dreave's blood was cold as ice. He pulled the trigger again.

Dreave staggered back and swayed on the spot, a second dark hole oozing fresh blood from his chest.

'This won't change anything,' Dreave said. 'Your Path is set.'

'It makes me feel better,' Lake told him, and loosed off another shot.

Still Dreave remained upright. Lake put another three shots into Dreave's torso.

Dreave slammed against the rear wall of the office, then straightened up and said, 'I'm beginning to feel a little under the weather.'

Four more shots, but Dreave withstood them.

'Perhaps you need a silver bullet, Nathan. Or a stake through the heart. What do you think?'

Panicking, Lake fought the desire to run away. In time, Dreave might collapse and die, but he needed to see it happen. He squeezed off a couple more rounds, clean through Dreave's neck.

'Have you got a Strepsil, Nathan? I think I'm developing a sore throat.'

'Shit.' Lake looked frustratingly at his weapon. How many bullets left?

'I haven't been counting, Nathan, but the Glock has a double-stack magazine. You might still do it.'

Lake glowered at his agent.

Gurgling a bit now, Dreave said, 'I know about firearms.'

Lake stepped forward, pointed the gun at Dreave's heart and pulled the trigger.

The impact spun Dreave around one-eighty degrees. With his back to Lake, he spoke quietly: 'That one hurt.'

'Just die, you fucker.'

'Now, now, Nathan. Patience, remember?'

Lake aimed a shot at the base of Dreave's spine. Dreave spasmed and crumpled to the floor, face down, paralysed.

'The end is nigh,' he spluttered into the carpet.

'Thank God for that.'

'But I'll see you soon, Nathan.'

Lake levelled the muzzle at the back of Dreave's skull.

'To hell with you,' he said, and blew his agent's brains out through his face.

EPILOGUE

London. December once again. The dark month.

The light was fading fast and a heavy fall of snow was offering a brief visual salvation to a sick and dirty town.

The couple with the world at their feet and the press at their door hurried into Langan's Brasserie to escape the cold.

Their glistening overcoats were taken from them. Nathan Lake brushed the melting white flakes from his hair and Sherry McCall popped off to the washroom.

Lake was shown to a conspicuously reserved table in the centre of the restaurant. Famous faces nodded at him. His own famous face nodded back.

He and Sherry had been an item for three months now, since the British release of their film had brought her to London for publicity purposes. They had fallen into bed within the first hour of meeting again. A week later they were engaged. It seemed as though destiny had been drumming its fingers, just waiting for it to happen. Subsequently, their film had been a smash hit and was already nominated for several prestigious awards. Everything was moving in strict adherence to his promised future.

Whether or not he loved Sherry he didn't know; he thought he did, but Dreave had told him that love was impossible along the Dark Path. Perhaps he did love her, but she could never truly reciprocate. Perhaps she was only in lust with him and it would all end in tears. But so what. He would take what happiness he could find for as long as it lasted. It would all end in tears soon enough anyway.

227

Tomorrow he was flying to Los Angeles with her. In two weeks their film would enjoy its Stateside release, and the publicity machine over there was all geared up to take them aboard.

He was leaving town and he wasn't coming back. London was too full of bad memories.

Of course, Sherry herself was a constant reminder of his true nature; they had met only because he had murdered Brigit Kelly. But he didn't want to forget what he was, what he had done, and his recurrent nightmares of the Dark Land would not have allowed him to.

Once, she had asked what had happened to his agent; Lake had raved about the man while on location in the Maldives. Lake simply said there had been a falling out. Why Dreave's body had never been reported when Lake had left it on the office floor had remained a mystery for all of one second. Someone, or something, had been dispatched to recover it. When she asked, as she often did, why he had not yet sought another agent, he replied that there was no rush, that patience was a virtue.

Ironically, after all that had occurred, patience remained a thoroughly alien talent to Lake. It was only his healthy bank balance and present fame that had kept Dreave's Method dormant. Lake prayed nightly that when these were all used up, some better part of him would still refuse to indulge the evil within his grasp. Only time would tell. But nearly every day during the eighteen months since Dreave's passing, the small, gaping cut in his right palm had literally itched to be used again.

Despite harbouring some deep moral qualms, Lake had decided to go ahead and star in the police series, *Gun Runners*. Now showing every Monday night, it had unsurprisingly leapt straight to the top of the TV ratings.

To the outside world, his life was perfect. Fame, fortune, a beautiful fiancée. How was anyone to know? He didn't complain. He put on a happy face – a brave face – and got on with it.

Yep, life had granted his every wish. Death, however, would leave a lot to be desired.

Funnily, he thought little of Suzy these days. After she dropped by his flat that night with the gun, he never saw her again. She had just disappeared, cleared clean out of town. He imagined she was in another city, another land perhaps, rebuilding her life. He liked to think so. She deserved to be happy. She was a good person.

'Have you ordered us some drinks?' Sherry asked as she took her seat.

Lake broke from yet another bout of his regular self-contemplation.

'Uh, no,' he said. 'I thought I'd wait for you.'

'OK.' She hailed the waiter. 'You know, I just met a friend of yours outside the bathroom.'

'Yeah? Who's that?'

The waiter arrived. 'Could I take your drinks order?'

'Dry vermouth for me,' Sherry announced, 'and—' She looked to Lake.

'Lager.'

'Any particular type?' asked the waiter.

'Strong.'

'Certainly.' The waiter went off to the bar.

'So which friend?' Lake asked.

'Some theatrical agent who knows you. Said to say hello.'

Lake swallowed hard. His eyes began to fill up with frightened, burning tears. He blinked repeatedly to stop them.

Sherry said, 'You OK, darling?'

He tried to sound casual. 'Something in my eye. This agent—'

'Yeah?'

He swallowed again and found he could barely speak. 'It wasn't a tall man with blond hair?'

'No.'

'Oh, Jesus!' He began laughing with relief. 'Must be Billy you met. Billy Banbury, my old agent.'

'No, no,' Sherry said. 'This was a woman.'

'A woman?' Lake pondered. 'An agent? Doesn't ring any bells.'

'Said she's just finished having dinner with a new client, a young actress fresh out of drama school.'

Lake shook his head. 'No . . . no, can't think.'

'Well, she knows you.'

The drinks arrived. Still searching his memory, Lake absently picked up his glass of lager and put it to his lips.

'Hey,' Sherry said, 'don't drink yet. Let's make a toast.' She raised her glass. 'To your happiness in your new home, our happiness in our future together, and to continued success in our careers.'

They clinked glasses and drank.

'Mmm—' Sherry interrupted her gulp. 'There she is, your friend, coming out of the bathroom.'

Lake turned in his chair and choked on his mouthful of lager, spraying it through his teeth. In that first confused moment of seeing her, joy and horror spun as one in his gut.

It was Suzy, but she had changed.

Then the nature of those changes sunk in, and there was no longer any joy inside him. His eyes flared and the burning tears sprang again, and this time he knew he couldn't staunch them.

'Nat? What's wrong?' Sherry asked. 'What is it? What's the matter?'

Lake didn't hear. He only saw.

Suzy ran a hand across her shorn blonde scalp and smiled at him. He believed she might also have winked, but he couldn't see her eyes behind her black wrap-arounds. Then she gracefully twirled on the spot, showing off her new cream business outfit.

He wanted to believe it was some kind of sick joke, but he knew it wasn't. It didn't make any sense. She was a good person. He knew her.

'Nat?' Sherry persisted. 'What is it?'

'Christ, no,' he said. 'No . . . please.'

He watched as Suzy went to her table and collected her client, a pretty, raven-haired young soul. He was about to dash over and drag the actress back from the abyss, when he sensed a dark communion with her and knew she had already gone over the edge.

At the doorway, before she stepped into the street, Suzy turned around to face him. Standing beneath the glare of a ceiling spot, she tapped her black glasses an inch down her nose for two seconds, then pushed them back up.

Anyone else would have dismissed what they saw as a trick of the light.